LEAGUE OF LEGENDS

LEAGUE OF LEGENDS

REALMS OF RUNETERRA

VORACIOUS
LITTLE, BROWN AND COMPANY
NEW YORK   BOSTON   LONDON

MELCHER
MEDIA

TO RIOTERS

*It is an honor to be surrounded daily by folks with
such a deep dedication to excellence. The passion, patience, and
perseverance that runs in the lifeblood of Riot is what has
made this world (and this book) possible.*

*If we can dream it, we can do it. Thank you for saying,
"Yes, and…" every day.*

TO PLAYERS

*Although this book may focus on the fictional world of
League of Legends, know that all of you
are at the center of our universe.*

Thank you.

Voracious
Little, Brown and Company
Hachette Book Group
1290 Avenue of the Americas
New York, NY 10104
littlebrown.com

First Edition: November 2019

Voracious is an imprint of Little, Brown
and Company, a division of Hachette
Book Group, Inc. The Voracious name
and logo are trademarks of Hachette
Book Group, Inc.

The Hachette Speakers Bureau
provides a wide range of authors for
speaking events. To find out more, go
to hachettespeakersbureau.com or call
(866) 376-6591.

ISBN 978-0-316-49732-9

LCCN 2019948238

10 9 8 7 6 5 4 3 2 1

WOR

Printed in the United States of America

To friends, old and new... Welcome.

For some, this may be your first encounter with the League of Legends universe. For others who have wandered with us over the years, opening this book may be just the yordle portal you've been searching for.

At the time of writing, it has been just over four years since I began my own travels through the realms of Runeterra. The stories I've been a part of have let me surf the sands of Shurima, chase augmented criminals through the corroded back alleys of Zaun, and solve the mysterious death of an elder master in Ionia.

When I joined Riot Games, I was told that, within the world of League of Legends, there is something for everyone. At first I was doubtful a fictional setting could be that robust—but as I started to become more familiar with it all, I realized there really was no limit to the characters we could meet, or the stories we could tell.

Now and always, Runeterra is for all of us.

Today, you might be a Noxian warmason, claiming new territory for the empire's expansion, while I might be a treasure hunter seeking mystical relics on the haunted shores of the Shadow Isles. Tomorrow, perhaps we can both be young recruits in the Demacian military, taking our oaths to join the ranks of the Dauntless Vanguard? Or maybe we'll just celebrate as Freljordian warriors, and toast "a good day" under a brilliant, celestial aurora? No matter where our curiosity takes us, I know there will always be something new to discover.

This book is meant to serve as a friend and guide as you navigate the wilds of Runeterra. More than just a collection of art and stories, this is the beginning of an exploration into civilizations and cultures touched by fantasy—this is a shared dream made real. Imagination really is the best story-toy-tool-game in the proverbial box, and it is my sincere hope that this glimpse into the world contained within these pages sparks your imagination as much as it has mine.

Wishing you magic and adventure on the journey ahead,

—Ariel "Thermal Kitten" Lawrence
Head of Narrative, Riot Games

THE FRELJORD

NOXUS

42

DEMACIA

68

96

◇

CONTENTS

Composed of both the material and spirit
realms, Runeterra is all that separates the
celestial powers of creation from the abyssal
threat of all undoing. This is a magical world
unlike any other—inhabited by peoples both
fierce and wondrous. Consider this volume
an invitation to explore its farthest reaches,
through accounts of each region, as well as tales
that bring to life the adventure and mystery
that exist across the realms.

TARGON

8

IONIA

16

PILTOVER & ZAUN

120

BILGEWATER

162

IXTAL

158

SHURIMA

224

SHADOW ISLES

190

To better understand Runeterra, one might start with Targon, where legends of the world's creation often begin.

Like any place of myth, it is a beacon to dreamers, pilgrims, and seekers of truth and enlightenment, such as the hardy tribes of the Rakkor who call the mountains home. Mount Targon itself is the mightiest peak in Runeterra—a towering pinnacle of twisted, sun-baked rock that seems to reach ever upward toward the stars.

For millennia, mortals have been drawn to climb Mount Targon, even though they cannot always explain why, and the ascent is known to be all but impossible.

THE SOLARI

While nearly all Rakkor worship the sun, those who completely devote their lives to it are known as the Solari. As the dominant religious sect on Mount Targon, the Solari believe the sun is the source of all life—all other light sources are false, and a threat to the future of their people. Disciples are guided in the strictures of their faith by temple priests, who preach that if the sun was ever to fade, the world would be swallowed by darkness. Accordingly, Solari warriors stand ready to fight any who would extinguish its holy light.

MOUNTAIN

THE LUNARI

Branded by the Solari as heretics, the Lunari worship the silvery light of the moon. They practice their beliefs in secret, hiding from those who seek to rid Targon of their influence forever—even though some claim that, long ago, the two groups lived in peace, worshipping the heavens as one people.

TAMU

Flocks of tamu are raised by the Rakkor. Their lush coats are sheared twice yearly, and woven into warm clothing and other textiles.

RAKKOR

The migratory Rakkor tribes have chiseled markets, seasonal homes, and ceremonial chambers into the mountain itself.

THE FAREWELL

In a sacred farewell ceremony before climbing the mountain, those beginning their ascent are celebrated. This day marks the moment when the fate of their souls is placed into the hands of Targon. Most will likely never be seen again.

PILGRIMAGE

PATTERNS OF THE DEAD

The mountain's sheer flanks and treacherous conditions make climbing it incredibly difficult. It's a grueling test of every facet of an aspirant's strength, resolve, willpower, and determination. They sometimes think to start out in groups, to assist one another on the way—since when a climber is exhausted or hurt, there is no hope of rescue from below.

The bodies of the dead do not tend to decay at such heights, but seem to gradually meld with the rock, becoming twisted into the circular patterns and ridges of the mountain.

OTHERWORLDLY PERILS

The most dangerous thing about Mount Targon is not the incredible altitude, but the way in which it challenges the very character of each climber. The Rakkor regard the ascent as a trial of an aspirant's spirit, as the inevitable solitude becomes unendurable and they suffer maddening, distracting visions of other times, places, and personal regrets.

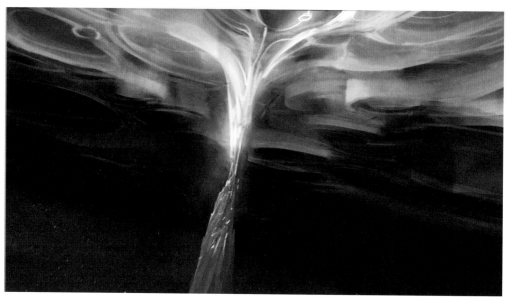

REACHING THE SUMMIT

In the rare event that a mortal reaches Targon's peak, the heavens open before them in a dazzling display of cosmic aurorae. Few ever bear witness to that radiant sight, far above the cloudline and beneath the glittering stars, where it is said that timeless, godlike beings dwell in a wondrous city of gold and silver.

HEAVENS

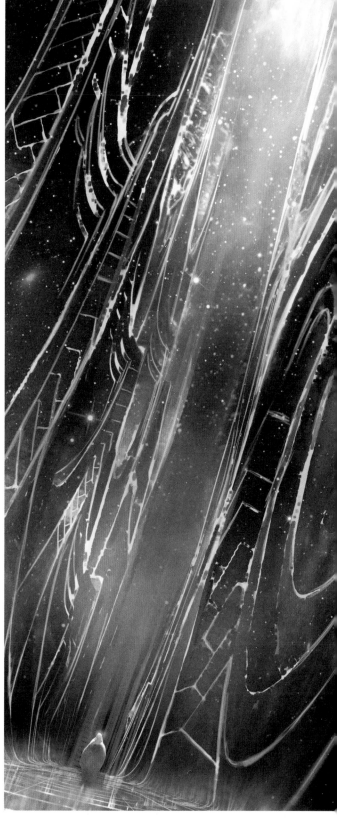

TOUCHED BY THE ETERNAL

The skies around Mount Targon shimmer with celestial majesty—the radiance of sun and moon alike, fiery comets streaking the darkness, and constellations of stars that can be seen from nowhere else on Runeterra. The Rakkor have long held all of these to be Aspects of great and unknowable stellar beings, powerful and ancient on a scale beyond mortal imagining.

Indeed, once every few generations, one of these Aspects may descend from the mountain within the body of a climber they have deemed worthy. Such an occurrence is the stuff of legend, and it is likely that these divine creatures shaped the destiny of the world in ages past.

IONIA

Surrounded by treacherous seas, Ionia is composed of a number of allied provinces scattered across a massive archipelago, known to many as the First Lands. Since Ionian culture has long been shaped by the pursuit of balance in all things, the border between the material and spirit realms tends to be more permeable here, especially in the wild forests and mountains.

Although these lands' enchantments can be fickle, its creatures dangerous and fae, for many centuries most Ionians led lives of plenty. The warrior monasteries, provincial militias, and even Ionia itself, had been enough to protect them.

But that ended twelve years ago, when Noxus attacked the First Lands. The empire's seemingly endless warhosts savaged Ionia, and were defeated only after many years, and at great cost.

Now, Ionia exists in an uneasy peace. Different reactions to the war have divided the region—some groups, such as the Shojin monks or the Kinkou, seek a return to isolationist pacifism and pastoral traditions. Other more radical factions, such as the Navori Brotherhood and the Order of Shadow, demand a militarization of the lands' magic to create a single, unified nation that can take vengeance on Noxus.

The fate of Ionia hangs in a delicate balance that few are willing to overturn, but all can feel shifting uneasily beneath their feet.

THE FIRST LANDS

Magic suffuses every part of Ionia—its people, its history, and most of all the land itself. All aspects of life here hang in a balance, with still so much left to be discovered and explored. Those who call this vast continent home strive to find harmony among the diverse races and habitats, far older than most others on Runeterra.

NATURAL BEAUTY

Ionia is home to many rare and ancient spirits and animals, hidden away from the world and seen by only a lucky few. Even the seas teem with magical life, existing in a state of constant change and renewal.

TITANS OF THE PAST

It is certain Ionia has a much longer and richer history than any living soul could claim to know. Indeed, in the more remote and mountainous highlands, the landscape is still littered with evidence of great wars from ages past—but instead of clearing the ruins, the Ionians choose to respect what remains, even if they no longer fully understand what it represents.

MYSTIC ALLIES

The people of Ionia's many provinces have always seen themselves as part of the natural world, and adapted their ways to live alongside all manner of fantastical flora and fauna. To outsiders, such a close relationship may appear strange, but it is through this interdependence that both the land and its inhabitants have thrived for countless generations.

LIFE IN EQUILIBRIUM

The pursuit of balance is central to Ionian beliefs and culture. The peoples living here measure their deeds against the world around them—they live as one with nature, rather than bending it to their needs.

THE GREAT MONASTERIES

Though the birthplace of many specialized forms of martial arts, Ionia maintains no standing armies. Rather, the ways of battle are tied to differing philosophies, passed on with reverence and care. In the northeastern mountains, the monastery of Hirana has long been a sanctuary for those seeking to better understand their connection to the spirit realm.

Due to the uniquely thin boundary between realms, natural magic and spirits suffuse every aspect of the land and culture. Ionians have generally embraced that relationship, though there have always been those who, at times, would seek to turn it to their own benefit.

The land and weather—and all their related spirits—respond to both positive and negative stimuli. Those in tune with the earth can harvest bountiful crops, while those who live as one with the tides will always find their nets full. Invading armies, however, can expect the Spirit of Ionia to resist them.

Ionians' lives, and their notions of permanence, are often substantially different from other Runeterrans'. Even the most mundane seasonal tasks can be radically transformed by this—these landfishers collect grains and fruits throughout the long summers, by attuning themselves to ever-changing magical currents in the Rivers of Grass.

HARMONY & BALANCE

Ionia's millennia of isolation has meant that this balance-attuned culture places a high value on keeping up healthy traditions. These customs and attitudes often manifest in Ionian architecture—the structures built here are characterized by a sense of natural flow and grace, aspiring to reflect the ethereal beauty of the land. Also, grand, open spaces ensure that one is never fully divorced from what organically existed there before.

LIVING ARCHITECTURE

ARCHITECTURE BY INFLUENCE

Ionians try to avoid cutting down trees, so as not to offend or harm the trees' spirits. Instead, woodweavers magically persuade them to grow into the shapes needed for the structure being built. However, the trees are still alive, and will continue to grow, which can lead to certain unplanned changes to a home over time.

AN ARTISAN'S MASTERY

Some temple houses in the highland valleys are shaped into the rocky hillsides, with living whipwillows serving as archways and support columns. The transitions between the walls and other elements of these sacred buildings are smooth to the touch, with few hard edges or corners.

A ROOFTOP GARDEN

Ionian architecture often includes organically curved tiled or shingled roofs. Here, branches extend outward from the trees within this building.

RURAL LIFE

Living in harmony with the land means that form tends to follow nature. Farms and villages sit gracefully within the environment—their floors, doors, and walls echoing the rise and fall of the earth and sky.

Ionia is home to countless schools and temples, which train disciplined students in ancient martial arts and esoteric philosophy. Deadly and graceful, these fighters, mages, dancers, and scholars spend years in training, hoping to master their craft.

During and after the Noxian invasion, many of these traditions were shaken. Extreme, hardline interpretations of their former beliefs are becoming more prevalent, as each practitioner struggles to make sense of the world in the aftermath of all they have witnessed.

THE PATH TO ENLIGHTENMENT

While it is true that harmony is sought by most in Ionia, few are so far along this path as to be considered truly enlightened beings. Their ideals are lofty, but not all can live up to them, and Ionians can be just as driven by hate, lust, anger, and love as any Runeterran.

From Hirana to the Placidium of Navori, there are places of sanctuary open to those trying to better understand themselves.

SCHOOLS OF LEARNING

THE KINKOU

This serene order is dedicated to preserving a balance between the physical world and the spirit realm, without showing a preference for either. They follow a single leader bearing the title of the Eye of Twilight, who is charged above all with the solemn duty known as Watching the Stars.

THE ORDER OF SHADOW

These assassins have taken it upon themselves to defend Ionia from all outsiders, and to move aggressively toward the total militarization of their homeland. Members of the Order traditionally spend several years learning the forbidden arts of shadow magic.

THE VASTAYASHAI'REI

In an age lost to myth, the harmony of the First Lands was shattered by war between mortals and a race of titans that had come from the skies above. Calling upon the wisdom of their ancestors, the most enlightened mortals took the power of the spirit realm into themselves, becoming *Vastayashai'rei*—deathless shapechangers who could wield the natural world itself as a weapon.

The titans were eventually defeated, and the Vastayashai'rei were hailed as the heroes of the age. Even so, they refused to put themselves above their mortal kin, choosing instead to live among them as equals.

MYSTERY OF THE VASTAYA

The vastaya are mystical, chimeric beings, neither mortal nor truly immortal, who are greatly attuned to the magic of Runeterra. Descended from the Vastayashai'rei, they long ago formed their own tribes. For thousands of years, the vastaya have sought to uphold their own spiritual legacy, even when it would bring them into conflict with one another.

More recently, as humans have continued to disrupt the currents of magic in the world, relations with many of the vastayan tribes have soured. No new vastaya have been born in several mortal lifetimes, and it could be that this ancient race now perceives another time of great change approaching.

THE GREAT STAND

Located in the heart of Ionia, the Placidium of Navori is a symbolic location, steeped in tradition. As such, it was a tempting target for the Noxian general Jericho Swain, who knew the Ionian resistance would never willingly surrender unless their spirit could be crushed.

But Ionia was far from united in its defiance of Noxus. Swain had secured the loyalty of disaffected vastaya who wanted to protect their ancient magical forests from future destruction or conquest, and these unlikely allies helped the Noxians take the Placidium's guardians prisoner.

Although far fewer in number, their superior position allowed them to draw the Ionian reinforcements into a trap. The courtyards and causeways of the Placidium became a fierce battleground, until the general himself was brought low by the outraged warriors he had originally captured. The Noxians were routed and their vastayan agents slaughtered as they fled along with them.

THE BLADE DANCER

The rumor that Irelia, a young blade dancer from Navori, had cut down the Noxian general quickly turned into a rallying call for Ionians everywhere. While some still urged meditations on balance, more began to fight back—with magic, with blade and bow, or by stealth and cunning. The people of Navori in particular were drawn into endless running battles with the empire's remaining warbands, and Irelia soon became their reluctant figurehead.

Though this battle turned the tide of the war, the sanctity of the Placidium had been marred by horrendous bloodshed, its tranquility lost forever. Noxus had left its mark on Ionia, and a land once united in balance had become broken and divided.

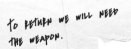

TO RETURN WE WILL NEED THE WEAPON.

ORCHID'S BLOOM

by MICHAEL YICHAO

J ing breathed deep.

The scent of orchid petals wafted on the air, carried by the breeze that danced through the open doors. Outside, bamboos swayed in the wind, their clatter a soft underscore highlighted by the twittering of birdsong. A small smile flitted over Jing's face as the sweet taste of spring danced just off the tip of her tongue. She sighed and stood, a weathered hand grasping the bamboo cane beside her, and tapped her way across the room.

A thousand familiar creaks and groans of the teahouse surrounded her. Sandaled feet carried her from window to window as she opened each shutter with practiced, steady hands. Some petals drifted in as she did so, sweeping past her with a quiet rustle. She didn't mind. After all, they were the teahouse's namesake. A few stray petals scattered indoors brought her small joys and called to mind sweeter memories of bygone times.

Sounds of footsteps drew her attention back toward the main entrance. Unexpected, as it was still early in the season for travelers in these parts. For a moment, Jing's breath caught in her chest. The muted taps of cloth shoes on stone. The whisper of loose clothing. *Could it be...?* But no. The cadence was wrong. The stride too long.

A patient smile replaced fleeting disappointment on Jing's features. She leaned into her cane, stood up straighter, and faced the door, feeling the warm sun on her face.

"Hello, *O-ma*," a voice called from the path. The honorific surprised Jing. Strong. Clear as it carried across the entryway. And faintly familiar—though Jing could not immediately place from where or when she knew it. Perhaps a voice she had not heard for many a year—or perhaps just a trick of faded memory.

"Welcome, traveler," she called in response. The creak of age in her own tones never failed to catch her by surprise. How quickly the years danced by! How time settled and clung heavy to bone and tissue, its gravel and weight inescapable.

"Seeking a respite from the road?" she asked.

"Indeed," the voice replied.

"Please, come in," Jing said. She turned toward the back room as she heard the traveler enter. The scrape of a bench. The faint clatter of metal on wood. *An armed wanderer. From the sound, likely a swordsman, blade at his side.* Her practiced hands picked up a small teapot, filled it with fresh water from the urn, and set it on the hearth.

It wasn't unusual for travelers to be openly armed in this part of Ionia. Indeed, an unarmed traveler would have signaled a potential for greater danger—hidden daggers, or a mage, or perhaps someone well protected enough not to need weapons themselves. Far more unusual was that the traveler was alone.

Once, long ago, the teahouse saw many guests passing through. But in the years following the Noxian invasion of Ionia, the paths that crossed near the teahouse saw fewer and fewer travelers. Caution and mistrust, as well as rising threats of bandits and aggressive factions that rose in reaction to the war, meant fewer folks who braved these particular roads. Yet in spite of this, Jing still opened the teahouse every season, steadfast in her devotion. Only time, care, and patience could restore the balance and broken trust.

And here was a lone traveler—though more likely an exception than a sign of restored tranquility. His voice sounded road-weary, yet he greeted Jing with the dialect of this region. Jing's hand hovered over the tea leaves. She passed over the traditional blend she served and opted instead for a white tea—primarily composed of the *Xaolan*, the gossamer flower, obscure to most but favored by the villages that dotted this part of Ionia.

The whisper of the wind. The crackle of the hearth. The whistle of the boiling water. She assembled the tea service quickly and returned back to the room, tray in one hand, cane in the other.

If it weren't for the traveler's faint breath, Jing would have thought he had left. Yet Jing sensed his meditative stillness, radiating a subtle, quiet calm. With a bit of focus, she could also *see* the faint outline of his spiritual presence. She crossed to him and set the tray down at his table. "Tea is served."

"Many thanks, O-ma."

The pouring of water. A fragrant bloom. Deep inhale. A surprised, then satisfied sigh. Jing smiled.

"The orchids bloomed early this year," she said, taking a seat at a nearby table.

"The Xaolan trees, too," the traveler replied.

So he does know the flower by name. Jing nodded. "Not quite the season when they are expected. An unannounced surprise."

"Unannounced arrivals can create quite a hassle," the traveler opined.

"Or bring unexpected delights." Jing held her cane in her lap. "Shifting winds often carry many treasures to the doorstep."

"Some strays bring no delight."

The traveler's words came as a muttered breath, steeped in far more bitterness than the tea. Jing raised an eyebrow at the acrid bite. The lingering aftertaste. The thin film of regret over his words.

"Hard for the petal in the wind to judge his part in the gale," she remarked.

The traveler said nothing.

Jing stood and stretched. "Ah! Please forgive an old woman for prattling on about nature. Could I get you some food, perhaps?"

"Is it just you here, O-ma?" the traveler asked.

The traveler's inquiry prickled Jing's sense of caution. But the words were spoken with kindness—and even more so than before, she felt certain she knew that voice. However, the memory still eluded her, an itch just out of her reach.

"My helpers are not set to arrive for another three days or so," she replied. "Technically, you're the first customer of the season."

"I am honored." Jing heard the smile in his words.

"The delight is all mine," Jing replied. "What winds are sweeping you through these roads? Returning home, or leaving?"

A brief pause. "Neither, I'm afraid." The levity evaporated from his voice. "A fool has no home."

Jing considered this for a moment. "How very dark and serious of you," she finally replied.

She heard the surprised stutter and flabbergasted chuckle that escaped the traveler and suppressed the satisfied grin that threatened to overtake her. "I think I will bring you some *kiwa* fruit. That always helped my son soak up all of that solemness whenever he got too melancholy."

Jing again walked toward the back room, leaving the traveler to his thoughts.

The quiet *tap, tap, tap* of her cane. Opening the cellar door. Down old, rickety stairs—pretending the creaking was all the wood and not at all her bones. Wrinkled hands found the kiwa tucked away in the cool. Fingers danced on the thick skin, ears listening for the hollow song of ripeness. Back up the stairs. A kitchen knife, slicing through. Peeling, cubing, as she had many times before.

The new voices reached her before she finished. Bawdy. Loud. Laughter, but empty of mirth. Jing wiped her hands on her apron. Carried the bowl of fruit back out.

Several others had joined the traveler. Well, *joined* perhaps was a strong word. They sat at a central table, a raucous bunch. Four, five voices. The dull clatter of weapons thrown carelessly down. An orchestrated performance meant to intimidate. Boots thudding on the table as their wearers leaned back in their seats.

The wind has indeed brought many strange and unexpected surprises today.

Jing headed to the traveler, setting down the fruit. His hand met hers as he took the bowl. "Thank you, O-ma—"

"Oy, oy! Can we get some service here or what?" A brutish woman's voice cut the traveler off.

"You're welcome," Jing replied, ignoring the interruption. "Anything else I could get for you—"

"You deaf, old woman?" the voice called out.

The room fell quiet. Clearly, the woman shouting led these newcomers—or at least spoke for them.

Jing continued to ignore her.

"Anything else?"

"… I am well, O-ma," the traveler replied. His voice was a spring, coiling with tension. Jing frowned. *May there be no need for it to find release.*

Finally, she turned and approached the rowdy newcomers. The *tap, tap, tap* of her cane punctuated the strained silence. She smiled as she reached their table. "Welcome, travelers."

"What you got to drink?" the leader's voice growled.

"At this teahouse, we have tea," Jing said.

The sound of spitting. "Nothin' stronger?"

"Black tea," Jing replied.

She swore she could *hear* the traveler smile behind her.

"Tea it is," the leader muttered.

Jing bowed slightly, then walked toward the back room. *Quite an unexpected day,* she thought.

When she returned, tea service in hand, the room was again quiet of voices. But the rustle of the newcomers gave them away—awkward scratches, adjustments of clothing, nervous sways, little coughs. Strained. Waiting.

Jing sighed, fairly certain of what was to come. At least it seemed the traveler had left—Jing no longer heard his breath from the far table.

Sure enough, as she approached, a sudden *pfft* sounded as one of the gang shifted a foot out to trip her. Jing stumbled forward before catching herself—but the teapot shifted on the tray, and she heard a few drops slosh onto the table.

Immediately, the figures leapt up. "You spilled hot tea on me, oaf," a young man's voice shouted. Jing suppressed the urge to roll her eyes at the performative anger.

"Careless fool," another said.

"My apologies," Jing said, with a slight bow of her head.

Jing heard the leader step in. Felt her lean close. Hot breath bearing down. "You hurt Bran," she said. "How are you going to repay that?"

Jing turned to face the leader, her face impassive. "This seems like a lot of effort to get one free pot of tea."

"Insolent relic," the leader snarled. Clatter as hands found weapons. A din as the group pressed closer. Jing's grip tightened on her cane.

"Insolence does indeed fill this house. But it does not pour forth from O-ma."

Jing turned, surprised. The traveler had *not* left. His voice rang out, clarion, from his seat. Yet Jing had not heard a single sound—nor felt his presence at all—just a moment ago. *A master of stillness. Who is this man?*

"This doesn't concern you, wanderer," the leader snarled. "Lest you wish to extend your stay here *permanently*, I encourage you to walk away."

Jing sighed again. She felt several gazes turn back on her. "You must be new at this, my child," she said to the woman. "To tell a wandering swordsman to walk away? All but guarantees he stays."

"She is not wrong." Amusement laced the tension in the traveler's voice.

"At the same time, I must agree with my other guests, young man," Jing said, turning to the traveler.

"Oh?" the traveler said.

A rough hand grasped Jing's shirt and pulled her around. "Oy! Don't ignore us," the leader fumed.

The metallic *shing* of drawn swords rang out around her. From the traveler's table, she heard a much softer *shhk*—a blade, loosened ever so slightly from its tie.

"One does not manage a teahouse by oneself this many years without seeing a few exciting days," Jing said, still turning her head toward the traveler. "If you stepped away, you'd be doing this old O-ma a favor."

"I said. Do. Not. Ignore me." Flecks of spittle flew across Jing's face as the leader snarled.

"Sorry, my child. You were saying?" Jing gave the woman a pleasant smile.

"New plan. You come with us." The leader turned to go, pulling Jing with her, the gang around her already moving toward the door.

But Jing did not budge.

The leader jerked back, unable to move

Jing. Jing heard her mutter in surprise. Felt the woman's grip adjust and tighten on her shirt. Felt a hand seize her arm. Felt the leader again try to pull her—and again fail to move.

"I'm so sorry, my child, but I cannot leave." Jing shook her head sadly. "You see... I am waiting for someone."

Other hands grasped her and pulled, muscles straining. Jing deepened her breath, focusing motes of spiritual power to her legs, strengthening her stance. She remained frozen, immovable against the grunts of effort.

"Cut her legs. He only said bring her back 'alive,' not 'well,'" panted the leader.

Two of the gang approached—and that's when Jing *felt*, almost before she heard, the traveler dash into motion.

A gust of wind cut through the crowd. Jing felt the breeze of the two thrusts slide deftly by her, followed by the delayed howls of their recipients. The metallic smell of blood washed over her. At the same time, Jing raised her cane, bringing it crashing against the three closest bodies to her, hard enough to hear bruising cracks and the snap of a fractured rib. She spun inward toward the traveler, her stance keeping her feet grounded on the floor, gliding in flowing arcs as her grip shifted on her cane to hold it as a short staff.

The maneuver took mere seconds but left the five attackers spread around the two in the middle, battered and bruised.

"Impressive swordplay. Unimpressive listening skills," Jing admonished.

She felt the traveler shrug. "Apologies, O-ma."

Before her, one of the gang let out a scream and charged. Jing scoffed—how undisciplined to give away his one advantage before his attack. She led with an easy parry using her cane, leveraged a gentle shift to send his momentum careening past, and followed through with a casual spin leading to a smack across his rear.

Behind her, she heard heavy strides as three of the others lunged toward the traveler. Jing listened as the traveler's footsteps pattered like rain. He danced between his foes, mobile in his stance, the song of his blade in constant flow as it glanced off their assailants' weapons and opened light grazes in flesh.

"Well, this is indeed an unexpected delight," Jing said as she blocked blows from two attackers.

"Do you often find joy in attempted kidnappings?" the traveler asked.

"Not every day an old lady gets to stretch her limbs," Jing said, "much less with such a natural with the blade."

"You honor me," the traveler said.

Jing brought her bamboo cane cracking across a kneecap and heard a foe fall with a stifled cry. "I haven't heard footwork such as yours in many a season," she remarked. "And your blade sings quite a unique song."

"I am but a humble student before O-ma," the traveler deferred.

"Quit prattling." The leader's voice cut through their conversation as her sword cut through the air with her lunge.

"Noisy storms rattle the shutters, demanding attention." Jing sidestepped, then followed on a feint with her cane.

"But gentle rains are more likely to inspire the poet seated inside."

"What does that even mean?" growled the leader as she swung her blade to parry. In the resultant opening, Jing shifted her stance inside the leader's reach.

"It means you're loud," Jing said, bringing her weapon down to rap the leader on the head. "And that you should consider being less loud," she concluded.

The woman stumbled back two steps, cursing. Jing leaned her weight back, shifting into an empty stance, cane held low. She listened to the soft groans around her. One would-be attacker moaned from the floor. Two more were scrabbling to their feet. The woman and the last attacker breathed heavily in front of her.

"I'm a little concerned, O-ma," the traveler said.

"Oh?"

"If they do not desist soon, I worry my blade will spill blood in your lovely teahouse." Jing heard the stranger's stance shift. Heard the steel in his voice. "My sword style is far less cordial than O-ma's staff; it seeks to end conversations, rather than extend them."

Jing nodded, impressed. From seeing a handful of exchanges, all while sparring with his own foes, this traveler had correctly identified the defensive nature of her style and strikes—then let her know his observation, while obfuscating it within a threat and warning to their opponents. *Who is this traveler?*

"Arrogant fool," the leader snarled. "We kill you first. Then we take her."

The leader muttered some brief incantation—and suddenly, the temperature in the room plummeted. At the same time, Jing heard the traveler adjust the grip on his weapon. *Whatever is happening isn't good.* Jing took a breath, centered inward, and opened her mind's eye.

Before her bloomed a range of vibrant colors as she peered into the spirit realm. Tendrils of spiritual energy tangled into every living thing, each pulsating with its own rhythm and flow. Next to her, the traveler blossomed into view, a wild swirl of focused power and harnessed wind. Jing's jaw clenched in recognition. *Of course. I'm a fool for not realizing it earlier.*

But it was her opponents that made her blood run cold.

The energy of the four remaining assailants turned light blue as their stances shifted. The spiritual energy from their forms extended through their swords, igniting their weapons with the soft glow of elemental frost. The four advanced, their feet never fully leaving the ground, their swords shifted to chest height.

Their stance. The formation they took. *That is* my *technique.*

"Who sent you?" Jing asked, already knowing the answer.

"Bao Lan requests your audience," the leader sneered.

Jing's grip on her staff tightened. "Tell my son if he wishes to see me, he must return home."

The leader laughed. Cruel. Mocking. "You will soon get to explain to him in person why you made this so difficult."

Jing sighed. "I see. My son has not returned, but his anger and his folly have."

The leader snarled at the insult. The four attacked.

Jing blocked the first strike with her cane. Immediately, ice formed and clung to her weapon. The second assailant struck for her exposed side, and though she twisted to evade, the aura of shocking cold robbed her of her breath. Beside her, she saw the other two press the traveler hard, swords shimmering with her frost technique.

They moved with her footwork—decent mastery, strong form—but the use of bladed weapons and the aggressive gambits of their strikes deviated from her teachings. Jing felt a bitter twinge in her chest. *How far have you meandered off the path, my son?*

Jing continued to parry and block, feeling her weapon grow heavier and slower as each strike sent more cold through her.

Beside her, Jing felt the traveler dodge and evade, clearly aware from the first parry that stopping blows with his blade slowly sapped his energy and heat. Her spiritual sight also revealed him drawing his own power, the wind surrounding him sharpening with every movement. *He's building toward something big,* Jing realized.

I better end this first, Jing thought. *Lest he cuts through half my teahouse.*

Breathing out, she dropped her spiritual sight. Breathing in, she drew upon her own magic. Spiraling out from her, ice crystals encrusted all surfaces at a miraculous pace. The temperature within the teahouse plummeted. With a spin, she gripped her cane with both hands near one end. She heard the assailants' frantic steps as they all charged her, trying to stop her from finishing her move.

Smart. But too slow.

Jing brought her cane down on the floor with force. *"Cease."*

From the epicenter of where her cane struck, sheets of ice burst forth with a roar, engulfing everyone and everything before her. Silence. Stillness.

Jing broke her cane free of the ice. She set it back down on the floor and leaned on it, catching her breath.

I am getting old, she thought. *That should not have winded me like it did.*

"I apologize, O-ma," the traveler said beside her. Jing took satisfaction in the slight chatter of teeth that accompanied his words. "I should have trusted you when you requested I leave," he said. "Clearly, you did not need my meddling."

"Only a fool would deign to make demands of where the wind would go," Jing's words broke short and curt.

An uncomfortable silence followed. The traveler started to respond—

But that was when Jing heard the ice crack.

She turned and flared her spirit sight  just as the ice before her shattered, shards exploding outward. Jing stared, shocked, as a blur of a blue aura dashed toward her, tinged black by a growing heart of shadow. The leader let out an inhuman, guttural growl, and Jing felt the sword tip pierce her abdomen, pouring biting cold into her body before she could even raise her cane.

"Hasagi!"

A whirlwind blasted her assailant back, sending a gale crashing against the ice. Frozen debris cascaded out the front door of the teahouse as the leader bounced once, twice on the ground, then finally lay still.

Jing raised a hand to her stomach and felt the wet of blood. She stumbled to one knee, her cane slipping from her other hand and clattering to the ground.

Immediately, the traveler swooped to her side. "O-ma, you are injured," he said, one hand under her arm, the other on her back.

Jing held up a hand. "I will be fine. The cut was not deep." She pulled away from the traveler's assistance, clutching her shirt to the wound to staunch the bleeding. She drew her other hand in a circular motion before her chest, coaxing the cold magic creeping through her veins out of her body.

"I was slow," the traveler said, voice tinged with concern. "I almost failed you."

Jing shook her head. "Always blaming yourself. You haven't changed one bit, Yasuo."

Jing heard the traveler straighten slowly to standing. "I suppose the wind technique gave me away."

Jing let loose a singular laugh. "I'm a bit embarrassed it took this long for me to identify Elder Souma's star pupil. Even after all these years, you're still quite famous in these parts." Jing released the pressure from her wound. It appeared the bleeding had almost stopped, though her shirt was surely ruined. *A pity,* she thought. *It was one of my favorites.*

With a practiced hand, Jing cast about and picked up her cane. Behind her, she heard a tense shift in Yasuo's stance, a soft clatter as he raised his sword.

"Oh, stop being so melodramatic. I'm not going to try to kill you," Jing said. She took her cane and tapped her way to a chair. "Besides, I've heard you've been acquitted. Exonerated. That a foreigner, an invader, was found guilty of his death."

"The guilt is still mine to bear. My negligence meant I was not there to protect him." Jing heard the raw pain in his voice. "I could have saved him."

Jing sighed. "How arrogant of you to assume so."

"I could have tried. I should have been there. And instead, he is dead. And the stranger who also bore the wind technique, whose weapon he shattered, now shoulders the guilt that I should have prevented."

"For a disciple of air, taught to dance light upon the empty breath, you sure are eager to take on all the heaviest burdens," Jing said. "So. Here you are. Yasuo. The brooding wanderer, haunted by guilt. The leaf blown in the wind. The 'fool with no home'. Will you continue running? Denying your birthplace?"

"Do you expect me to find peace, O-ma?" The gravel of anger edged into Yasuo's voice. "I cannot forget my actions. I cannot deny my past."

"I would not ask you to do either," Jing said. She took a deep breath. "I could not. I would be lying, Yasuo, if I told you that I harbor no resentment toward you. Elder Souma was a close, dear friend. I knew many of his students well. I knew your brother well." For the first time, Jing heard Yasuo's breath lose its calm. She shook her head, sadness gripping her heart. "But you cannot journey forward to atonement if you cling to your past failings."

Silence settled over the room. Jing stood and began shuffling toward the back room.

"What are you doing, O-ma?" Yasuo asked. Jing waved him off.

"Please. Call me Jing. If I hear O-ma one more time, I am in real danger of crumpling to dust before your very eyes," she said.

"Elder Jing," Yasuo began. Jing heaved a dramatic sigh. "… Jing," Yasuo amended.

Jing turned back toward him. "I'm grabbing my broom to start cleaning this mess." Jing gestured at her clothes. "Also, I need to change out of this shirt. I'm sure it looks just dreadful."

"You look fine," Yasuo said.

"You're terrible at lying," Jing said.

Yasuo walked toward Jing. "I could help," he offered. "With the cleaning."

"These are my responsibilities," Jing said. "Especially *them.*" Jing gestured out across the teahouse. "I'll need to thaw them out, wake them up, and send them back on their way."

"You're… letting them go?" Yasuo asked, incredulous.

"Well, not the one you cut with the wind,"

Jing said. "She seems fairly dead from the thousand slashes you administered."

"But they tried to kidnap you—"

"They are disciples of my son," Jing replied. "Misguided as he is. They all have lost their way."

Yasuo spoke, his voice hard. "Errant branches should be pruned, not nurtured."

Jing raised an eyebrow. "A surprising assessment from one many would call an errant branch." She continued speaking over Yasuo's protest. "I am the one responsible for my son walking away from the righteous path."

"You cannot blame yourself for the actions of your children," Yasuo said.

"Have you ever taken a pupil, Yasuo?" Jing's voice tensed for the first time.

"Not as formally as such, but… yes." Yasuo's reply came tentatively.

"If they strayed, would you not feel responsible? Would you not be responsible?"

Yasuo's silence was answer enough for Jing.

"Children. Students. We love them, even when they err. Perhaps most of all when they err." Jing's voice softened as she spoke. "My son has lost his way. The Noxian war… changed him. Broke his heart. Made him… *impatient.* And angry."

Jing tapped her way back to Yasuo and turned her face up toward his.

"I have failed him as his teacher—and as his mother. I waited for him to return home, hoping his broken heart would heal. But now, it is clear that I must find him. Speak with him. Remind him of the path to balance."

"He sent these brutes to take you. Do you not worry that when you meet again, he would be consumed by malice?"

"If we must first speak with staff and blade, then so be it." Jing patted Yasuo's shoulder. "But you shouldn't waste your energy worrying about an old woman such as me. You have your whole life ahead of you—and plenty of your own demons to contend with."

Jing turned her face toward the open teahouse door. Breathed in the scent of orchids. "These are uncertain times in Ionia. Self-reflection must be balanced with actions outside the self. Perhaps we both will find greater clarity within when we seek answers outside ourselves."

A breeze again set the bamboo clattering. Tentative birdsong slowly returned, breaking the silence that had followed the fight.

"I do not know where to go next," Yasuo said. Soft and underspoken, but Jing heard the heartbreak beneath.

"You are a man of strength who knows the meaning of loss," Jing said. "There are plenty of folks who lack both. Instead of drifting in the wind, perhaps you can harness it to lead you to those in need— wherever that may be." Jing lifted her cane and gave a light tap on Yasuo's forehead. "But for now, you should get out of my teahouse. I have much cleaning to do."

Jing listened as Yasuo stood and retied his blade to his side. "Thank you, Jing. And thank you for the tea. It was… nice to have a taste of home."

"Home is home," Jing replied. "No matter past trespasses, nor how far you may roam."

"I hope your son realizes that," Yasuo said.

Jing smiled, bittersweet. "I do as well."

NOXUS

Noxus is a powerful empire with a fearsome reputation. To those beyond its borders, it is brutal, expansionist, and threatening, yet those who look past its warlike exterior see an unusually inclusive society, where the strengths and talents of its people are respected and cultivated.

The Noxii were once fierce barbarian tribes, until they stormed the ancient city that now lies at the heart of their domain. Then, under threat from all sides, they aggressively took the fight to their enemies, pushing their borders outward with each passing year. This struggle for survival has made modern Noxians a deeply proud people who value strength above all—though that strength can manifest in many different forms.

Anyone can rise to a position of power and respect within Noxus if they display the necessary aptitude, regardless of social standing, background, homeland, or wealth. Those who are able to wield magic are held in particularly high esteem, and are actively sought out in order that their special talents may be honed and best harnessed for the benefit of the empire.

But in spite of this meritocratic ideal, the old noble houses still wield considerable power. Some fear that the greatest threat to Noxus comes not from its enemies, but from within.

Noxians respect strength above all things, and the only way to remain strong is to be constantly tested. They relish the opportunity to compete with one another, for fear of growing weak, and even those at the peak of power must always seek new ways to challenge themselves— or they will not remain in power for long.

It is not just physical or martial strength that Noxians admire—those who demonstrate expertise in politics, craftsmanship, and trading all help to create a stronger Noxus.

Noxus has one of the largest armies in the known world, composed of elite troops such as the Trifarian Legion, as well as hundreds of individual, localized warbands. Led by their own chieftains, marshals, and captains, each warband is unique, with its own culture and hierarchy. They fulfill specific roles as part of a much larger warhost, perhaps fighting as frontline shock troops, heavy infantry, scouts, assassins, or cavalry— whatever best suits their skills.

The most elite, respected, and battle-hardened military force within the Noxian empire, "the Legion" is led by the Hand of Noxus himself. The soldiers are not only the best, but also the most loyal, utterly devoted to the empire and its leaders.

OF STRENGTH

There is little uniformity in the rank and file of Noxian warhosts. The empire embraces a warrior's natural talents and specialities, rather than forcing them to conform to a particular way of waging war. This tends to carry across into all aspects of Noxian life, since they believe in discovering what you are good at, and finding a way to utilize it to make the empire stronger.

Grand General Jericho Swain established the council that currently governs Noxus, with each of its three members representing one of the vaunted Principles of Strength. Swain speaks for Vision, while Darius, the Hand of Noxus, embodies Might. Finally, a cloaked and anonymous individual represents Guile, keeping political opponents outside the council guessing as to their true identity.

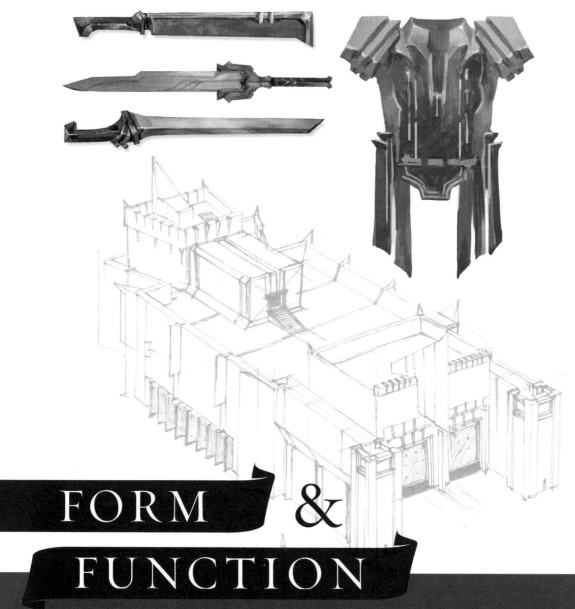

FORM & FUNCTION

IMPERIAL ARCHITECTURE

Noxian cities are characterized by imposing structures, claustrophobic streets, crenellated buildings, steep-sloped walls, and immense gateways. They emphasize the strength and dominance of the empire, and are highly defensible—an enemy attempting to take a Noxian city by force can expect to be fought and resisted at every turn, for even the humblest home is built like a fortress.

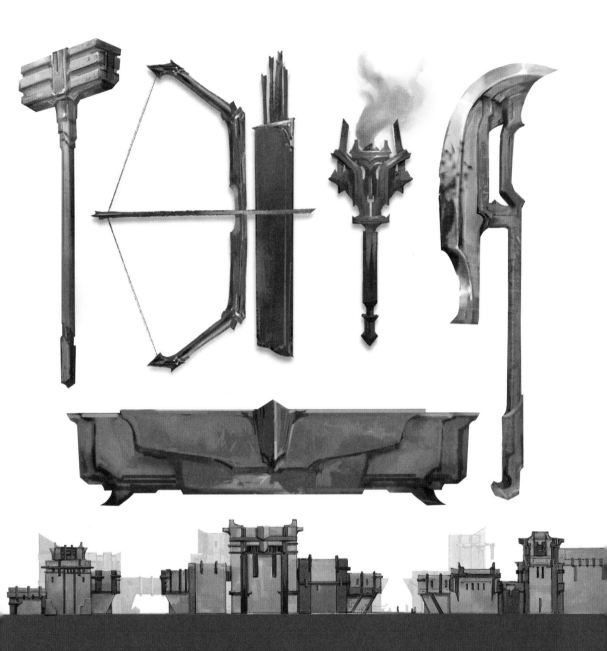

A CONQUEROR'S ARSENAL

The forges of Noxus never cool, churning out swords, axes, and armor in vast quantities for distribution to the warhosts. The empire values function over form, their designs often enabling additional uses, such as hooked handles to unhorse mounted enemies.

In recent years, Noxus has begun to experiment with crude black-powder weapons, and chemtech from Zaun—though the results are often as destructive to friend as they are to foe.

BUILDING AN EMPIRE

Noxus is aggressive and expansionist, always looking to widen its borders by conquering new lands. It does not always do so by violence—indeed, many are the nations that have taken the knee before the Grand General, seeing a chance for greater stability and security in joining the empire. Those who defy Noxus, however, are crushed without mercy.

WARMASONS

These resourceful individuals are scouts, engineers, and warriors all at once, who design and oversee the construction of roads, bridges, and fortifications. Often the first indication of Noxian expansion is not the sight of troops on the march, but a lone warmason surveying enemy territory for possible invasion routes.

NOXTORAA

Whenever Noxus is victorious, the warmasons immediately set to work stamping the empire's authority upon the newly acquired territory. Gateways of dark stone are raised on every road leading to or from the capital—and these towering structures leave approaching travelers in no doubt as to who holds the reins of power.

NOXIAN BASILISKS

onstrous reptiles from the jungles of eastern Shurima, basilisks are fierce predators that can grow to gargantuan sizes. Juveniles are prized riding beasts, and few can stand against their charge. After they become too large for a rider to control, they are put to use as beasts of burden, or sometimes as living battering rams to smash down the walls of besieged cities.

As Noxian armies conquer more and more of Runeterra, their capital city has sprawled far outside its battle-scarred walls. Old Noxus retains its forbidding character, but the structures beyond its original fortifications grow ever more varied, as the diverse peoples of the empire are drawn to the capital by the promise of wealth and glory.

CONSTANT UPHEAVAL

Due to the very real threat of political coups, assassinations, and sundry other intrigues, property and holdings change hands often within the capital. Since this gives the sense of nothing being permanent, it has given rise to a haphazard maze of new structures being built around—and on top of— the old.

THE

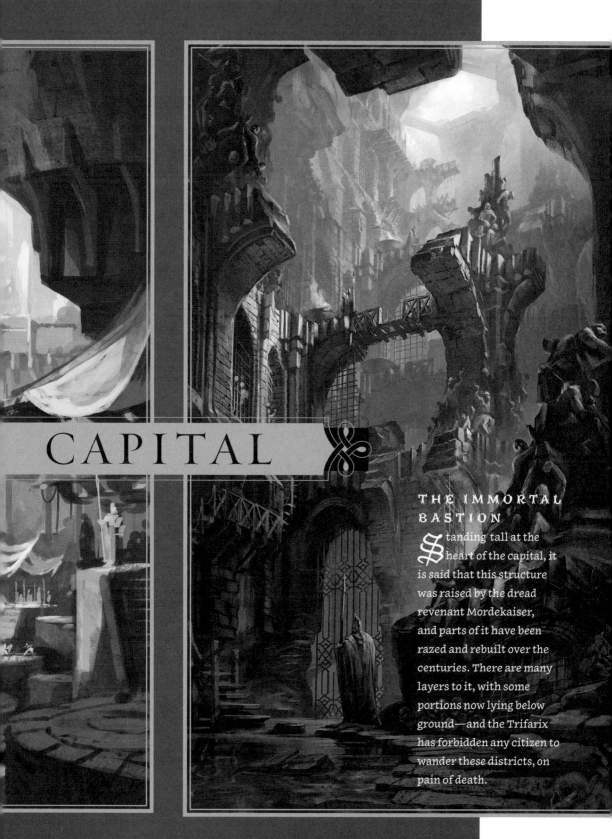

CAPITAL

THE IMMORTAL BASTION

Standing tall at the heart of the capital, it is said that this structure was raised by the dread revenant Mordekaiser, and parts of it have been razed and rebuilt over the centuries. There are many layers to it, with some portions now lying below ground—and the Trifarix has forbidden any citizen to wander these districts, on pain of death.

AS STONE

by DANIEL COUTS

Noxus arrived at Kimir's gates before the remains of its ragged army had time enough to bury their dead. Colm Onren, captain of the Kimiran guard, watched from the walls as two long, rectangular military tents went up on either side of their gates. In those short hours he could detect no fanfare, no celebration. Just an industrious bustle, ants building a colony.

"Fewer than I expected." Marsh Daya, his second-in-command, glowered at the sight. The morning frost hung loose around them, shrouding the nearby hills.

Colm rested rough hands against the battlements, wrought of fine stone. These walls had been hewn and laid by Kimir's progenitors, a reminder to both of them of their home's worth.

"Most of their warhost rode on to the next battlefield," Colm replied, watching as a pair of soldiers muscled out a trough large enough to water a dozen horses. He'd expected to have to invite Noxus in, to feed and house them as they negotiated terms. But this

army carried home on their backs and transformed the bare patch of ground outside the city gates into a safe harbor with unmatched speed.

"Pity," Marsh spat more than said. Colm hoped his companion's remarks were just that, but the darkness of bitter loss shadowed his words. The two men sat in silence for a while, staring down at the harbingers of empire.

Marsh erupted in caustic laughter. "Strength is all they respect. Perhaps we could—"

"We laid all our strength on the hills," Colm interrupted, "and it wasn't enough to keep the flood of Noxus at bay. The battle's over, Marsh."

Marsh, eyes narrowed, swept a hand over the stone wall. "Stayed free of 'em this long. Take this advantage and rout 'em, eh? If we show we're not afraid, maybe they'll give us the respect we deserve."

A lifetime spent in the quarries had taught Colm a simple lesson: you broke the stone, or the stone broke you. Noxus had crashed against Kimir like swell against shore; all that remained for the captain was to make sure at least some of Kimir wasn't washed away with the tide.

"No," Colm told Marsh. "Kimir has watched Noxus's border inch closer for decades. Terrain advantage and our willingness to trade generously kept us free this long. Now, we simply endure."

Marsh shifted and grew stony, defiant of the resignation in Colm's voice or afraid of that same future. Colm stood, stretched, and walked back to the stairs to meet his new masters.

⸻

By midmorning the fog had lifted, replaced by the melancholic languor of Kimir's soldiers, shuffling one by one toward the Noxian commander's tent. Colm stood at the gates, silently greeting each pair of eyes as they filtered into neat rows. He'd been their captain just long enough to feel a twin sense of duty and failure toward them all; acknowledgment was the least he could offer.

Marsh wandered out close to last, clustered with a group of career soldiers. For Kimir that was mostly trackers and trappers, their battles fought in skirmishes, each engagement a planned retreat. Colm felt a sudden chill at the strange light in his companion's eyes, the conspiratorial nod of a head. The group kept silent, but resentment stirred in the air at their passing. He settled in shoulder to shoulder with the others and waited to be judged.

The commander's tent flaps drew aside, and the Noxian warleader stepped forth, cheerfully inhaling the brisk morning air. She was dressed against the cold in a heavy, red fur-trimmed robe, and her head was shaved, except for a long ponytail flowing from the top of her skull. Age lined her face, green eyes adding warmth to a beaming grin. Her wide frame bounced with energy, limbs ever eager to spring into action.

The Noxians she passed straightened, whether with pride or fear, and even from a distance Colm felt her aura of control. She stood and faced the rows of Kimir's finest, all of them too tired to consider why they were here.

"They grow you folks big out here," she said, looking around those assembled with a bark of laughter. Ironic, since, tall as they were, most still had to look up at her.

Pride forced Colm's spine straight as he spoke, projecting his voice from the middle of the crowd. "Everyone who can drive a pick takes a shift mining stone from the quarry. Been that way for generations. Keeps us healthy."

She looked his way, and his throat tightened. He swallowed hard and resisted the urge to shrink down.

The commander nodded. "You'll excel on the front line."

Colm suppressed a growl. She moved toward the next candidate, but he raised an objecting hand.

"Our people aren't made for the front line," he said. What little chatter there was ceased as his voice rang out again. "We're sculptors and miners, not soldiers. Traps, terrain, disguise—these are our weapons."

She shouldered past the first line of Kimirans to stand closer to Colm than was comfortable, but there was play in her eyes as she spoke. "I know what kind of fighters you are. My people tell me you led yours in battle. Colm, is it?" The warleader's voice was cheerful and rough with use.

She looked him over, sharp eyes digging into every fiber, appraising his battle readiness. Colm sensed her measuring his shoulders, straight and heavy from years of wielding a quarryman's pick. His hands, grown steady beneath the watchful eye of a master sculptor. Gait, made stealthy by a childhood of adventurous tiptoeing along a quarry cliff's edge. *Just as I feared. All they see are soldiers for war.*

"Only briefly," he said with a nod. "I took command after our elder fell. Maybe five days ago."

A long moment passed, and she fixed her gaze to his own. Her next words were loud, chin raised. "It took our warmasons a good while to break through your defenses, rock breakers of Kimir. The resistance we saw these past days made our attacks as shovel against stone. Noxus cannot be resisted, but I am your witness: you defied as well as any!"

A thunderclap sounded on her last word—the work of each Noxian soldier, driving the butt of their spear into the ground in unison.

"Heh. Taught 'em that one myself," the commander said before clapping a hand on Colm's shoulder. She tightened her grip, and he saw a flash of something in her eyes—recognition, understanding, maybe. "Name's Hama. I'm your new warleader. And you're my new lieutenant." She released her grip and beckoned him forward. "Let's go. We're marching out soon, and there's much to put in order."

Kimir's founders had raised its long-hall many generations ago, not far from the quarry whose stone laid its foundation. Competition over herds with other tribes transformed into trade negotiations and border skirmishes. The stone lent the founders strength, walls, industry. They passed traditions to children, stories to families. From the quarry's wellspring, Kimirans developed a sense of self.

Colm could see that to the Noxian chief warmason, it was just a collection of rock.

"And you've yet to strike groundwater?" the warmason asked, voice high and eager. He was tall but reed-thin, and he abandoned warm clothes and armor for a simple tunic and a bandolier of tools, which hung loose around his chest and shoulders. His energetic aura was more than enough to stave off the cold wind blowing past them over the quarry's edge.

Kimir's oldest quarry was unequaled in the north. It was nestled between a trio of high foothills, the inverted ziggurat slowly biting into their height. From where Colm and the warmason stood atop one hill, they could see the mountains to the east, the forest to the north, and the city's walls just a short trek southwest.

"There's an aquifer nearby," Colm replied, pointing across the quarry to a grouping of wells on a hilltop. "We're careful. We've cut a few quarries further east—a few have flooded."

"Marvelous, marvelous. And you mine mostly...?"

"Soapstone, alabaster, clay, limestone, and slate. We've staked out a few spans of granite, but they're too close to the aquifer for us to safely mine."

"Pah! There's not a flaw in this whole pit. You've got the skill for it." The warmason knelt down and leaned over the quarry's side, running long fingers against the stone. He closed his eyes and took a deep breath, as though absorbing the quarry's knowledge. After a moment he stood. "We'll stop digging here. No need for soft rock—but a quarry of granite this far north will be quite the boon to the war effort!"

Colm shared neither his eagerness nor his laughter. "That soft rock is our livelihood; even Noxus buys our stonework."

"Well," the warmason said, eyes serious despite his laughter, "be sure to point out the best to me. Crafting the noxtoraa that mark our every road is an art of its own, and I can always use more skilled masons."

"I've seen your monuments," Colm replied. If the warmason felt the hard edge Colm put on that last word, he ignored it with the cold. "Tall, simple things. Our masons are *artists.* That work would waste them."

But the warmason was already moving, heading back toward the trail. "All the better! Such masons can turn artistry into industry and double the output of the uninspired. I've seen it done!"

A risky new quarry so close to the city, half his masons out crafting monuments to the empire. Colm frowned, but said nothing more as they began their descent back to the walls. *Is this Kimir's future?*

"What grows here?" A thin wooden pointer thrust toward the map neatly rolled out onto a table in Kimir's longhall. Colm stared at the document, his home etched in ink and smooth scrollwork. The map was accurate to the cobblestone, tight lines and neat script reducing locations to their defensive value and precise worth of stored resources. Colm wondered how long the Noxians had hidden a warmason here, passing as a merchant or traveler, while recording details for the time when Kimir would belong to the empire.

Colm regarded the pointer's wielder, a long-haired woman wearing a long leather coat—locally sewn, by its cut—with a traveling case stacked with documents and quills. Her eyes held a single-minded tension, poring over the map as an owl over a field, hunting for mice. Distrust stirred within Colm, more here than even on the battlefield, at this woman who held his shrunken home in a leather map case.

"Flowers," he responded after a minute's silence.

Her brow raised with interest, and she bent a little further over the map, her pushed-out chair long forgotten. "Medicine or spice?"

"We've cordoned off a few acres for medicine and herbs. Everything else is just flowers."

"Decorative?"

Trade with Noxus had always been its own sort of battle, fought with bluff and barter, need and scarcity. But here was a master, her trade not in meager coin or sacks of grain. Cities, walls, borders—these were her currency. With his city splayed naked on the table, Colm turned to knowledge, the last remaining weapon in his pillaged armory.

"Mostly we use them for dyes, but the flowers themselves can mean different things. It's difficult to grow them this far north, so they're coveted by our neighbors. My great-grandfather would tell everyone who listened of the time a well-placed bundle of blue stargazers won the war with the city of Morrin before it began." Colm had learned his passion for dyes from his father, and his own private garden was regarded with envy and awe. Or it had been, until he'd neglected it to go to war.

He pointed to several spots on the map and began explaining—where particular strains of flowers grew, how many generations it took to grow this color or that, which flowers produced dye that would hold its luster when painted on limestone, which on shale. He impressed upon the warmason the value of this knowledge to Kimir and to its trading partners. She listened without complaint, her fierce owl eyes absorbing all he had to say.

When he was finished, she drew a stick of chalk from her case and scrawled a note. "You're right to be proud," she said. "This is good land, quite rare this far north. We'll use it to grow medicine."

Colm's lips formed a thin line. "This has been our work for generations. It would take as long to teach others our craft."

"There are regions south of the capital where dyes grow in the wild. You'll import from them and grow medicine here, where it's easier to ship along our border."

Noxus should have used a chisel to carve its mark in the foundations of Kimir—instead, it wielded a mason's hammer, shearing valuable seams with each swing to get at the gemstones within.

"Changing this one part of Kimir will affect the rest," Colm said. "Noxus would gain more if you let us use our strengths as we have for so long."

The trader opened her leather case with a snap and expertly rolled the map back into its place. "You're part of the empire now. You are part of Noxus, and Noxus is part of you. I'll put to rest any work you do here that could be more cheaply done elsewhere. It will be to your city's benefit."

To your city's benefit. This had been the response to his offers of knowledge, suggestion, compromise. Marsh's words rang in his head. Perhaps Noxus felt it had nothing to gain from a defeated people. That their own strength bred unassailable

knowledge. He wanted nothing more than to resist, to abandon his attempts at cooperation and stand up. To say, *No, paper soldier. We'll grow dye as we always have, we'll celebrate our hard-earned spring growth as did all the generations before us. You can't put a price to this piece of our souls.* Colm could see only one way to make such a declaration, and that road led to more war.

If the trader witnessed any hint of this struggle, she took no pleasure in it. Colm stared a moment longer, then stalked from the hall.

Kimir's walls were not high, but the ground surrounding the city was uneven, so they seemed to tower as Colm led a group of his former soldiers down a pebble-strewn path along the city's eastern edge. Their graveyard was cut into a low valley just outside its ramparts, surrounded by statues of the past. His father's sculpture stood here, and so did that of Marsh's beloved wife. Before they marched, they would add new ones and bid their fallen farewell.

"So we teach the bastards all we know, give 'em our best cutters, our best stone, and dig where *they* tell us. What do we get out of it?" said Marsh, in step beside Colm.

Colm's laughter was helpless, unintentional. Where Marsh felt anger, he now felt only resignation. "To live, I guess."

Marsh laughed too, the bark deep and hot with violence. "To live as Noxians, fodder for their armies. Not enough, my friend. I want us to stand proud as Kimirans or not to stand at all."

"Trader says we won't need to sustain ourselves alone, that we'll benefit by being part of the empire."

Marsh snorted. "'Til what, we stop hunting food ourselves, too busy fighting another land's war?" The bigger man bent to scoop a handful of pebbles from the path and dashed them against the wall in frustration.

Colm had been turning the same idea in his head. "It's more than that. We've become their northern border. They'll have us turn our defenses toward the tribes of the Freljord, waiting for their marauders to test the weak spots in Noxus's crawling wall of expansion."

He, too, took a pebble from the ground, rolled it in his palm, its rough bevels smashed down to size by hammer rather than riverbed. "They'll take what they can learn from us, spread it across their empire, and put what's left of our home into their imperial coffers, another coin they may spend."

Colm imagined a future, not far from now, when Kimirans proudly declared themselves Noxians first, competed with one another to join their militaries and scrabble for rank and power. He didn't give voice to the deeper fear, the future fear.

What happens should Noxus fall?

A long silence followed, broken only by popped knuckles as Marsh clenched his fists. "You're too calm."

An accusation. A spark of his friend's anger nestled into Colm's heart. "What else can I be, Marsh? I've negotiated, I've explained all I can."

"If they wanted to trade, they would've traded! They marched, weapons loosed, because that's all they know. All they *respect!*" Marsh's shout echoed into the valley, scattering birds into the clear sky.

Funerary statues peeked into sight along the hill. Ahead, the path was flanked by dozens of Kimir's broadcloth-wrapped fallen. In front of those, piles of dirt straddled a long cut in the earth. A dozen Noxian troops toiled with shovels, digging a large, shallow hole. They looked up at the approaching Kimiran warriors, and Colm felt the spike of lethal tension drive its way into the valley.

"You Noxian curs," Marsh roared, his steps throwing pebbles into the air. "What do you think you're doing?"

One of the Noxians in the grave struck his shovel into the ground and leaned on it, squinting up at Colm's approaching band.

"Folks at the gate said your soldiers refused to leave before burying your dead." The Noxian gestured toward the shallow grave, and Colm saw it already contained several of his fallen. "We've got orders to take care of it so we can march. You're welcome."

Colm put up a hand toward his band, and they stopped behind him.

Marsh pushed past him nonetheless, making for the hammer looped threateningly at his hip. Colm jogged forward to catch his arm and pressed a hand against his friend's chest.

"This isn't the way," he said in a low voice, then turned to the Noxians, speaking up. "We need time to carve their likeness, and for their families to—"

"You are needed elsewhere now," the Noxian replied, his patience spent. "Warleader Hama granted you the time to organize your departure. If you're done with that..." He pulled up the shovel and offered it, and with a smirk jerked his head toward the bodies in the dirt.

The spark in Colm's heart turned to flame before even Marsh could react. He sent his old friend stumbling backward and grabbed the Noxian's collar, heaving him from the grave. In an instant, he was surrounded by red-clad Noxians, eyes dark. Colm slugged the shoveler with enough force to topple him into another. Hands reached for him, but a familiar howl rent the air and Marsh crashed to his side, leading the rest of his band into the fray.

It wasn't enough that they'd lost, that he'd shown the conquerors how to reshape the city to their tastes. He'd spent the day with the Noxians, helping them imagine their future while his people's own dwindled into twilight. Soon, their sculptures would be left to crumble to dust.

No more. Noxus values strength. I will show them strength.

He didn't know how long he had lost himself to violence when a series of guttural commands pierced the din of combat. As one, the Noxian soldiers retreated and reformed in a clean line at attention. Disrupted by this sudden beat, Colm, Marsh, and their band stumbled to their feet and clustered defensively. Several limped, sporting bruises and bloody faces. Hama and a group of fresh Noxian soldiers stood in a ring around them.

"I don't mind a little combat practice." The warleader's words remained playful but carried the edge of threat. Her eyes were bright. She turned to her own bloodied soldiers. "Locals teach you something new?"

Colm strode forward. Defiance still burned in his breast, and his narrowed eyes burned as bright as Hama's. "We'll not see our people dropped into a grave like this." He gestured at the jagged hole, at its promise of ignoble afterlife.

A short, sharp laugh, genuine despite its condescension. "Impossible. We're marching tonight. Leave it to your families, if need be."

"They fell with *us*," Colm replied. "*We* will see them off. That is our tradition."

"Tradition, huh? And you're willing to fight for it. Still." Her voice carried a distant note of something like nostalgia. Colm nodded, unblinking, and she met his gaze. "Good enough for me. Noxus has tradition, too, and you're one of us now."

Her grin widened. "I'll teach you what that means."

Hundreds of Kimirans lined the walls above the city gates, gazing down at the pair of command tents—at the spectacle

unfolding between them in the chill evening air. Colm and Hama, stripped bare
but for loose pants and bands of cloth
tightly wrapped around their upper bodies, stood facing each other in the cold.
Noxian and Kimiran soldiers alike stood
around them, forming a wide circle.

"This is your tradition?" Colm
called, his face as serious as Hama's was
relaxed.

Hama shrugged. "It's the opposite of
your burial rite. Acknowledge the dead,
bid them farewell. Here, we acknowledge life." She slapped a hand across
opposite shoulders, drawing the crowd's
attention. "First to push the other from
the ring wins. *When you lose*, remember
that you chose this fight."

Colm set himself into a wrestler's
stance. "Noxus's border came to greet
us. We did not seek it." He crouched into
position.

"Try not to look so serious!" Hama
called with a wild smile and crouched to
match him.

They stood, stone-still.

Colm breathed in the cold air, put the
battle at the graveyard from his mind. He
had lost hope for Kimir's future. Now he
would fight for its present one last time.
He charged at Hama with sudden ferocity.

The Noxian commander found the upper
hand immediately, driving a rigid palm
into Colm's hip. He turned to weaken the
blow, and her foot snagged around his calf.
Hama kicked up, forcing his leg from the
ground, and grabbed it with her free hand.

He gripped her shoulder, struggling to
stay upright, and the two locked in a
battle of strength, quarryman against
warleader.

"You think we're here to grind you
into the dust of history," Hama said,
tightening her grip under his knee.
Colm resisted the urge to cry out, doubling down on his efforts to shake her.
He kicked his leg up, earning a strike
against her ribs and a brief gasp of pain.
They stepped a breath away from one

"That's—" he began, but cut off as she strode forward.

"A fine strategy. Noxus respects strength," she said, raising her fists into a ring fighter's pose. Hama launched a series of jabs as he swatted her away with a heavy arm, giving himself more room. "The next warhost would be double the size of the one that defeated you. After that, triple. Noxtoraa already tower over roads right up to your gates. The plans to expand northward past your city have existed for years."

She landed a hook on his jaw, and Colm lost sight of her as his head snapped back. "You were conquered by Noxus long ago. I'm just here to show you that."

Colm's vision swam, making Hama's grin dance side to side in front of him. He had strength enough to lift and shape the earth. But he knew no pickax sharp enough to crack this iron empire or its iron ambassador.

"So we die, then." He slowly raised his fists in defiance. Resigned or proud, he could no longer tell.

Hama's smile at last became a sneer. "If you wish to die today and consign yourself and your home to oblivion, then so be it." Arms shot past Colm as the warleader stepped fully into him, absorbing his meager counterstrike and squeezing his whole upper body in a vise grip.

Her words were a whisper in his ear. "You cherish your burial rites, Colm. Do you wish to be buried?" He felt himself being lifted up and over Hama, and

another. "That choice is always up to the conquered."

"What choice? *Submit or die?*" Colm's words were obsidian-sharp, and he charged before she could respond. Hama brought her forearms up to resist his flurry of punches, then suddenly accepted one on the jaw and swept his legs out from under him. He hit the ground, and half a heartbeat later Hama's elbow spiked his stomach. He let out a gasping cough.

Hama's voice was soft, carrying none of the rigor of combat. "You and your friend saw an opening. You rose against my warband. You rebelled to reclaim your home." She dug her elbow further into his gut, then abruptly rose and stepped away from him. He stood, gulping breaths, as she straightened over him.

sensation turned to light as an explosion at his back stole his senses.

Years could've passed between one breath and the next. By the time he coughed back to life, he was being dragged by the arm toward the circle's edge. "Those too proud or rigid to change are forgotten."

Her words washed over him. Noxus built itself, each day, for war. While Colm's mother had taught him to swing a pick, his father to carve a relief, Hama learned to swing a blade, to scatter a line. The Noxians carried war on their backs, set it at their table with bread and meat. To defeat something like that, any who opposed them would have to give all of themselves.

Colm was born of stone, of the very bedrock of the world. He closed his eyes, let Hama drag him another step. He pulled against her grip—she tightened it, and he smiled a victor's smile. He turned with all his strength, wrenching his captured arm from its socket, dug his toes into the earth, and drove beneath the warleader's bulk. He pushed, bracing to pile her across his shattered shoulder and throw her from the ring.

But if Colm was stone, Hama was the ocean. He drove forward without gaining an inch, his roar of effort turned to unbearable pain. Hama brought a fist down into his spine, and he scrambled backward, hunched, arm hanging limp from his heaving frame. Hama's lined face creased into satisfaction, cold eyes alight.

She gave him a solemn nod. Viper-quick, an uppercut forced his body straight, and a heel drove into his stomach, launching him from the ring.

A deep quiet filled the evening air, the stillness of earth after quake. Colm dropped to a knee, eyes closed tight against the agony of his ruined shoulder, of reality. He wouldn't drive a pick again.

"You're not much of a fighter," Hama said, not caring to suppress her mirth as she crossed to tower over him. Colm squinted against her presence. "But you asked for a fight and gave yourself to it. The best of yourself, judging by the twist in your shoulder. I respect that."

She stuck a hand beneath his good arm and pulled him to his feet. He cried out as a starburst of pain clouded his vision. But Colm would not bow his head. Not while his people watched. He took a deep breath and met those cold eyes.

"We will *serve*, warleader. We will watch as Kimir crumbles into dust, replaced by a Noxian warpost."

Hama's laughter was a sharp clap in the still air. "Some of you will serve," she said, nodding toward Marsh and his followers, who were fuming in angry silence that seemed likely to break sooner than later. "But you, Colm? You're no soldier. You made yourself into one because Noxus came to your doorstep. Because your people needed you to be one. Now they need a leader."

Colm looked to Marsh. Colm's own anger, the furious beat of his heart, his clenching fist, had dissipated. He'd thought Kimir shattered by Noxus. He fought to shelter its broken pieces from being lost forever. But water didn't shatter stone; it shaped it, wore it smooth, carved furrows and troughs. Kimir was not broken, it was simply swept up in the currents of history. Colm could guide that flow, could shape its course. He looked back to Hama, her gaze appraising, as if waiting for the pledge he was about to force from himself.

"I'm no soldier. And Kimir is no warpost," Colm said, his breath steadying against the weight of his words. "Kimir can offer much. But it stands as stone, and its silent, hard edges will resist." He kept Hama's eye as he gripped the bicep of his shattered arm, ignoring the surge of pain as he raised an outstretched hand.

"Let me be your chisel, and Kimir will serve Noxus to its fullest."

Whatever secret hopes Kimir's people held as they stood atop its walls this day, that perhaps their leader would find a way to resist, to expel Noxus, to dam the flood, were dashed with Colm's offer of fealty. Mere moments after Marsh and his soldiers had been promised rebellion, here was Colm embracing defeat. Perhaps they would struggle with his decision, the way they had struggled against Noxus. But *that* was a fight he was prepared to win.

Hama regarded his offered hand for a brief eternity. Colm didn't let his gaze waver, allowed her to savor the result of her lesson. Finally, she grasped his arm

with hers, crushing strength sending waves of shooting pain across his shoulder, as she pushed his shoulder back into place. But she grinned, and he returned the expression through tears streaking his dusty face.

"You are a fine leader for your people, Colm of Kimir."

The warleader took a step back, and her soldiers stood to attention.

"Take the night. Bury your fallen. In the morning, send me a warband with fighters—real fighters—on the double. Give me your best, and I will teach them war."

She stepped back from Colm. "Lead. And make Kimir strong. For Noxus and for your people." With a final thunderclap of staves against stone, Hama and her troops departed for their tents.

The quarrymen's song carried into the morning air, their rich voices mixing with the crunch and heave of the day's work. Apprentices pushed carts of debris, stone, and dirt up and out of the way while the hearty men and women of Kimir put pick to stone all around the nascent quarry's first level.

Colm stood in a row with two others, pick in hand, looking thoughtfully over a rectangular chalk outline. He rolled his shoulder—it had healed well, but the sting had never quite left him. The other two took a nervous step back. Colm lifted the pick into the air and, with his whole body, twisted and crashed it against the stone, right along the chalk border.

Layers of cobble and lime fell away with the strike, revealing the telltale mottling of granite. His two companions clapped, and Colm couldn't hide a grin, though he kept in a sigh of relief that he hadn't been sprayed with water.

"And here we all thought your mining days were behind you," a voice called, rough as earth. Colm turned to see his general, Marsh, red cloak and graying beard making him almost unrecognizable. "They kick you outta the elder's chair already?"

"If only," Colm said, eyes bright. He passed his pick to his companions and held out a dusty hand, which Marsh gripped easily. "A few more days locked up with those Noxian architects, and I would've torn the place down."

Marsh grunted appreciatively and pulled his old friend into a crushing bear hug. Both men laughed.

They strode up the slope toward the quarry's entrance. The pair stood apart from the bustle and noise, looking out toward the hillside.

"How're things at home?" Marsh asked.

"Found our third source of granite. Might need to double the caravans coming in from the south and, with that, find folk to ride alongside."

Marsh nodded. "Had the chance to put up one of your noxtoraa. Hama wanted me to pass on her compliments. Says the arches are better off with a little imagery on 'em."

Colm paused, almost imperceptibly.

"Right," he said. "Give me the news."

Marsh reached into a pouch at his side and produced a sky-bright silver pin, worked into the shape of an eagle, and a tattered wreath of twine and blue petals. "Morrin surrendered. Took a hell of a fight."

Colm nodded. Their neighbors were as proud as Kimir, prouder maybe. For all their rivalry, they'd always been allies against the threat of Noxus. "And Elder Mati?"

Marsh was quiet.

Colm cast his eyes downward. "Ah."

"Made it quick. Took his best into my warband. We'll treat the town well enough. Host of folk on their way here now."

"What for?"

"Hama called 'em slow learners."

"So we show them how to be useful members of the empire."

Marsh nodded.

Colm looked out toward the sloping hill, covered in statues of the past, rising up to meet Kimir's wall. Beyond the wall he could see their flowering acres, blue stargazers in full bloom.

"They're Noxians now. I'll teach them what that means."

TIMELINE OF RUNETERRA

With territories spread across Runeterra, the empire of Noxus has united and assimilated countless smaller nations over the course of centuries. Aside from its obvious military strength and stable, central governance, Noxus takes great pride in "bringing the calendar" to every corner of the globe—indeed, it is difficult to imagine a more pleasant euphemism for martial conquest.

But to be Noxian is to subscribe to their notion of the world's history, which begins long before the Rune Wars that gave rise to the empire. Since many historical records were lost in those dark times, the precise details of anything earlier are likely based on conjecture, or popular myth.

-9000
THE FIRST LANDS
Across the island continent now known as Ionia, a great war raged between mortals and a race of sky-giants. Only by the intervention of the Vastayashai'rei—legendary beings of immense power, existing in both the material and spirit realms simultaneously—was victory eventually won.

-8000
WAR OF THE THREE SISTERS
After they defeated the old gods of the north, a feud developed between the sisters Avarosa, Serylda, and Lissandra, and quickly escalated into open conflict. The final battle was fought at the gates of Lissandra's citadel, where she sacrificed many allies to entomb her enemies in True Ice.

-6000
A WESTWARD MIGRATION
Bringing all their ancient knowledge and wisdom with them, settlers from the forgotten lands of the distant east reached the shores of Shurima and Valoran. In time, their descendants would come to rule some of the greatest civilizations Runeterra has ever known.

-5000
THE RISE OF THE GOD-WARRIORS
Guided by the divine Aspects of Targon in preparation for some unknown future war, the ancient Shurimans used the Sun Disc at Nerimazeth to create the first Ascended. These noble beings were worshipped as living gods, and the empire they forged would endure for millennia.

-2500

ICATHIA REBELS AGAINST SHURIMA

In a desperate bid to secede from the tyranny of the empire, Icathia unleashed the Void in battle. Their own capital city was instantly destroyed, the land tainted and corrupted beyond all recognition. Even the mighty Ascended Host could do little to combat this horror, and Shurima was forced to abandon Icathia for good.

-2000

AZIR'S FAILED ASCENSION

Denied godhood by a base act of treachery, the last Shuriman emperor, Azir, was lost, along with the Sun Disc itself. The people, filled with fear and sorrow, looked to the remaining Ascended to protect them.

-550

THE GREAT DARKIN WAR

Bereft of purpose, and scarred by what they had endured in facing the Void, many of the Ascended became twisted in body and mind, naming themselves "Darkin" and raising hordes of mortal warriors to conquer the world. Eventually, the Aspects who had inspired their creation were forced to intervene, imprisoning the Darkin within their own accursed weapons.

-400

REIGN OF THE IRON REVENANT

Deceiving the mages who had resurrected him, the warlord Sahn-Uzal was reborn as Mordekaiser, and set about conquering the material realm from his Immortal Bastion. Though it took almost three centuries, he was eventually defeated by an alliance of the Noxii tribes, who inherited the empire he had built.

-25

THE RUINATION

A terrible accident occurred in the arcane vaults beneath the city of Helia, hidden away on the Blessed Isles. With the barrier between the material and spirit realms shattered, the souls of the dead were trapped in eternal torment within the coiling Black Mist, and the newly dubbed Shadow Isles were abandoned by all right-thinking mortals.

-13

THE RUNE WARS

With Helia lost, dangerous magical artifacts soon began to find their way into the wrong hands. On the fields outside Khom, the renowned mage Tyrus and his apprentice Ryze witnessed the first devastating attack in the Rune Wars—a sight that would haunt Ryze's nightmares for the rest of his unnaturally long life.

0

NOXUS ENDURES

The Rune Wars escalated across most of the known world. After a decade of almost apocalyptic battle, the last of the Noxii were forced to retreat inside the Immortal Bastion for shelter from the magical fallout. When they finally emerged, the land beyond had been ravaged, but they survived. They were alloyed as a single people, no longer Noxii but Noxus, and have marked their calendar from this date ever since.

292

THE DEMACIAN CROWN

Far to the west, the nation founded by the great champion Orlon crowned its first king. Originally settled by refugees from the Rune Wars, it was declared that Demacia would be a sanctuary from magic, now and forevermore.

349

NOXUS BECOMES AN IMPERIAL POWER

After a series of forced annexations and the fall of the Drakkengate, the strength of Noxus grew to match its ambitions. The noble houses swore, though it might take a thousand years, to unify all the nations of Runeterra beneath a single banner, and elected a Grand General to lead their warhosts to victory.

772

TRAGEDY ON THE RIVER PILT

Merchant clans controlling the trade routes between Valoran and Shurima accelerated construction of vast accessways and conveyors—however, excavations for these "Sun Gates" undermined the ancient port of Zaun, plunging whole portions of the city into the lightless caverns beneath.

787

BILGEWATER

With more and more bedraggled fortune seekers washing up on their shores, missionaries from the Buhru granted these *paylangi* outsiders refuge in the southern island bays. While there were many years of cultural confusion—even including the name of the Serpent Isles—this settlement would eventually grow into a bustling port city in its own right.

984

THE INVASION OF IONIA

Following many years of scouting and preparation, Grand General Boram Darkwill ordered a large-scale occupation of Ionia by Noxian forces. Though initially met with little resistance, the warhosts' brutal advance across the provinces soon gave rise to fierce retaliation from various Ionian militias, which became more organized after the infamous Battle of the Placidium.

989

JERICHO SWAIN SEIZES NOXUS

In spite of his dishonorable discharge from the military, former General Swain enacted a coup within the Noxian capital, deposing and killing Boram Darkwill. In less than a year, Swain had ended the occupation of Ionia, vastly reduced the influence of the noble houses, and established the Trifarix council to govern the empire.

DEMACIA

Demacia is a strong, lawful kingdom with a prestigious military history. Its people value the ideals of justice, honor, and duty most highly, and are fiercely proud of their cultural heritage.

Founded as a refuge from sorcery after the nightmare of the Rune Wars, this largely self-sufficient nation was built upon the riddle of petricite—a peculiar white stone that dampens magical energy. From the capital, known to all as the Great City of Demacia, the royal family and attendant nobles see to the protection of the rich and fertile land.

In spite of all this, Demacia has become increasingly insular and isolationist in recent centuries. Indeed, those who dwell beyond the heavily guarded borders are often viewed with suspicion at best, and many former allies have begun to look elsewhere for protection.

Some dare to whisper that the golden age of Demacia has passed, and unless its people are willing to adapt to a changing world—something many believe they are simply incapable of doing—that the kingdom's decline is inevitable. And all the petricite in the land will not protect Demacia from itself.

CARVED IN STONE

THE GRAND PLAZA

This wide, open space lies at the heart of the Great City, and frequently welcomes crowds gathered to applaud those honored by the crown.

THE PALACE GARDENS

A favorite of the late queen, Lady Catherine, these well-maintained and orderly gardens allow for moments of quiet reflection.

THE CITADEL OF DAWN

The royal family of Demacia resides in the Citadel of Dawn, a palace whose majestic design is said to reflect the splendor of the ruling Lightshield dynasty.

1. The Last Gate
2. Military district
3. Noble family residences
4. King's Rock
5. The Mageseeker compound
6. The Grand Plaza
7. Silverwing aviaries
8. Sepulchral halls
9. Harbor

OUR PEOPLE REPORT GOOD PROGRESS BEING MADE IN ALDERBURG.

TEMPLE OF THE LIGHTBRINGERS

One of the oldest structures in the capital, this temple honors the legend of the Winged Protectors—embodying the Demacian ideals of duty, honor, and tradition.

SWORD AND SHIELD

The smallest formation of Demacian soldiers is called a Shield. The warriors in each Shield are armed and armored almost identically. Battalions are composed of differently armed companies of Shields, and will often have units of specialists seconded to their command element—such as scouts, raptor riders, or duelists. The most prestigious battalion is undoubtedly the Dauntless Vanguard. At full strength, it numbers over two thousand soldiers—currently, it is led by Garen, nephew of the High Marshal Tianna Crownguard.

While vastly outnumbered compared to the many warbands of Noxus or the combined tribes of the Freljord, the prowess of Demacia's military is renowned across Valoran, and its disciplined culture informs much of daily domestic life in the kingdom. From a simple shield-sergeant to decorated sword-captain, officers are expected to lead from the front, by example, and their warriors to follow with unwavering loyalty.

DEMACIAN STEEL

Sometimes referred to as silver steel or rune-steel, this alloy is highly regarded across Runeterra. It is rumored that Demacian armorers quench the metal in blessed waters, to offer protection from magic in battle.

JARVAN IV

As the king's only son, Prince Jarvan is heir apparent to the throne of Demacia. Raised to be a paragon of his nation's greatest virtues, he is forced to balance the heavy expectations placed upon him with his own desire to prove himself on the battlefield. An exceptional warrior in his own right, Jarvan also inspires his troops with fearsome courage and selfless determination, raising his family's colors high and revealing his true strength as a future leader of his people.

GAREN CROWNGUARD

Though born into the noble Crownguard family, Garen earned his place in the shieldwall through courage and skill. When the previous sword-captain of the Dauntless Vanguard fell in battle, Garen found himself put forward for command by his fellow warriors, and the nomination was unopposed. To this day, he stands resolute in the defense of his homeland, against all foes. Far more than Demacia's most formidable soldier, he exemplifies all the most noble ideals upon which it was founded.

THE MYTHS OF MAGIC

Demacia has always had a complicated relationship with mages. One of their oldest myths, the cautionary tale of the Winged Protectors, tells of the founding of Demacia—over the centuries, it drove the creation of the kingdom's laws and values, but also caused many to fear the unpredictable power of magic. More recently, the infamous Mageseeker order has been tasked with suppressing all knowledge and practice of sorcery.

HIDDEN IN PLAIN SIGHT

In the past, objects of warding or focus for magical power were often disguised in various ways, to avoid the attentions of the Mageseekers. In time, the true purpose of these objects may even have been forgotten, since they were handed down as innocuous family heirlooms, such as canes, staves, or scepters.

THE VEILED LADY

Another enduring myth is that of the Veiled Lady—a pariah whose dark outbursts and preaching of redemption led to her exile. Even so, some Demacians still create totems to her memory when seeking guidance on matters of family and forgiveness.

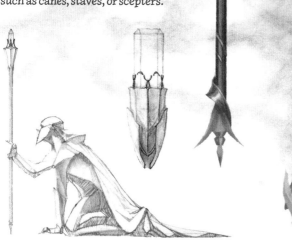

All this talk of swords and wings... why isn't they talk of cruelty this...?

II - The Coming of the Twins

Born beneath the vault of stars,
one in Light, one in Shadow.
Kayle and Morgana,
Sisters by Fate, joined hand in hand.
To Demacia's fair lands they came.
A land untouched,
 a kingdom yet to be.
Though magic raged across the world,
it broke upon her wooded shores.
A Haven amid the Raging Storm.

XIV - Coda

Of Morgana, only myth remains.
Veiled secrets and hidden shadows.
Yet the legacy of Kayle burns bright,
in all our hearts and minds.
The wind whispers of her return.
When Targon's beacon shines anew,
and night falls on the world,
look to the south on that day.
And pray for all Demacia.

—Excerpts from
*The Canticle
of the Winged
Sisters*, an epic
poem held in
the Crownguard
family library,
High Silvermere

PRECIOUS GEMS

Some primal, elemental magic made its way into early Demacian hands in the form of precious gems. These were fashioned into jewelry such as pendants, brooches… and even crowns.

Petricite is not infallible. When magic is not nullified properly by the stone, it can cause it to flake and torque most unnaturally.

WINGED PROTECTION

Wings and feathers are almost as common in Demacian art and architecture as swords and shields. While they recall the aspirational ideals of freedom and transcendence, they also highlight the kingdom's connection to the Silverwing raptors—some of the most impressive hunters found anywhere in Valoran.

BIRDS OF PREY

Native to the high crags of the Demacian mountains, raptors are rare and voracious predators known to attack lone farmers, and occasionally even armed convoys of soldiers. Nevertheless, particularly exceptional individuals have made an art of building rapport with these noble beasts, forging such a bond that the raptor may permit itself to be ridden. These riders serve in the Demacian military, scouting ahead or harassing the enemy advance.

RAISED TO SOAR

Silverwings hatch from the egg with yellow and light blue feathers, only gaining their signature silvery hue—and deadly attack speed—as they reach maturity.

QUINN & VALOR

Sponsored by the noble Buvelle family, Quinn is a ranger-knight of Demacia who undertakes dangerous missions deep in enemy territory. She and her legendary eagle, Valor, share an unbreakable bond, and their foes are often slain before they realize they are fighting not one, but two of the kingdom's greatest heroes. Nimble and acrobatic when required, Quinn takes aim with her crossbow while Valor marks their elusive targets from above, making them a deadly pair on the battlefield.

HONOR & TRADITION

Every Demacian child knows the expectations and responsibilities placed upon them. No matter how humble, Demacians consider it their duty to help strangers as well as family, and to demonstrate courage, respect, justice, and mercy in all things.

Since mighty Orlon led refugees from the Rune Wars to the land that would one day become Demacia, its people have held to the values that brought them safety and prosperity in those earliest days.

KING'S GAMBIT

Far from being the humorless, duty-obsessed bores that outsiders sometimes mistake them for, Demacians dance, sing, and play as often and as enthusiastically as anyone else. One especially popular game, played by families, comrades, and new friends alike, is King's Gambit.

A variant of the ubiquitous tellstones, King's Gambit is considered a duel of minds, where each player tries to commit the movements of the stones to memory while also trying to confuse and outwit their opponent.

THE WEIGHT OF EXPECTATIONS

by AMANDA JEFFREY

Cithria hacked at the ground with the mattock, her shoulders burning with the exertion. The ground was heavy with clay and resisted her efforts to dig out the trench surrounding the camp. She'd been awake since two bells before dawn, and her whole world had narrowed to the tool, the dirt, and the ditch. She scraped the now-loosened earth to the ditch wall and almost jumped out of her skin when her universe of dirt and iron was invaded by a pair of boots.

"Good work, recruit. Durand couldn't do better." The voice seemed unfamiliar for a blink. Cithria looked up to see the boots were attached to Proctor-Corporal Pell, the officer overseeing her testing for the Dauntless Vanguard. In the dust and evening light, her gold armor and halo looked beautiful—a broad-shouldered guardian with an offset nose and enormous grin.

Or I'm so tired I'm hallucinating.

"It's no East Wall." Cithria's mouth felt gritty and dry after hours of silent work.

Beyond, fresh shifts of soldiers were digging the rest of the trench, but Cithria had been here, with scant rests, all day.

"Come on. Leave the rest to the regulars," said Pell. "You still have sunset watch after this—time to eat before then." Pell vaulted out of the ditch and held out a hand. Cithria took it gladly and let Pell pull her up, long past caring that her stinging red hands were covered in clay. She was about to start walking back into the camp when Pell caught her shoulder and shook her head.

Oh. She'd forgotten her pack.

Cithria reached down for her backpack and, without even the energy to resent it, hauled it on her back. Inside were simply rocks, but recently the pack had been her constant companion as much as Corporal Pell had been.

Every time in the last two weeks when Pell had ordered that she march, walk, or run, through mud and rain and worse, the testing required that she bore half her own weight on her back. Weighed down like that, Cithria and her fellow aspirants had endured meltwater river crossings, unannounced night runs, and retreats across "enemy" territory with the much larger Pell posing as an injured comrade on an improvised litter.

Each rock had been signed by a soldier in the Ninth Battalion— each one a friend and former comrade of hers. That first week, she'd fantasized about "losing" one or two, but seeing their names there, knowing the Demacians they represented... they felt a little lighter after that.

But not a *lot* lighter.

Her trials had magnified since then, but if she could make it—if she could become one of the legendary Dauntless Vanguard, well, her heart ached when she thought about how *proud* her family would be.

Pell strode forward, and Cithria followed obediently. They stepped aside to allow a surveyor and a column of soldiers carrying gateposts past. When Cithria first signed up to become a soldier, she found the commotion of army camps over-whelming, but now it filled her with pride. Hardworking Demacians with clear goals and a shared vision of this tiny pocket of a safer, more orderly Demacia—a haven against the dark.

As they reached the messfield, Cithria saw soldiers dunking hunks of fresh bread into bowls of steaming hot stew handed out by boisterous war chefs. The smells were intoxicating, and Cithria's stomach raged, but Pell wasn't slowing down. Cithria locked her eyes forward and followed—how could she prevail in battle as a Vanguard if *stew* could threaten her focus?

Pell pointed out a Vanguard standing next to a crowd of soldiers. "Eyes up, recruit. The fellow over there is called Bunder. Knowing him, there's a stones tournament in play already."

Cithria could see two players sitting around a table at the center of the commotion. *Huh. So even Demacia's finest enjoy a game of tellstones.*

The Corporal gave Cithria a sideways look. "Are you any good?"

Cithria thought back to countless games played with her father, how she'd practiced and practiced until he had confessed he'd stopped letting her win a long time ago. She'd been known as the one to beat in her last squad with the Ninth.

"I do all right."

Cithria finally got her bowl of rich, dark stew and immediately burnt her tongue trying to spoon it into her mouth.

"Easy, recruit. Sit down to eat, at least." Cithria must have looked skeptical, so Pell reassured her. "I swear, I'll not interrupt your supper."

Cithria fought the impulse to wolf down the entire portion. While Pell had put her through near-constant hardship these last two weeks, she'd never lied to her. Maybe faith in her comrades was part of the testing too.

With as much restraint as she could muster, she put her spoon down and instead filled a flask with water before heading toward a log bench. Nearby, a raucous game of tellstones was just finishing around a makeshift table fashioned from a tree stump—one of the war chefs was winning at two points to one against a raptor-scout. The other cooks were making faces and clanging pans to try to distract the lean salt and pepper–haired rider. She sat poised, missing nothing despite their bluster. Cithria noticed the scout's lips faintly moving as she silently recited the order of the stones to herself.

"What do you think, folks? Time for a little peek?" the young chef called.

"Peek, peek, peek," the crowd chanted back.

With great pantomime, he picked up a stone and showed it to those standing behind him, feigning shock. Cithria caught a glimpse, and her heart sank for the scout—she was repeating the wrong sequence of stone names. The match didn't last very long after that. Cithria hid her disappointment behind mouthfuls of dinner.

Two new players took a seat at the center of the crowd. Bunder, the Dauntless Vanguard from Pell's squad, was a lanky young man with mousy hair. He had challenged another Vanguard soldier with wiry muscles and a scar on her cheek. A new game started, but this was not the tellstones Cithria was used to—the two opponents stared silently at each other with an intensity Cithria had never seen. The crowd around them was growing much larger and mirrored their silence. It took a moment before Cithria even realized the game had begun.

Without a word, the two soldiers broke eye contact to flick their gaze down at the stones, silently prompting their opponent to carry out the game's moves. It was faster than any match she'd ever seen, and it didn't seem to follow the rules she was used to. Pieces were added, moved, flipped, and identified without words. Startlingly, the scarred woman rapped the top of the tree stump once, looking up to stare coolly into Bunder's brown eyes. He breathed the name of the stone while simultaneously revealing it.

Cithria realized she'd stopped eating, holding her spoon halfway to her mouth in awe. Convinced she'd shatter the players' concentration if she put the spoon back in the bowl, she silently took the mouthful of cold stew.

Back and forth. Knock and whispered response. Expressionless and blindingly fast.

The woman's knuckles rapped twice on the log.

Nothing happened.

The players' stares froze. There

were no glances, no movement of stones. Cithria tried to see what they saw, but not a muscle moved. Still as petricite statues.

Finally Bunder stood, face flushed with what seemed to be sudden fury, before breaking into an enormous grin. The crowd cheered, and both received slaps on the back in celebration. Bunder laughed and slowly applauded his now smiling opponent, the apparent winner of the match.

Pell appeared behind Cithria, almost making her drop her bowl.

"Ready for a match? You said you do all right, after all."

Cithria shoveled the last cold spoonful of stew in her mouth and made an apologetic shrug. "*Mmffmmff.*" She couldn't be less ready.

Pell laughed. "Fine, fine. I said you could finish eating—after that, we're teaching you how the Vanguard play."

She sat with a dull thump on the log bench, Pell's hand firmly pushing her down. In front of her was another stump table, rough-hewn and fresh from clearing for the camp, with a set of tellstones pieces laid out on top of it. An acutely important detail dawned on her— she was sitting opposite *Sergeant Merrek*. He was the leader of the Dauntless Vanguard's First Shield and the long-standing mentor and second-in-command to Sword-Captain Garen Crownguard himself.

Cithria sat bolt upright, the backpack digging into her lower back, trying somehow to stand to attention while sitting on a log.

Merrek watched her, a stern craggy face thoughtfully taking her measure. Cithria fixed her eyes forward, uncertain of what was expected of her.

Pell crisply saluted Merrek. "She's all yours, sergeant."

"Thank you, Proctor-Corporal Pell. I'll take it from here."

Pell hunkered down at Cithria's eye level, an uncharacteristically reassuring expression on her face. "You're going to do fine, Cithria, it's just a game. But in case you were wondering—this is most *definitely* part of your testing to get into the Dauntless Vanguard. Good luck!"

Cithria's mind raced, remembering all the stories she'd heard since joining the army. Of the legendary Merrek hacking his way free of an augerbeast's grasp—he'd tracked it for close to a month after it had destroyed four fishing vessels and finally caught it during a night storm. Or when he and Garen had fought back-to-back—

"It was *three* months." Merrek interrupted her thoughts.

Cithria started.

"About now, even sleepfogged, you're going over what they've told you about me. Things I've done, battles I've won. I'd say you'd have gotten to the augerbeast tale by now—it's written on your face."

Cithria felt her cheeks redden.

"But we're not here to discuss what I've done, soldier. We're here to see what *you* might do. What you're capable of." Merrek's words hung heavy in the air.

He nodded, once, seemingly to himself.

"Can you follow orders, soldier?"

"Yes, sergeant!" Cithria's voice cracked, and she winced.

Great, now he thinks I'm some nervous raw recruit staring at her feet.

"Look at me," Merrek ordered.

Cithria blinked in bafflement for a second before looking up. Her eyes took in his worn but perfectly maintained armor, old scars hatching the skin below.

"No, soldier. My eyes. Lock eyes with me. That's an order."

Cithria felt her cheeks burn. Trying to look into the sergeant's eyes made her want to bolt from the camp and return to her old comrades in the Ninth.

Maybe I should quit now. Would suffering the Ninth's disappointment be easier than the Vanguard's pity?

No. She could do this. Fiercely determined not to fail, she fought all her urges to look away.

Merrek was doing something with the game pieces. Without looking, he had picked them up, clicking and clacking as he shuffled them from hand to hand.

Again, she fought the temptation to break eye contact.

She saw him slowly holding up one of the stones, close to her line of sight, the tile's face pointing in her direction.

"Keep your eyes on me. What tile is this?" Merrek's voice was quieter now, calmer.

Cithria scowled. She knew the tellstones icons of course; she wasn't a child. But being asked to look *without looking* seemed absurd. She let her eyes relax their focus as she tried to concentrate on the edge of her vision. She could make out that it was a narrow shape, longer than it was wide—that could only mean…

"The Sword, sergeant." She felt a tiny surge of triumph.

Hah. Because identifying a game piece means I'm ready for the Vanguard.

Merrek didn't even nod—he immediately placed the tile on the table, faceup between them, with a clack. He brought up another tile and another. Cithria identified them as the Scales and the Shield. Clack, clack.

I'm actually getting the hang of this.

Her weary eyes were drying out, and she reminded herself to blink.

"I'm going to look down at one of the stones on the table, and I want you to tell me which one I looked at. Understood, soldier?"

This is too easy. Is he playing a trick on me?

She nodded. "Yes, sergeant."

A moment passed. Very deliberately, his eyes glanced down to her right and then, with a leisurely blink, returned to look back at Cithria.

Her mind raced. *The Sword is in the center, I'm sure—then the other two on either side.* It had to be the Scales, the Sword, the Shield, from her left to her right. So if he'd

looked to her right, then it must be the Shield stone. She hoped.

"The Shield," she said, with more confidence than she felt.

Merrek rumbled a quiet grunt of approval and nodded almost imperceptibly. "Again."

His eyes flicked down to the middle of the table and back up to Cithria. She was ready this time and responded immediately.

"That's the Sword, sergeant."

He reached out to the tile and she watched him flip it facedown.

"Eyes up, soldier," Merrek admonished.

Ugh, just when I thought I was beginning to appear competent. I've got to focus!

Cithria adjusted herself on her log and solidly planted her feet, bracing her tired body and her ever-present burden. She met his gaze once more.

Without a word, Merrek reached down and, from the sounds, seemed to be turning the other two tiles facedown. Even if she looked now, it would be no help.

Quick as a blink, he glanced down to Cithria's left and then back at her. She had been waiting for this and almost stumbled over her immediate response.

"Scales, sergeant."

He then looked, quite deliberately, off to the right edge of the table—far beyond the three stones. He returned his gaze to her and slowly raised a questioning eyebrow. He'd clearly not looked at the Shield, Scales, or Sword, and he had been very obvious in what he was doing.

This was, as Pell had told her, part of the testing.

She felt a frown forming on her brow, from frustration or concentration she couldn't quite be sure. If it wasn't the three stones in front of her, what could it be? Suddenly, she remembered that Merrek had left the other unused stones off to the side.

"The pool, sergeant?"

He took a moment before replying, measuring her in some way she could only guess at.

"Aye. More specifically, the Hammer. That'll come with practice." His gaze never wandered, never became a stare. "What do you think I'm doing this time?"

Barely daring to blink, Cithria still almost missed his glance—this time straight down the middle, then snapping immediately to her left. Had he changed his mind on what stone to pick? She stared and stared at his eyes without really seeing them, as her mind raced and she considered what he'd done.

"The... the Sword... *and* the Scales?"

The corner of Merrek's mouth rose a little, and his cheeks creased—an unexpected smile—and he broke eye contact, freeing her eyes to do the same. She breathed a sigh of relief.

"Not bad, Soldier Cithria," Merrek mused. "You can tell when I glance at a single stone—what move in tellstones, if you know the game at all, do you think that could signify?"

Despite her newfound freedom to look anywhere she pleased, she found herself gazing at, or more specifically through, one of the stones on the table as she wrestled her exhausted mind to find an answer. The only information a single glance gave was about that lone piece, and so far she realized he hadn't looked at a facedown piece.

"I would say you're trying to give the *hide* command, sergeant, because there's not enough information for it to be anything else."

Merrek focused on gathering up the pieces, purposely not looking at her. "Go on."

Cithria continued, "When you glanced at two stones, that could have been the *swap* move, and when you looked at the pool, well, that has to be the *place* move, where you add a stone from the side. You're able to communicate the game moves without even speaking!"

Merrek neatly laid the stones on the side of their impromptu table, arranging them in a neat row before sitting back on his log and taking in the messfield around them both. He seemed in no hurry to acknowledge her revelation.

"Where do you hail from, soldier?" he asked out of nowhere.

"Cloudfield, sergeant," she replied, surprised at his question.

"Cloudfield. Didn't they celebrate Yellow Spring Festival recently?"

How did he know that? Cithria's mind raced. "Yes, sergeant—usually I'd have missed it, but the hills bloomed early this year, and I was still on leave."

"And your family?" Merrek seemed honestly interested, casually leaning forward with one forearm on his knee. "They still live there?"

"They do, yes, sergeant. My niece was one of the flower-bearers this year, and my father kept busy running around after her with her basket. He was so proud of her. I was too."

Merrek was nodding, and Cithria realized she felt much better. The lump in her stomach was gone. Hardly anyone outside Cloudfield even knew about the Yellow Spring Festival, but somehow Sergeant Merrek did.

"There are two varieties of tell-stones in the Dauntless Vanguard," Merrek said. "Drawing the Lines, and the silent training version you saw earlier. Drawing the Lines is reserved for more serious disputes, so Cithria of Cloudfield, let's play some Silent Stones."

"Yes, sergeant!"

"While we're playing, you can just call me Merrek." A smirk crumpled his wrinkled face. "Though if I catch you doing so *outside* of the game, you and your corporal will be on half rations until the physicians stop smiling."

Cithria must have blanched, because Merrek laughed at her reaction.

"Is this still part of my testing?" Cithria hoped she didn't sound nervous; she just wanted to be clear.

"Perhaps. As Proctor-Corporal Pell wisely likes to say—consider every moment of this month to be part of the testing and, like all of us, every day in the Dauntless Vanguard another test to prove you're worthy of our mantle." Merrek's expression was somber once more, and Cithria felt the weight of his words keenly.

He paused, then asked, "Any more questions before we begin?"

Bunder's game flashed through her mind—most of it she now understood, but a few moments remained unclear. Replaying the game in her mind, she found her hand moving, mirroring what she'd seen.

She rapped once on the tree stump.

"That's the *challenge*." Cithria spoke slowly but with certainty. One remained.

She looked back up at Merrek and knocked twice on the stump.

"And this is the *boast*," she stated. "But after that… Soldier Bunder just gave up?"

Merrek made a most undignified choking sound, and his eyes widened half in shock and amusement. "Gave up? Bunder?" He looked around at the nearby soldiers and found who he was looking for.

"Corporal Pell!" he called, and she hustled over. "Soldier Cithria here says she observed, during an earlier game of stones, Soldier Bunder giving up. Can you confirm this?"

She stood at attention, but Cithria watched as Pell's face twitched wildly to suppress a smile that threatened to rampage across her face. "No, Sergeant Merrek, I cannot."

"Then can you explain what Soldier Cithria saw?" Amusement dripped from Merrek's every word.

"Soldier Bunder evaluated the situation, his own capabilities, and the capabilities of his opponent and concluded that a protracted engagement would not result in victory or

honor, sergeant. He opted for an abbreviated conclusion and preserved his strength for more worthwhile future encounters." Pell seemed to have this well rehearsed, and managed to keep a straight face through most of it.

"Very good, Corporal Pell. You may return to poorly spying on our game."

"Yes, sergeant." Pell made it several paces before her stony facade collapsed and she broke out in a grin, returning to a nearby bench where she sat laughing with a few others of the Dauntless Vanguard.

Merrek explained to Cithria: "Soldier Bunder is a Dauntless Vanguard through and through—I'd stand shoulder to shoulder with him against a hundred Freljordian raiders and consider it good odds."

His voice lowered, somewhat conspiratorially. "He has, however, been known to be *stubborn*. What you saw as giving up is a rare victory in a war he's been fighting for years against his greatest opponent."

The sound of Merrek's knuckles hitting the log stump startled Cithria. "One knock. That's to indicate you accept the boast, and they get a point." He rapped twice. "Two if you want to turn the boast back on them. And if you want to call their bluff, simply sweep the table with your gaze, indicating all of the stones, forcing them to name them all correctly or lose the game."

Merrek leaned back on his bench. "Now, let's play! Pell said I should go easy on you, but I don't think I need to give any quarter to the *four-time tellstones champion of the Ninth Battalion*." He raised a fiercely bushy eyebrow as he watched her reaction.

Ah. Yes, I suppose the Yellow Spring Festival wouldn't have been high on the list of things he could have heard about me.

"Captain Eldran would take it as a slight on the battalion's honor, I assume, if I underestimated you?"

"Yes, sergeant, she would." Cithria adjusted the pack on her back. "I'm ready to play."

They settled into the first turns of the game, Cithria focusing for all her worth on holding Merrek's gaze. Stones were placed, hidden, and swapped and, while nowhere near the blistering pace she'd seen the sergeant's squad play, she hadn't made a fool of herself quite yet.

Suddenly, an out-of-breath soldier interrupted her concentration to report to Merrek. Cithria stubbornly refused to let her gaze wander, the order of the pieces wriggling away from her like a line in rough seas. From the edge of her vision, the sergeant acknowledged the runner's update and effortlessly picked up his turn where he left off.

"What do you think of this version of the game, soldier?"

Don't break eye contact. Don't break eye contact.

"It's… strange. Much harder, but it seems…" She hesitated to speak. It felt treasonous to voice these thoughts.

"Go on." His voice was relaxed in spite of the tense game.

More stones placed, another pair swapped. She was having to concentrate on so much at once. There was the order of the stones, the turns, the new way of playing moves, an especially sharp rock— probably Eldran's—in her pack digging into her spine, and having to keep her eyes in check. In the end, she just blurted it out.

"It feels *uncivilized*." Her face fell at the shock of what she'd just said. "I mean, I don't…"

There was no way to unsay it. Not honestly, and he'd immediately see through any attempt to weasel her way out of it. His hand moved suddenly, and she was so tense she almost flinched. He knocked on the log stump. Cithria was so flustered, she'd missed which stone he'd glanced at. Her fist flexed reflexively in frustration. She just shook her head. She took the *peek* action and glanced at one of the stones. Merrek waited, expecting her to look at the other two that were her due after a failed challenge, but she refused to move.

She didn't deserve it.

"Uncivilized, eh?" he said, placing the last stone. "Why do you say that?"

"It's impersonal. Brutal. Not like *play*." All the stones were hidden by now. Cithria felt her palms starting to sweat.

"Impersonal," he said, maintaining his gaze for longer than usual between turns. "I can see how it might seem that way to others. I was raised to believe that honesty and openness are two of our greatest strengths, and sometimes it can be easy to hide intentions behind noise and distraction. The eyes tell you so much about a person, what they're thinking, how they feel. I think I know you better now than if we'd played a hundred normal games, Cithria."

He held her bare gaze for just a second more before he returned to the game. Stones swapped places, and she struggled to focus through the realization that she'd felt like she knew and trusted him more than she'd ever expected.

The game was becoming ever more complex. They'd not seen a stone's face for a dozen or more turns now, and the score was at one point apiece. If this were a normal game, she'd be ready to call a boast, but now… She couldn't put her finger on it, but Merrek's eyes told her it wasn't time yet.

A flurry of turns followed—she faintly recognized that there was a real crowd around them now, hushed for the most part, but she let them fade into the background. How much of her selective focus was intentional and how much was exhaustion she couldn't spare the time to decide.

A pair of engineers arrived with a quandary for Merrek about the location of the Fifth and Eighth Shield campsites, and again he responded patiently.

"You said it was brutal," he said in the middle of a flurry of swapping stones. "Demacia was forged in a brutal time. We train, we fight, and we protect so that we never have to suffer that brutality again. This game might appear brutal compared to other ways to play, but it's only a game, Cithria."

"Of course, I—"

"It's *important* you understand the Dauntless Vanguard must face brutality, violence, sorcery, and horror that no Demacian, not even other soldiers, should ever have to suffer. Every Vanguard understands that they might die in lands foreign or near, at the claws of some terrible beast or even the hand of their comrades, if they find themselves turned into something unnatural. Every soldier who wears this armor knows their ultimate purpose is to give their all, even their life, so that Demacians can build homes and raise families and enjoy their own Yellow Spring Festivals."

Cithria flushed.

"I know, Sergeant Merrek. That's why I'm here. I've read the stories, and I've seen more than most of my squadmates can stomach. But all it makes me feel is angry! Angry that there are Demacians suffering and dying because we weren't there. Angry that *I* wasn't there."

Cithria felt her heart thumping in her chest and ears, and her hands were in fists.

"All right." Merrek nodded slowly, and she saw something like approval in his eyes. "It's your move."

She took a deep breath and forced herself to calm down.

Is he trying to get me to lose control? Testing if I can keep a cool head or if I'm Soldier Bunder without his better qualities? Well, I have better qualities too.

Cithria flicked her eyes down to call for two of the tiles to be swapped, and they were back into the game, faster than ever.

Yet another soldier hustled over with questions for Merrek, and Cithria found herself irritated at the interruptions. While the soldier droned on, she heard Pell's voice whispering from behind her. "We've got your back, recruit."

Confused, Cithria actually *listened* at last to the soldier... who was apparently speaking nonsense.

"... so obviously, sergeant, the Second Shield's new swords will stay under the smith's *hammers* for the night—we simply can't *scale* production without... ah, I can't do it! Crown! Knight! Scales-Hammer-Flag-Sword-you-can-do-it, Cithria!"

Another laughing soldier elbowed the distracting soldier in the ribs and dragged him away, still yelling random stone names at Merrek.

Merrek grinned. "It seems you already have allies willing to fight with you—even against me!"

They got back to the game. Cithria realized she wasn't entirely sure if the Shield or the Flag was where she thought it ought to be. It was definitely one or the other, but keeping it straight in her head was getting harder the longer they played.

"We play this game to know and trust each other. That's why it's a game of war," said Merrek. "But not in the way you might think."

Cithria thought she heard a moment of hesitation, the faintest pause in his otherwise steady speech. *Is he starting to falter?*

"Can you tell me why the Dauntless Vanguard plays it this way?" His question seemed casual, but Cithria reminded herself that this was part of her testing.

Why *would* the Dauntless Vanguard play this strange silent version? Even as she thought about it, tiles were moving and swapping—every move inscrutable to outsiders.

"It's practice for communicating with your comrades without alerting the enemy," she said, confident in her answer if not the location of the Shield tile. "If I can warn you or command you with just a glance, well, maybe we can save lives in the field."

Cithria felt not exactly comfortable, but like she had a handle on this way of playing the game at last. It was difficult, but she knew what she was doing.

"And it goes further than that, I think," she continued. "I used to think tellstones was a game of memorization. It was when my father taught me. I practiced every day—working hard like a Demacian ought. When I played in the Ninth Battalion, I realized that it wasn't just about that—it was about planning your actions and anticipating your opponent."

Merrek nodded again. The stones danced between them.

"But it's not just that either, is it?" she asked.

He answered her question, and no hint of his earlier hesitation remained. "It's about courage. Your courage, my courage. Skill is important, but skill without courage is nothing. For example…"

He reached out and knocked twice on the tree stump.

The boast.

Someone in the huge crowd around them gasped before being shushed by their neighbor. The sun was low on the horizon, and raptors were crying in the distance. Silverwings, far from home. Merrek's blue eyes sparkled and held her gray-eyed gaze steadily. Cithria searched for the doubt she thought she'd seen before. She searched her heart for her own courage and finally found plenty—born of the skills that she'd honed for years.

She raised her hand and responded—one knock, two.

It was now his turn to decide whether he believed Cithria knew the stones as she claimed. She willed every last grain of certainty into her eyes for him to read.

He smiled and slowly swept his gaze across the tiles, demanding she prove it.

She reached for the tiles in order, left to right. "Hammer. Scales. Sword." She named them just before turning them faceup, each one a testament to her skill. "Banner. Knight."

Again, she was right, but somewhere in the last two were the Shield and the Crown, and for all her practice, skill, and determination, she wasn't sure which was which. She hesitated.

"Well?" Merrek's voice betrayed nothing.

Her hand resting on the sixth piece, she took a deep breath and called "Shield."

It was the Crown.

The crowd around them erupted into cheers and commiserations, outrage and disbelief. Cithria herself sat stunned, her stomach as heavy as the backpack of rocks engraved with her comrades' names. People she'd failed. Friends she'd just let down. She'd proven unworthy to carry their names.

Merrek leaned over the table, stern voice clearly audible over the commotion.

"Played with courage. Played like a Dauntless Vanguard. I look forward to our next game."

THE MARCH

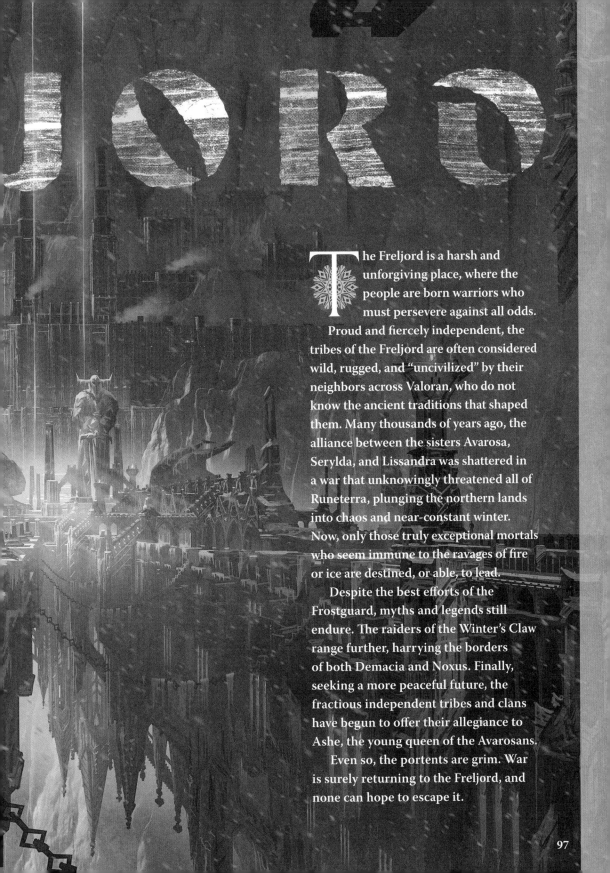

JORD

The Freljord is a harsh and unforgiving place, where the people are born warriors who must persevere against all odds. Proud and fiercely independent, the tribes of the Freljord are often considered wild, rugged, and "uncivilized" by their neighbors across Valoran, who do not know the ancient traditions that shaped them. Many thousands of years ago, the alliance between the sisters Avarosa, Serylda, and Lissandra was shattered in a war that unknowingly threatened all of Runeterra, plunging the northern lands into chaos and near-constant winter. Now, only those truly exceptional mortals who seem immune to the ravages of fire or ice are destined, or able, to lead.

Despite the best efforts of the Frostguard, myths and legends still endure. The raiders of the Winter's Claw range further, harrying the borders of both Demacia and Noxus. Finally, seeking a more peaceful future, the fractious independent tribes and clans have begun to offer their allegiance to Ashe, the young queen of the Avarosans.

Even so, the portents are grim. War is surely returning to the Freljord, and none can hope to escape it.

THE FROZEN WATCHERS

Deep in the Howling Abyss, ageless and monstrous intelligences rage at the veil between worlds. Long have they observed Runeterra from their prison of True Ice, but now, against all reason, that ice has finally begun to melt.

ANCIENT MAGIC

Though many of the old songs have been forgotten, some Freljordians still dare to whisper the names of forbidden demi-gods: Ornn, who wrought the land; Anivia, who dies and lives anew; or even the Volibear, who cleaves souls from flesh.

And by the hearth-fire's light, there is no divide between magic and belief that a song cannot bridge.

LIVING MYTHS

CORRUPTING SECRETS

The malevolent power of the Watchers—and the abyssal realm from which they come—has seeped into the True Ice around them. The result is Dark Ice, inky-veined and heavy with inverted elemental power. Though foul beyond mortal description, the ice carries great cultural value for those who know its origin.

THE ICEBORN

Though a rare phenomenon indeed, the blood of the tribes has been known to carry the power of an ancient and terrible bargain. From mother to child, the Iceborn are stronger, tougher, more resistant to cold—and they alone are capable, with great effort, of wielding weapons of magical, unmelting True Ice.

THE AVAROSANS

AVAROSA'S LEGACY

While little is known for sure about the Three Sisters who first conquered the wild north, it is the name of Avarosa that is most often invoked, in these times of darkness and uncertainty. Her palace of True Ice, and her battles with foes beneath the earth and beyond the stars, are an inspiration to all now united in her name—those who hope and pray she will fulfill her promise to return, and unite all the tribes once more.

THE FROST ARCHER

The Avarosan tribe is commanded by their Iceborn warmother, Ashe. Stoic, intelligent, and idealistic, yet uncomfortable with her role as leader, she taps into the ancestral magics of her lineage to wield a bow of True Ice. With her people's belief that she is the reincarnation of Avarosa herself, Ashe hopes to unify the Freljord once more by retaking their ancient, tribal lands.

THE WINTER'S CLAW

THE WINTER'S WRATH

Sejuani is the brutal, unforgiving warmother of the Winter's Claw, one of the most feared tribes of the Freljord. Her people's survival is a constant battle against the elements, forcing them to raid in order to withstand the harsh winters. Sejuani herself spearheads the most dangerous of these attacks from the saddle of her drüvask, using a True Ice flail to freeze and shatter her enemies.

UNRELENTING RAIDERS

Death stalks the ice in a thousand guises—some with fangs, some with blades, some bringing numbing frostbite, and others bitter starvation. To survive is to fight every death, crush every threat, steal every advantage.

Each new dawn brings a choice to the Winter's Claw: Do whatever it takes to survive, or die. To the Winter's Claw, that is no choice at all.

THE FROST GUARD

THE ICE WITCH

Many among the Frostguard believe their reclusive leader, Lissandra, is a living saint, bringing healing and wisdom to the tribes of the Freljord. The truth is perhaps more sinister, as she uses her elemental magic to twist the power of True Ice into something dark and terrible, entombing or impaling any who would reveal her deepest secrets.

STORY HUNTERS

Most of the Freljord's cultural history is passed on in a rich oral tradition, though this was not always the case. With her seemingly benevolent Frost Priests accepted in most of the tribes, Lissandra has long sought to purge certain *uncomfortable* details from the oldest tales, separating the legendary past from a bleak and austere present. Only time will tell if the Frostguard themselves can continue to deny the truth, when they are eventually confronted by the horrors that lie hidden beneath their feet.

A GOOD DAY

by ANTHONY REYNOLDS

Vrynna gritted her teeth to stop them from chattering and forced herself on, trudging through the thick snow. The wind whipped at her, ice and snow stinging her face, but she did not shy from it. She would not show weakness in front of the others.

Her clan was part of the Winter's Claw and could endure anything the frozen north threw at her.

The dark sky was lightening in the east behind them as it grew nearer to midday. It was midwinter, and the sun would barely make it over the horizon before it retreated again. Further north it wouldn't rise at all.

There were five of them on this hunt. The three cousins were with Vrynna—Halgar, Shiverbones, and Rylor—spread a ways off to the right, while the fifth scouted ahead, unseen.

"There's nothing out here," muttered Halgar, the closest of the others. "This is a waste of time. We're all going to starve. The tribe should've turned south months ago."

Vrynna rolled her eyes. Had they been feasting, with all the food and mead they could desire, Halgar would have found something to complain about.

"Still your tongue, cousin," snarled Shiverbones, "or I'll still it with my blade."

Halgar scowled but didn't say anything further. The hard-eyed leader of the hunt,

Shiverbones was not given to idle threats, nor known for his patience.

Vrynna prayed to the gods Halgar was wrong, but she felt it in her bones that today would be another hard day. It had been more than a month since there had been a successful hunt, and the salted reserves—meant to last the whole winter—had run out weeks ago. There had been a minor respite after they ambushed a Storm Crow war party, far beyond their usual hunting grounds, but the food their enemies had been carrying didn't go far. The tribe was starving.

They continued on, unspeaking, the only sound the crunch of snow underfoot. Vrynna used her spear like a walking staff, stabbing deep into the snow with each step. Her bow was slung across her shoulders, her arrows at her hip. Not that there had been any opportunity to use them yet. They were four hours out from camp and had seen no sign of prey.

Her stomach growled—it had been days since she'd eaten anything more substantial than weak bone broth—but she did her best to ignore it. The wind was picking up, and Vrynna pulled her fur-lined cloak in tight as she walked. Above her, the clouds thickened, slowly obscuring the stars and making the day darker, even as they approached the midday dawn.

Despair began to claw at her, insidious and subtle. Doubts wormed their way into her mind, whispering to her.

We're all going to die out here, frozen and alone, they said.

Vrynna shook her head to dislodge them. Before her, shadowy, jagged rock forma-tions rose in clumps from the snowpack like giant frostbitten fingers. Out this far, there were no trees, no signs of life. It was a desolate frozen wasteland, extending forever in every direction.

Occasionally, far to the north, lightning flickered. Time seemed to slow as they advanced across the icy tundra, minutes blurring into hours. Vrynna's whole existence became focused on simply keeping moving, one foot in front of the other, her senses dulled by hunger and tiredness.

Lost in this fugue state, Vrynna took half a second to react when a figure loomed out of the darkness, appearing suddenly right in front of her.

She jolted in shock, taking a step back and scrabbling to ready her spear, before realizing it was Sigrun Ice-Runner, their scout.

Ice-Runner had been standing within a cluster of rocks, utterly motionless, her mottled, pale cloak drawn close. It had only been when she had stepped into Vrynna's path, less than a dozen paces ahead, that she'd become visible.

Ice-Runner's tightly braided hair had long gone to silver, and her face was well worn, with deep crevices to either side of her eyes from many years of squinting against the frozen glare. Though she was one of the oldest living members of her clan, perhaps even the entire Winter's Claw, she still had a fierce vitality about her, and there were few who could withstand her withering gaze. Even the warmother's bloodsworn were cowed before her unblinking appraisal. Tall and wolf-lean, she looked at Vrynna with iron-hard eyes.

"You sleepwalking, unscarred?" said Ice-Runner. "If I were an enemy, you'd be dead."

Vrynna cursed under her breath and looked down, cheeks reddening. Ice-Runner's eyes still reminded her of the raid. *After all this time.* Halgar, Shiverbones, and Rylor crunched over to join them. One glance at Halgar's smirking face told her they had heard Ice-Runner's rebuke.

"Jumped like a scared snow rabbit, unscarred," Halgar said. "You wet yourself, too?"

"You didn't see me either, Halgar," snapped Ice-Runner, turning on him. "I just expect more of her."

The tribesman grinned back through his icy beard. "No one *ever* sees you, Ice-Runner."

"You've found something?" asked Shiverbones.

Ice-Runner stared down Halgar for a moment, just long enough for his grin to falter and for him to look away, before she turned to the leader of the hunt with a nod.

"Tracks, half a league ahead," she said. "Just over the rise, heading northwest."

"Elnuk?" said Rylor. The expression behind the knot-work tattoos covering his face was serious, as ever. Vrynna wasn't sure he was even capable of smiling.

Ice-Runner shook her head, the ghost of excitement in her voice. "Thunderhorn. Big one, too."

Vrynna's eyes widened, and Rylor murmured in appreciation. Even Halgar had nothing negative to say to that.

"How far?" said Shiverbones.

"Tracks are fairly recent," said Ice-Runner. "I'd say it came through here a couple of hours ago."

Vrynna's exhaustion was suddenly forgotten. Even a young thunderhorn would feed the whole clan for a month or more. Her mouth began to water in anticipation.

The party looked to Shiverbones to make the call. The long-haired hunter held his totemic bone necklaces for a moment, cocking his head to one side, as if listening to voices no other could hear. Many of his bone fetishes were carved in the likeness of gods and spirits of the north, and Vrynna wondered if it was they that spoke to him. Some of those gods she recognized—the Ice Phoenix and the Seal Sister among them—while others she did not, such as a ram holding a hammer and a two-headed raven.

Shiverbones held the totems close, staring up at the sky. There was an ugly scrawl of clouds overhead, and the winds were beginning to howl more fiercely. It was nearing noon, but this was the darkest it had been all day. Nevertheless, a thunderhorn was a prize that could not be ignored.

Shiverbones gave his totems a shake, making them rattle, then opened his hand to look upon them.

"Two hours in front?" said Shiverbones, glancing at Ice-Runner.

"Maybe less."

Shiverbones nodded, thinking. "We give chase," he said, eliciting a sage nod from Rylor and a savage whoop from Halgar. "But we have to move fast. This storm looks bad."

"Think you can keep up, *unscarred?*" said Halgar.

Vrynna glared at him. "I won't slow us down," she said.

"We wouldn't wait for you if you did," he snarled in reply. "You'd be left to die, and the clan would be the stronger for it."

"I won't slow us," Vrynna said, clenching her fists. Halgar smirked and walked away.

Vrynna felt eyes on her and turned to see Ice-Runner nearby. She'd clearly watched the exchange, and Vrynna reddened, her shame redoubled.

"It was my youngest who first called you unscarred, wasn't it?" Ice-Runner said, her voice softer than before.

Hrolur.

Vrynna nodded. "It was," she said.

"I miss him," said Ice-Runner.

Vrynna looked up at the older woman. Ice-Runner's expression was somber.

"I do too," Vrynna said.

When Halgar called her unscarred it was as an insult, as one unproven in the eyes of the tribe, yet to have faced an enemy with axe or blade. But when Hrolur used to say it, it had made Vrynna laugh.

He was Ice-Runner's youngest son and only a year older than Vrynna. He'd been just as untested as she; that was why they'd both found it so funny.

"*Ah, but I bear the mark of a blooded reaver!*" he had declared, gesturing proudly to the jagged scar on his left cheek. "*Let all who look upon me know the true meaning of fear!*"

"*The true meaning of clumsiness, more like,*" Vrynna had said, laughing.

It had been midsummer, the two of them just children. The scar Hrolur boasted about had been made when he'd tripped running to a feast the week before and hit his head on a stone. Not exactly the tale of a mighty hero, and they both knew it. Their own private joke.

The ambush came that winter—Storm Crows, driven by hunger and age-old rivalry. Most of the tribe's warriors were out raiding or hunting at the time.

It had been a massacre.

Vrynna's mother had hidden her beneath a stack of furs, then killed three reavers before she was taken down by an arrow in the neck. Vrynna lost her sister in that raid as well, leaving her without any family.

Numb, tears running down her face, she had stumbled away from her tent. That was when she found Hrolur, lying on his back in the snow, a spear through his chest.

Vrynna had been kneeling beside him when Ice-Runner and the others returned, drawn by the smoke of the burning camp. Ice-Runner shed no tears for her son, though Hrolur had been the last of her children; she had never borne a daughter, and her other sons were dead, lost to raids and sickness. Ice-Runner's bloodline would end with her.

A war party had been gathered for reprisal, and faces smeared with blood and ash. Vrynna had wanted to go with them, the desire for retribution strong, but she was too young. Ice-Runner placed a hand upon Vrynna's shoulder.

"*Your mother was a fine warrior,*" Ice-Runner had said. "*A true daughter of winter. And I know my son was your friend. Our kin are in a better place now. We'll see them again, one day soon, and we will hunt with them across the endless ice plains beyond.*"

Then Ice-Runner had melted into the darkness with the others and was gone. They had returned a day later, having exacted a bloody toll of vengeance upon the Storm Crows. Ice-Runner had nodded to Vrynna, but no more words were spoken between them… until today.

"Time to hunt," ordered Shiverbones, breaking Vrynna from her painful memories.

Ice-Runner nodded to Vrynna, both their hearts clearly in the same place. Both of them had lost everything that day. Everything except for the tribe.

The five hunters loped into the darkness, moving like a wolf pack. Ice-Runner took the lead, ranging out in front, while Vrynna, as the youngest and least experienced of them, ran in the middle, with Halgar and Rylor to either side. As the leader, Shiverbones stayed at the back, ensuring no one fell behind and ever watchful for an attack.

Ice-Runner set a punishing pace. Vrynna was pleased to see she was not the only one breathing hard. Even stoic Rylor struggled to match their scout, who seemed to run without tiring.

The thunderhorn tracks led them on. Vrynna marveled at their size. Each was over two hand spans in width and almost as deep. This beast seemed content ploughing straight through some of the larger snow-drifts in its path, without slowing. It truly must be massive. Fast, too; the hunters were gaining ground on it, but not at a rate anyone seemed happy about.

Snow began to fall, making Halgar swear. Vrynna didn't need to ask why. Not only did fresh snow make running more diffi-cult, even Ice-Runner would have trouble

tracking the thunderhorn if it came down heavy enough. The hunters picked up the pace, pushing themselves harder, in the hopes of catching up to the great beast before the incoming storm obscured its passage completely.

The wind was howling, whipping across the open tundra in bitingly cold waves. Vrynna was sweating dangerously from exertion beneath her leathers and furs, but her face was freezing, and ice clung to her eyebrows and lashes. Halgar's beard was frozen solid. If they stopped out here where there was no cover, exposed to this killing wind, they would not last long.

They continued on, but the storm was worsening. Still, Ice-Runner led them unerringly onward, though how she could discern where they were now going was a skill beyond Vrynna's understanding.

It became almost impossible to see more than a few paces in front. Vrynna could no longer see any sign of their quarry's tracks. She had lost sight of Ice-Runner completely, and could only just see Halgar and Rylor to either side of her. Lightning flickered, its thunder now close enough to hear.

A hand clamped down on her shoulder from behind, and she gave a yelp of surprise, though thankfully that noise was lost on the gale. It was Shiverbones, the sweeping horns of his mustache hanging like icicles around his blue-tinged lips. Vrynna came to a halt, and Halgar and Rylor closed in to join them. A moment later, the silhouette of Ice-Runner appeared, stalking out of the storm like an ice wraith.

"What's the hold up?" Ice-Runner shouted over the wind.

"See the flashes in the heavens?" Shiverbones shouted back, shaking one of his totems. "The Stormlord rages!"

"I can still track the beast!" shouted Ice-Runner. "We are closing in!"

Vrynna didn't doubt Ice-Runner, even though the tracks the hunters themselves had just made were almost completely obscured already. And yet Shiverbones shook his head.

"It is an ill omen!" he called. "We must turn back!"

Vrynna thought Ice-Runner was going to argue, but to her surprise she simply began walking back the way they had come. The others made no protest either, turning without a word. Vrynna was the only one who didn't. She looked at Ice-Runner, confused and disappointed.

"But we're so close!" Vrynna said.

Ice-Runner merely shrugged and kept walking.

Vrynna turned, shouting at the backs of the other four hunters. "We've come all this way! The clan is relying on us!"

"There's always tomorrow," shouted Rylor. "We'll hunt again once the gods' anger has subsided."

"But the clan is starving *today!*" shouted Vrynna, walking along in the wake of the others now. "It's been weeks since we've seen any sign of prey!"

"Go hunt it alone then, unscarred," snapped Halgar, over his shoulder. "I'll raise a cup to your noble sacrifice back at the fire."

"People will die if we don't make this kill," shouted Vrynna. Shiverbones stopped walking and turned to look back at her. The others stopped as well.

"So the weakest among the tribe go back to the earth," Shiverbones said. "That is the Winter's Claw way!"

"And if all of us die?"

"Then it is the will of the gods!"

Vrynna stared back at the others. Was it just that her pride was wounded at the thought of returning empty-handed?

"If we die in that storm," shouted Shiverbones, "the clan's lost five of its best hunters. That endangers everyone."

"Well, four of the best plus the unscarred," said Halgar, with a grin. Vrynna scowled at him, wanting to punch the smirk off his face.

She was not the only one irritated by Halgar's snide remark. Ice-Runner walked up and slapped him in the back of his head, making him stumble to one knee in the snow with a curse. He was on his feet in an instant, hand clenched around the haft of his war axe.

"I've killed others for less, scout!" he spat, his face red—and not just from the ice and wind.

"Then try it, little man," said Ice-Runner, staring at him unblinking.

Halgar licked his lips. His gaze flicked down to the pair of long hunting blades strapped at Ice-Runner's sides. She'd not made any move to grab them. Not yet, at least.

Shiverbones and the others stood unmoving, waiting to see how things played out.

At last, Halgar relinquished his grip on his axe, thinking better of taking on the renowned hunter. He turned away, muttering to himself.

"Doesn't change anything," he said. "Right, cousin?"

The leader of the hunt looked first at Halgar, then Vrynna, then Ice-Runner.

"You siding with the girl?" Shiverbones asked the scout. Ice-Runner shrugged.

"I can still track it," she said. "And you said it yourself—if we die in the storm, then such is the gods' will."

Shiverbones furrowed his brow and gave his totems a shake before nodding.

"We go on," he said.

They finally came upon the beast within a snow-covered stand of black rocks, and it truly was the biggest thunderhorn Vrynna had ever seen.

Almost as long as a wolfship from the jagged forehorn to the tip of its stubby tail, it would have put up a terrible fight... had it been alive.

The colossal beast lay sprawled on its side, and the snow around it was reddened with blood. More was splattered in wide arcs around the area, and the ground was churned and gouged deeply, as if this had been the site of some titanic battle.

The hunters approached carefully, weapons at the ready. They spread out instinctively, without a word. The wind howled mournfully, scattering snow in blustering eddies.

Vrynna clutched her spear in both hands, moving in a low crouch. She scanned the area, searching for enemies, but the fallen thunderhorn kept drawing her gaze. It was a true monster.

Its body was thick and heavy and covered in dark, ice-encased fur. The deadly horn jutting from its head was longer than the broad harpoons other clans of the tribe used to hunt mourn-whales. Its mouth was open, exposing surprisingly small, chisel-like teeth, and its pink tongue protruded in a silent death-bray. Its tiny eyes were wide and staring.

"What killed it?" Vrynna asked, an icicle of fear stabbing into her gut.

"Whatever did is likely still close," hissed Ice-Runner, an arrow nocked to her bowstring.

"And probably not best pleased with someone else claiming its kill," added Halgar sourly. He, too, had his bow at the ready and was turning on the spot.

Shiverbones approached the thunderhorn's carcass warily to inspect its wounds. Ice-Runner stared intently at the markings on the ground, eyes darting back and forth, reading them as a Frost Priest might read the totems. Vrynna, Halgar, and Rylor fanned out, facing outward, watchful for danger. Vrynna could smell the dead thunderhorn, a heady animal musk.

"Wounds across its flank," Shiverbones called out. "And its throat's been ripped out. This was not done by axe or spear."

"Yeti?" said Rylor.

The word sent a shudder through Vrynna. Her main fear when coming on this hunt had been tundra wolves, or running into a Storm Crow hunting party. She hadn't considered the possibility of encountering a yeti. They didn't range this far south…. *Did they?*

"Wait," said Ice-Runner, kneeling and touching her gloved hand to the snow. "This is…"

"What do you see?" said Vrynna.

A yeti would have been bad, but what Ice-Runner shouted was worse.

"Wildclaw!" she bellowed.

It came at them amid an explosion of snow, bursting from a drift with shocking speed.

Vrynna saw little more than a blur of pale fur and a flash of yellow eyes. She had barely begun to bring her spear around before the wildclaw slammed into Rylor, swordlike claws digging deep into his body. The beast drove him twenty feet back before landing, the warrior broken beneath its weight, his flesh riven by its talons. It bit down on him and ended his life with a savage twist of its powerful neck, sending a fresh spray of red across the snow. The wildclaw rounded on the other hunters, its tails lashing the snow, and let loose a terrible roar that made Vrynna's insides shudder.

It was big, likely an alpha, larger even than the drüvask ice boars ridden by the fiercest of the Winter's Claw. It moved with feline grace, lithe and powerful on its six legs.

Ice-Runner was the first to react, loosing an arrow that took the wildclaw in its neck, eliciting a snarl of pain. Swiftly, she drew and loosed another shaft, and again her arrow found its mark, thudding deep into the beast's flesh.

Then the wildclaw was charging, its narrowed yellow eyes locked on Ice-Runner.

It moved with staggering speed, covering the ground between them in two swift bounds. Another arrow—Halgar's—took the giant cat in its chest, but it didn't slow. Vrynna shouted wordlessly and lurched forward, spear lowered, knowing she was going to be too slow.

Ice-Runner dropped her bow and hurled herself into a roll, desperately trying to avoid the flashing claws. She was fast, but the years had robbed her of some of her speed. She avoided the worst of the slashing talons, but the wildclaw still managed to strike a glancing blow. Claws gouged across the small of her back, slicing through her leather jerkin and deep into the flesh beneath, sending her reeling.

The cat snarled and went after Ice-Runner again, moving with a speed no one could hope to match.

Nevertheless, it was distracted for a fraction of a second as Shiverbones launched himself at it, a war axe clasped in each hand, a war cry on his lips.

It was just enough of a pause to allow Vrynna to close the distance. She shouted in terror and defiance as she thrust her spear into the wildclaw's side, driving it deep with all her strength and weight. She felt the spear tip scrape between ribs.

The giant cat screeched and spun

away from Ice-Runner. The power of the movement ripped Vrynna's spear from her hands and dragged her off-balance. She fell to her knees in the snow as the wildclaw alpha turned.

Death stared down at her, and its eyes were yellow.

One massive paw, easily as big as Vrynna's head, swatted her across the face.

Blood filled her vision, and she fell.

Vrynna didn't want to wake up. She was warm and content, wrapped under a swathe of thick furs.

She frowned. She heard distant shouts and the snarls of some big creature, but they were faint, coming to her from a great distance. *Just a dream,* she thought, numbly, and tried to go back to sleep, burrowing deeper under the furs. The sound was insistent, however, and with a sigh, she opened her eyes.

She found herself staring up at a dark sky. Snow was whipping back and forth above her, as if in some wild, weightless dance no mortal could truly understand. It was beautiful the way each flake spun and whirled. She felt the snow settling upon her, but it didn't feel cold.

If this was a new dream, it was a good one.

She heard screaming and felt a flicker of annoyance. The sound was intruding on her peace. A roar, closer again. *What is that?*

She suddenly felt confused. She wasn't lying on furs… she was on the snow, yet she couldn't remember falling. She realized she couldn't see out of her right eye. Everything was darkness on that side. She reached up, thinking perhaps her hood or a blanket had slipped over her face. But no—when she moved her hand away, it was covered in blood.

Then the pain hit her, and the reality of her situation snapped into stark clarity with it. The last vestiges of her confusion shed away, like an ice-drake sloughing its skin. The shouts were from her fellow hunters, still locked in a desperate fight with the wildclaw that had smashed her aside and left her for dead.

But she wasn't dead. Not yet.

She scrambled to her knees, groaning. It felt like someone had rammed a hot poker into her right eye. Her whole face was throbbing angrily. She fought not to spill the contents of her stomach and steadied herself with one hand on the ice as her head spun. Thankfully the wave of nausea passed swiftly. Gingerly, she touched her face again. Blood dripped onto the snow. She winced as her fingers felt the deep lacerations crossing her skin from brow to cheek. She still couldn't see out of her right eye, but she didn't dare prod at the socket, too afraid she'd find it empty.

Vrynna staggered to her feet, vision wavering. She wobbled, staring toward the ferocious battle still underway.

The wildclaw, too, was bleeding, and arrows jutted from its body. Its tail swished angrily, and its ears were pinned back as it turned, snarling, its eyes wild. Blood caked the pale fur around its gaping maw.

Ice-Runner and Shiverbones circled it, while Halgar was down. He wasn't dead, but one of his legs was a ruin and twisted at a sickening angle beneath him. He fumbled with his bow, cursing and grimacing in pain. The body of Rylor lay in a broken heap nearby.

Both Ice-Runner and Shiverbones were injured, but the beast was limping too, its strength fading. The outcome of the battle remained uncertain.

They were not so different, the alpha and the Winter's Claw, Vrynna realized in a strange moment of clarity. Both were simply struggling to survive in this harsh frozen landscape that was their home. The alpha might have had a family of its own to feed, fighting desperately to keep the hunters from stealing its kill.

This was the way of things, as it always had been and always would be. All life was a battle. The weak perished, the strong prevailed.

Rage built within her. Rage at all the hard days her clan had suffered. Rage at her own fear, her own weakness. It warmed her, banishing the numbing cold. Her eye narrowed, fixed on the wildclaw. Snarling, she tore her hunting knife from its sheath at her hip and broke into a run.

If today was to be the day death came for her, then she would meet it head-on, with spear and blade, fighting till the last.

An arrow, loosed at close range, sank deep into the wildclaw's thick neck. It hissed and turned on Halgar, sprawled on the ground. The tribesman swore loudly and fumbled for another arrow. Ice-Runner leapt forward, stabbing with a spear—Vrynna's spear. As the immense cat turned toward Ice-Runner, Shiverbones darted in, hammering one of his axe-heads into its flank.

The cat swatted at Shiverbones, but the leader of the hunt rolled beneath the blow. As he did, Ice-Runner struck again, ramming Vrynna's spear deep into its side. This time, the wildclaw was faster to react. It caught Ice-Runner heavily in the chest with one massive, crushing paw. Vrynna cried out as the old scout was hurled through the air before slamming into one of the nearby rocks with a bone-snapping impact.

An arrow skidded off the cat's skull, tearing through one of its ears, and the wildclaw turned to face Halgar. It stalked rapidly toward him, body low, ready to pounce.

With a scream of fury, Vrynna leapt from a snow-covered rock, holding her knife high in both hands. She came down on the wildclaw's shoulders and rammed

the blade down hard. It sank to the hilt, and bright blood gushed.

The beast screeched and bucked, trying desperately to dislodge her. Vrynna clung on, keeping a hold on her knife with one hand while the other gripped the cat's thick fur. She tore the blade free and managed another two stabs before she was thrown aside, falling heavily to the slushy, gore-soaked snow.

The wildclaw roared down at her. Its hot breath reeked of fetid meat. From the ground, Vrynna roared back, matching the beast's fury.

Then an axe took the wildclaw alpha in the back of the skull, and it finally slumped to the ground.

It twitched a few times, then was still.

Shiverbones looked down at Vrynna. "Your face…" he said.

Vrynna shrugged.

"I'm alive."

Her gaze slid over to Ice-Runner, collapsed at the foot of the rocks. Shiverbones hauled Vrynna to her feet, and they staggered over to Ice-Runner's side. The scout was breathing, but her chest was caved in, and blood foamed at her lips.

Vrynna sank helplessly to her knees.

"Is it dead?" Ice-Runner growled.

Vrynna nodded. "Shiverbones landed the killing blow."

Ice-Runner coughed blood and smiled. Her teeth were stained red. "Good," she wheezed. "Would have been disappointing to die for nothing."

Shiverbones appeared at Vrynna's side, supporting Halgar under one arm. Vrynna looked up at them. Shiverbones' expression was grim as he looked down at Ice-Runner's wounds. He shook his head.

Ice-Runner reached out, and Vrynna took the dying woman's hand in both of her own.

"I'm sorry," Vrynna said. "It's my fault. I shouldn't have made us push on."

"Hush yourself," Ice-Runner chided. "Today is a *good* day! Our clan will feast, and I… I will see my sons in the beyond. Yes, today is a good day."

"But—" started Vrynna, but Ice-Runner interrupted her.

"It was the right thing to do," she said, clutching Vrynna's hands tightly. "The *Winter's Claw* thing to do. It is not our way to shy from hardship and danger. The tribe needs bold leaders like you."

"I am no leader," said Vrynna.

"You will be," said Ice-Runner. "And you are no longer unscarred."

Vrynna's face was throbbing, but the blood had ceased dripping. *Frozen, most likely,* she thought.

The worst of the storm had blown itself out, and a patch of clear night sky opened up overhead. In the darkness up there, luminescent bands of color were revealed. It was beautiful and peaceful; perhaps the gods themselves were paying their respects to the passing of a hero.

Shiverbones rattled his charms, murmuring under his breath.

Ice-Runner squeezed Vrynna's hands one last time. "I always wanted a daughter," she said.

Her grip weakened, and she let out a final, ragged breath.

Then she was still.

The clan ate well that night.

Vrynna and Shiverbones had dug Halgar a shelter, for he was unable to walk, and left him to guard the kill while the two of them had set out to make the long journey back to the tribe.

The Winter's Claw tribe built no permanent structures—they were a migratory people, constantly moving and raiding, hunting prey across the ice. And so, Vrynna's clan broke camp as soon as they received word of the successful hunt.

Vrynna half expected to find Halgar

dead upon their return and the kill gone, but all was well when they finally made it back, along with the rest of their people.

Vrynna's face had been bound by the clan's healer. Though the healer did not say, she knew she would never again see with her right eye.

She sat staring into the fire, her stomach full of charred thunderhorn meat, when Shiverbones found her. He had two horns of honey wine—the gods alone knew where he'd found it—and held one out to her. Vrynna nodded her thanks.

"You fought well today, *scarmaiden,*" Shiverbones said, as he settled down beside her. "Would you join us on the hunt tomorrow?"

It took Vrynna a moment for the impact of what he'd said to register.

Scarmaiden. It had a good sound to it.

It should have been a moment to savor, but she felt no stirring of pride within her. She felt nothing. The two hunters sat staring into the fire, sipping occasionally from their drinking horns.

"She was a mighty warrior and the best tracker I've ever known," said Shiverbones, correctly guessing where Vrynna's thoughts were. "It was an honor to have known her and to have fought alongside her."

"It was," agreed Vrynna.

"To Sigrun Ice-Runner," Shiverbones said, and the two of them drank.

Ice-Runner would be with her sons now, hunting and raiding across the eternal ice plains of the beyond. It gave Vrynna comfort to know that one day she would join them.

"We may die tomorrow, but today we survived," said Shiverbones. "Today, the clan eats. That is good enough for me."

Vrynna nodded slowly, finally realizing the simple truth in those words.

This was what it was to be Winter's Claw.

Every day was a fight for survival. And while every new dawn was one to be thankful for, it didn't matter if she joined Ice-Runner and her sons in their eternal hunt tomorrow or twenty winters hence.

All that mattered was right now, in this moment, her clan lived. And tomorrow, the fight for survival would begin again.

A deep sense of peace descended upon her. Finally, she understood.

"A good day," said Vrynna, raising her drinking horn high.

Those who pass will never know... The perfect silence, after the snow.

PILTOVER

The dual city-states of Piltover and Zaun
control the major trade routes between
Valoran and Shurima, but the divide between
their social classes is gradually becoming more
and more dangerous.

Home both to visionary inventors and their wealthy
patrons, Piltover is a thriving, progressive city overlooking
the ocean. Dozens of ships pass through its docks
every day, bringing goods from all over the world, and
allowing the resident merchant clans to fund incredible
endeavors—including artistic follies, and architectural
monuments to their individual power. With ever more

& ZAUN

artisans delving into the emergent arcane science of hextech, the self-styled City of Progress is fast becoming the destination for some of the most skilled craftspeople from across Runeterra.

By contrast, Zaun is the polluted undercity beneath Piltover—once united, the two are now separate, symbiotic cultures. Stifled inventors often find their unorthodox research welcomed here, but reckless industry has rendered whole swathes of the city highly toxic. Even so, thanks to a thriving black market, chemtech, and mechanical augmentation, the people of Zaun still find ways to prosper.

nce known as Oshra Va'Zaun, the slim isthmus that connects Valoran and Shurima has been a hub of mercantile activity since ancient times. Even after the fall of Azir, it continued to serve as a prosperous port and trade route, and became known simply as Zaun. But the steady growth of the area came at great cost to the community, when ambitious construction work resulted in the flooding and collapse of some of the oldest parts of the city. Undeterred, the powerful merchant clans moved their interests to the outlying districts of Piltover instead.

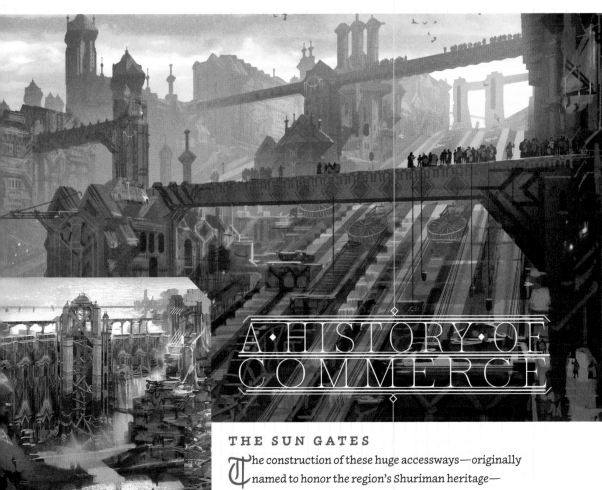

A·HISTORY·OF COMMERCE

THE SUN GATES

The construction of these huge accessways—originally named to honor the region's Shuriman heritage—brought unimaginable wealth to the merchants of Piltover. A shortened route between east and west has also enabled the rapid expansion of the Noxian empire along the coast, although Piltover charges truly staggering hazard rates for the transport of all military assets.

THE JUBILEE

A local festival dating back several thousand years, the Jubilee has been celebrated every quarter century to give thanks for the sea and the bounty it brings. For modern Piltovans, this is a quaint but happy excuse for traditionally themed feasting. For Zaunites, it has become a more somber observance.

MERCHANT·CLANS AND·INVENTORS

JAGO MEDARDA

The current head of Clan Medarda, Jago commands immense respect throughout Piltover. His family was instrumental in the construction of the Sun Gates.

THE FLOW OF COMMERCE

A council of the richest merchant clans forms the basis of Piltovan government. While a greater flow of traffic and profit may not be their sole motivation, more recently Clan Medarda has convinced them to invest a fortune into harnessing the power of hextech, to speed the opening and closing of the Sun Gates. Since the citizens tend to be keen and idealistic, to date there has been little opposition voiced.

A CULTURE OF INNOVATION

Piltovans are self-reliant, industrious, and always aspire to do better. They see an open and free market as essential to their city's continued prosperity.

SIGNS OF WEALTH

The merchant clans of Piltover each have their own unique sigil to identify their homes, workshops, shipments, warehouses, inventions, and places of business.

THE GREAT FUNICULAR OF CANTEXTA

The port of Piltover is always busy with ships from every major region. This funicular brings goods from the docks to the Commercia.

SIDEREAL AVENUE

The streets of the city are rumored to be paved with gold, but to the disappointment of many a hopeful traveler, that is merely a metaphor.

THE ECLIPTIC VAULTS

The interior of Piltover's buildings are no less ornate than the outside, and are often marvels of technological ingenuity in their own right.

ZINDELO'S INCOGNIUM RUNETERRA

The lifetime's work of Valentina Zindelo, the Incognium Runeterra is a device she claimed was able to locate any individual in the world. Since Zindelo's mysterious disappearance, many believe her alchemical formulae were stolen. The apparatus remains eerily dormant.

MONUMENTS TO·PROGRESS

Hextech is the newly emergent fusion of magic and technology, used to create exquisite artifacts that can be wielded by anyone—not just those few with a natural aptitude for the arcane.

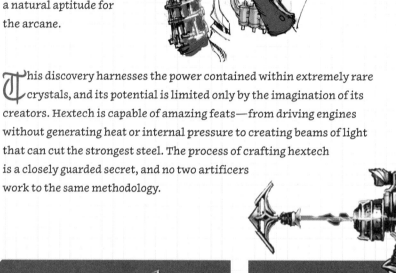

This discovery harnesses the power contained within extremely rare crystals, and its potential is limited only by the imagination of its creators. Hextech is capable of amazing feats—from driving engines without generating heat or internal pressure to creating beams of light that can cut the strongest steel. The process of crafting hextech is a closely guarded secret, and no two artificers work to the same methodology.

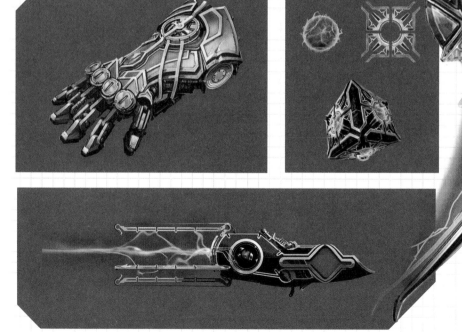

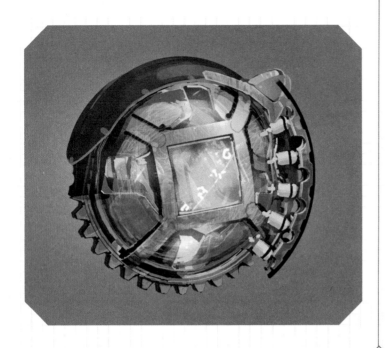

A man of means, pay heed, take note! Three yourselves stacked up in a coat!

$\mathcal{E}$ach item of hextech is a unique work of exquisite beauty, a bespoke creation that likely took years to craft.

THE DISC-RUNNER

HARNESSING HEXTECH

$\mathcal{A}$ combination of hextech, precision engineering, and visionary technology, this single disc-runner is capable of reaching dangerously high speeds, and takes great skill to control.

AN UNDERGROUND BUSINESS

A loose alliance of convenience exists between the chem-barons, powerful individuals who each control an area of the undercity. It is they and their thugs who keep Zaun from descending into chaos.

THE·WORLD BENEATH

BOUNDARY MARKETS

The levels between Zaun and Piltover are home to thriving markets and Commercia halls. These areas are the most cosmopolitan of the cities, where people from all walks of life and levels of society can be found.

HEXDRAULIC CONVEYORS

Travel between Zaun and the surface usually entails a long and tiring climb, but towering elevators do exist that allow for much swifter transit. The largest among the public descenders has been nicknamed "the Rising Howl" by both Zaunites and Piltovans.

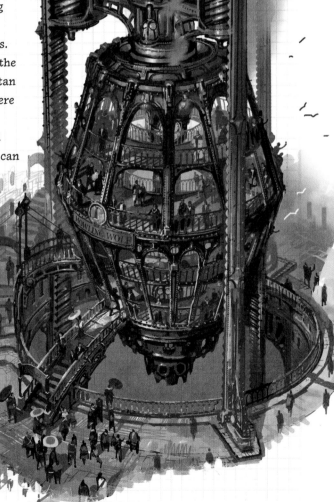

A CULTURE OF INVENTION

Though there is brutal functionality to the bolts and rivets of Zaun's structures, its inhabitants still manage to craft breathtaking wonders that pierce the smog and reach for the sky.

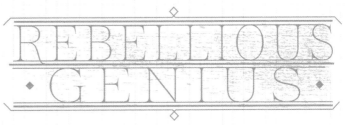

CHEMTECH RESEARCH

Denied the funds and means to craft hextech, Zaun's researchers instead use potent chemicals to power their creations. Chemtech performs like hextech, but is far more dangerous, toxic, and explosive.

REBELLIOUS · GENIUS·

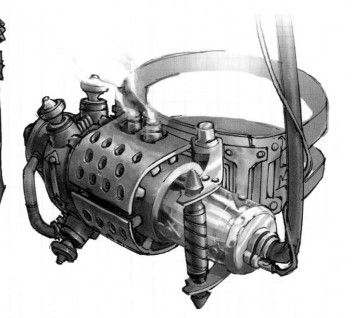

IRON & GLASS

Most of Zaun's larger structures are crafted from lattice ironwork, forged in seething foundries or wrought from scavenged material discarded from above. Even though the undercity lies far below the surface, it is far from gloomy—chem-lights, polished steel, and carved sunwells bring light to the depths.

THE GLORIOUS EVOLUTION

While many Zaunites choose to live in Piltover's polished but uptight shadow, Zaun is seen as the home of true genius. Some prefer to regard their bodies as tools, to be optimized and experimented on, to achieve their ambitions. They willingly opt in to powerful—and only occasionally monstrous—upgrades and prosthetics.

THE ZAUN GRAY

Zaun has few restrictions on its industries. To outsiders, the atmosphere of the undercity is thick and heavy, with a burning, chemical aftertaste. However, Zaun may not be completely to blame, since the production of synthetic Piltovan hexcrystals is rumored to be a heavy contributor to the Zaun Gray.

DANGEROUS ·LIVING·

SUMP-SCRAPPERS

Nothing is wasted in Zaun, and even the toxic hinterlands of the Sump can be churned for salvage. This environment is too hostile for unprotected humans, so the sump-scrappers make a modest living by wading through the waste looking for anything of value.

CHEM-PUNKS & SUMPSNIPES

The short life expectancy of Zaun's workers results in a great many orphans. Though the majority of troublemaking youth gangs form in the lower reaches of Zaun, their members come from every level of the city, and Piltover too. These chem-punks and sumpsnipes can be found begging, stealing, or earning a coin in places where their small size is an advantage. Despite the grime and hardship, the people of Zaun tend to be relentlessly hardy—proud of their home and their freedom to explore every avenue of invention.

THE SUMP

THE
JUBILEE
JOB

by IAN ST. MARTIN

It was on the eve of Jubilee, when all the undercity was awash in preparation, that Nikola's luck finally ran out.

His plan had been a good one, in truth. He had taken his time, casing and observing the spot he had chosen for the past two days. In that time he had tracked the inhabitants' rotations, sketched out his path, and worked out what the score inside was likely to be.

From all that, his guess was that it was quite substantial. Enough on hand for Nikola to put distance between himself and some particularly unfriendly debts, with a little left over to set down his lock-picks for a while in the Entresol, where he

could sleep with both eyes closed without fear of collecting a knife in his ribs.

Most importantly, the building was clear of the icons and markings of the syndicates. Nikola had pulled enough jobs to know that you steered clear of anything owned by the chem-barons, unless your desired end involved slowly dissolving in a caustic pool in the Sump. By all appearances, Nikola's score was a small, unaffiliated warehouse, the kind that played middleman to the many goods brought in by the sea as they moved to their new owners above and beyond the undercity.

He waited until the celebration was at the center of everyone's minds, when distraction was at its peak, and with one last encouragement from an increasingly empty stomach, Nikola made entry.

It was within a minute of doing so that Nikola realized his mistake—the only one he had made, but the only one needed to cast his plans to the fire and his wrists into irons. From the outside, there had been no sign of who the owner of the establishment was. Once within, though, it became abundantly clear.

Just a minute through the door, a strong hand on his shoulder was followed by an involuntary nap, and Nikola was off to see where his rotten luck had taken him.

A dull scraping noise finally roused Nikola to wakefulness, the sound of his boots dragging and catching against floorboards. His head throbbed, each blink sending a jagged wave across his skull as he struggled to get his bearings. He was somewhere else—the sounds of the warehousing district gone, replaced by the dull roar of industry.

The hands holding him up weren't hands at all, but clawed pincers of vertigreed brass and clicking clockwork. Footsteps thudded along on either side of him, ironshod boots sheathing what flesh remained, all glittering brass chemtech. One of Nikola's captors still had a man's face, blunt and scarred with a nose mashed flat. The other wore a helm styled into some likeness of a minotaur, with acrid emerald wisps of Gray wheezing from a twisted crown of exhaust pipes like horns behind his head.

Without ceremony, they dropped Nikola to the ground, sending fresh pain hammering through jangled nerves. He took a quick sidelong glance and saw a broad chamber of lethal opulence—half penthouse and half gangland master's lair. A spread of bottle-green glass domed the chamber, offering a view of Zaun spilling out across the canyon walls and floor, garish and deadly and alive.

A gout of flame from a nearby foundry tower flooded the room with light, casting the scene in front of him into stark relief.

Finally, Nikola's head cleared, and his eyes focused enough to see who held his life in their hands. Shining, silver hands.

Nikola's heart sank.

"Oh, just kill me now."

"Come, come now," said a voice, refined like an artful design etched along the edge of a blade. "Where would be the fun in that?"

Of all the chem-barons to steal from, it had to be him.

Nikola was dead. His heart just happened to still be beating for as long as his captor held interest. This captor was a man of reputation in the undercity, and not a benevolent one. Even the other syndicates kept their distance from him.

His captor was Karvyq the Silver-handed.

For all their bluster, most chem-barons in Zaun made no secret of their dependence on Piltover, just as the merchant clans and trade guilds above needed them. They went along to get along, a symbiotic relationship dating back to before the separation and before the Flood. Karvyq was a maverick among them, openly hostile to the metropolis of gold and light perched over Zaun and as fierce as he was unassailable. Had any other single syndicate or gang posed as much a threat to the stability between the cities, they would have been settled down in the Sump long ago. The Silver-handed, though, held control over the finest chemtech labs in Zaun, the mechanical limbs and breathing appa-ratuses he produced rivaling those of Piltovan hextech—supplying gifts that were sorely needed in the undercity. For this he was tolerated, even as he irritated the great merchant clans.

Karvyq the Silverhanded was a man free from consequence, and in Zaun that made him one of the deadliest men alive.

"Cheer up, my son," said Karvyq in his disarming drawl. "You didn't know who you were stealing from, and that's damn poor luck at the least. In fairness, you actually made it further along than most who try—the furthest in some time, in fact. You almost made it inside one of my shadow houses before Bakkens here nabbed you. How exhilarating, wouldn't you agree?"

Nikola knew better than to answer the chem-baron. *Better to let him speak,* he thought, *and maybe when he decides to get down to business he'll make it quick.*

The chem-baron was exquisitely dressed, his clothes spotless and tailored precisely to his tall, lean frame. Above his silver hands, which softly purred with every motion, his flesh was covered in tattoos. Elaborate patterns were barely visible through the thin white linen of his shirt, whorling up his neck and face—gangland marks and iconography whose significance was lost on Nikola. The thief wondered for a moment if the tattooing extended over his entire body.

The chem-baron bent down, cocking his head to the side as he studied Nikola with a natural pair of jade-green eyes.

"I respect a man of skill in this world,"

Karvyq grinned, his teeth the same brilliant silver as his hands. "And as low as your own luck might seem, I don't share your plight, because I just so happen to be in need of some skill at this moment. So much down here falls short and disappoints, but I see something in you. That's why you're here and why I'm going to offer you a choice. It is Jubilee, after all."

For a moment, Nikola's chest tightened. The pulse pounding in his ears intensified.

"Let's get to the crux of this, then," said the chem-baron, swiftly rising to his feet. "The choice: a quick job outside these walls, in and out, get you a little *sunshine*—or you take a not-so-quick trip downstairs. That option's only one-way, son."

The minotaur-headed thug chuckled behind Nikola, the sound like grinding asphalt.

"Bakkens is hoping for downstairs," said Karvyq.

Nikola swallowed, his voice barely above a whisper. "What's the job?"

"A trip upstairs to inquire about a member of the prestigious Clan Tariost."

The name fairly slithered off the Silverhanded's tongue, as though saying it was enough to elicit pain. Anyone paying attention knew the locus of the chem-baron's hatred was reserved for Tariost, a powerhouse in the shipping trade. No one knew why he hated them, only that he did.

"One of their family has recently passed, I'm afraid," said Karvyq, who now began pacing the floor of the chamber. "According to their traditions, the body is to be burned before the ashes are interred in the Clan Tariost vault. I need you to steal them for me."

Fighting through the throb within his skull, Nikola struggled to make sense of the request. What could a chem-baron want with a dead noble's ashes? Some last humiliation? Something even more ghoulish?

"You're probably curious why." Karvyq's pace quickened, growing increasingly erratic along with his speech.

"They have taken," he paused a moment, "a great many things from me—Gray be cursed, from you, from all of us in Zaun. Have you seen how they celebrate the Jubilee in Piltover? Such a joyous occasion to them, but then again, why wouldn't it be? The sea means beauty and endless wealth up there—they never see the dark side of it. After all, *they* aren't the ones that were drowned by their neighbors' hand."

In a blink, Karvyq rounded on Nikola, and the silver hands clenched his shoulders. The thief fought back the urge to cry out, hearing the soft purr as the fingers dug into his flesh. "So never mind what I need the ashes for—I need them!" The green eyes bored into Nikola. "Promises were made, and so promises will be kept. As for you... what's it going to be?"

Nikola's heart pounded in his ears like a hexdraulic hammer. Words failed him, so he gave a hurried nod, though the pain of it nearly made him pass out.

"Splendid!" Karvyq released Nikola immediately, standing as he flashed another grin of polished silver teeth. "Glad to have you on board, son. Now, time is of the essence, so we must move quickly. Though you need one more thing for this job. Volsk?"

The sound of a bone saw whirring into high-pitched life behind Nikola sent a wave of gooseflesh rippling over his body. Karvyq cupped Nikola's chin in a glittering silver hand, raising the thief's face to look up into his own.

"Courage now, boy, this is going to hurt. I'm afraid you are going to have to die for a little while."

This wasn't how he expected things to end.

Being born and raised in the Sump taught a boy to manage his expectations, to scrape out every bit of joy he could wherever he could find it and treat it like it was the last he'd ever see. More often than not, the chance was good that it would be.

Even so, Nikola had believed he would be different. He'd envisioned for himself a future beyond the caustic haze of the Sump, somewhere he could breathe and think and grow into a man he never would have the chance to be down among the snipes and the jacks and the barons.

There was so much more to Zaun than what Nikola had been able to see. The Entresol was the heart—vibrant, full of art, music, and expression... safe. And then there was the Promenade, up so high it mingled with Piltover, but without ever losing its own identity. To Nikola those places were the real Zaun, not the Sump. He was desperate to escape the shadows.

Desperation led to thieving. With never enough to go around and plenty looking to take it, it was the strong, the quick, and the smart who got by. Nikola had never been brawny, but as far as the other two were concerned, he was in luck.

Luck that had brought him *here*. Nikola had to wonder, as the bone saw lowered and an injection blurred his awareness to sleep, whether he should have stayed in the shadows after all.

The first thing he felt was a rattle in his chest, like too many birds in too small a cage, panicked and fighting to escape. The rattle gained momentum, building into a single, agonizing throb.... Then it grew again, and again, into some crude metronomic mimicry of a pulse. The pain spread like acid through his veins, filling every inch of him.

Nikola bolted upright but found himself restrained. The world around him was muffled, dark, and oppressively close. His hands pressed against the material surrounding him—a thin rubbery shroud. He felt around, searching for a seam, and, finding one, began to tear himself free.

Bright, cold light stung his eyes. Nikola recoiled, almost shrinking back into the relative safety of the stifling cocoon. He squinted, taking shallow, pained breaths as he waited for his vision to clear.

Everything around Nikola was different, clean and gleaming. He couldn't sense the familiar tang of chemtech, the earthy smell of steam, or the sour taste of corroded metal on his tongue. In fact, he couldn't sense anything beyond a cold, bleached sterility that was unlike anything he had ever experienced.

Nikola wasn't in Zaun anymore.

The realization sent a thrill through his body, bringing a sharp flare of pain that radiated out from his core. He took a shaky breath, his ribs feeling like they were humming. Something was very wrong.

With shaking fingers, Nikola felt along his chest, finding puckered flesh and thick sutures of fine wire. He looked down, blinking through tears, and saw a scar the length of his hand bisecting his sternum. A faint green glow throbbed beneath his skin.

A note dangled from the last of the sutures. With a grimace, Nikola pulled it loose, bringing it up close to his face to read:

Hey kiddo,

You're probably a tad confused, so allow me to explain. You see, trust is an understanding of a thing's nature, not a belief that it will do what you want. A thief's nature, for example, is to lie and to run. So in your case, trust is the new heart I put in your chest.

You have until twelve bells to get me what I want, or I make it stop beating. Don't fret, I left some hints on you that should help you on your way.

Now run along, your little clock is ticking!

—You Know Who

What little was in Nikola's stomach was emptied onto the spotless floor of the room. The retching and the panic only made the thrumming of his new heart worse, so he forced himself to breathe and calm down. He had to clear his head. He had to think.

Twelve bells? What time is it now?
I don't even know where I am!
Focus! He said something about hints.

Nikola read the note again, his vision now clear enough to realize that the heart was not the only change the chem-baron had made. Scrawled across the flesh of his arms and hands were tattoos, his skin still pink and irritated from their recent application. There were notes, blueprints, and maps all meticulously inked onto him.

The urge to scratch rose like a wave of dancing pins over Nikola's body. He took a second to breathe, trying to swallow the shock of what had been done to him. Together with the itching, he drove it from his mind, leaving only the job. The job.

All that matters is the job, he told himself. *Finish the job, save your hide.*

He glanced over the maps, seeing shapes and roads that were completely new to him. The clean smell, the unfamiliar room—suddenly it all came together.

They had really sent him to Piltover.

It was only then that he began to take in the full extent of his surroundings. The shock and horror of the past few moments dulled, replaced by focus as the thief in him took over.

Nikola wiped a hand across his face and slipped out of the shroud and onto the floor. The pale stone was cold on his bare feet, sending a shiver over his body as he gingerly stepped around his own vomit. The air was clear, cold, and almost sweet. It made him light-headed.

The chamber was full of shrouds like his, arrayed all around him in neat rows on slabs of enameled tilework. Nikola guessed by the vague impressions through the thin material that each of them contained a corpse. That must have been how they had gotten him here—as

a corpse. The thought sent another shiver up Nikola's spine.

A careful glance around the room located a large hamper. Nikola rifled through clothes and personal effects, finding himself what he hoped could pass for the garb of a regular Piltovan youth. Though Nikola was just shy of twenty, early years of privation in the Sump had kept him short and rail thin. He had used that, along with a baby face he had kept since childhood, to his advantage in more than one job. It looked like he would do the same today.

Moving quickly through the rows of shrouds, Nikola searched for the body of the noble from Clan Tariost. His hopes of an easy mark eroded quickly, as he found nothing but ordinary citizens of Piltover lying in their final repose. He should have known a high-ranking member of the clans would be kept somewhere more secure. Sliding shirtsleeves down over the tattoos covering his arms, Nikola turned his attention to finding an exit.

Along his right forearm was a blueprint of the mortuary chamber Nikola found himself in, as well as the adjoining rooms and corridors. A life of cat burgling had taught him to read a map, taking every detail into his mind no matter how minute. He ran his finger over his flesh, tracing the path that would lead him to the crematorium.

"Hey!" called out a woman's voice from behind Nikola. "What are you doing? No one is allowed in here!"

Without pause, Nikola shoved down

his sleeve and ran awkwardly toward the orderly, flailing his arms. "Oh please, don't let them take Papa!" Nikola squeaked, forcing tears to well up as he buried his face in the woman's smock. "He's just sleeping, I know he is!"

The orderly's anger at Nikola's intrusion melted away to nothing. "There, there now," she doted, placing a hand lightly on Nikola's head. "Hush, child, all is well."

Gingerly she guided Nikola from the mortuary chamber out into a corridor lined with somehow even brighter lights. Their sting aided in the thief's false tears. Together they sat down on a bench, Nikola pretending to cover his face with his hands as he scanned each person that passed them by.

"Where are your people now, lad?" the orderly asked.

"I-I dunno," Nikola sniffed, quickening his breathing as much as he could without going light-headed in the clean air. "It was j-just me and Papa. But I can't f-f-find him!"

"Oh, dear," the orderly sighed, gently stroking his hair. "Now you wait right here, and I'll fetch you some water. Then we'll see if you and I can find him together, eh?"

Nikola nodded, making a show of threatening to burst into another fit of tears.

"You stay right on that spot," she said, rising to her feet and turning right to walk down the corridor. Nikola watched her, waiting until she took a bend and broke line of sight, and started moving left.

Nikola walked quickly, though not so fast as to draw attention to himself. His eyes flitted left and right, taking in the spotless environment around him, and the equally spotless people who passed him by. The chemtech heart throbbed in his chest, and he heard a mechanical tone in the hall, echoing the distant tolling of a great bell.

Seven bells. Nikola had only five more to finish the job and make it back to the Silverhanded. His hand involuntarily clutched at the front of his shirt, praying that the light from the device didn't show through the fabric.

Unwilling to risk exposing his tattoos, Nikola relied on his memory for the path he needed to take, ducking into a shadowed alcove to check them only when absolutely necessary. The building's floor plan was organized into an elaborate geometric pattern, beautiful to behold but dizzying to navigate. There was a distinct absence of collapsed passages as well, a hallmark of the Sump and more often than not an excellent place to hide. He was out in the open here.

The crematorium was nearly in sight, just ahead, if Nikola remembered right. He shrank back into a doorway to confirm it, but as he rounded the corner he realized he hadn't needed to.

A pair of armed guards stood sentinel on either side of the door, clad in blue-and-gold armor and bearing the shining blade symbol of Clan Tariost proudly on their shoulders. Each cradled a rifle in a practiced grip, intricate things of coils and crystals and filigreed casings that were as much pieces of art as they were weapons.

All this Nikola took in at a glance as he walked past the crematorium. He watched the guards out of the corner of his eye, finding that neither of their visored helms moved to track him as he passed. With that entrance out of the question, though, he would have to improvise.

The beautifully inscribed plaque hanging on the next door marked it as a storeroom. Using a hairpin he had lifted from the orderly, he quickly picked the lock to slip inside.

The storeroom was cramped and utilitarian in comparison with the rest of the building. It was filled from wall to wall with iron racks and shelves holding tools, supplies, and containers of various shapes and sizes. Nikola navigated the narrow aisles between the tall shelves, his eyes darting intently from label to label.

He came to a halt at a row filled with simple clay jars about double the size of Nikola's fist. Urns for the crematorium next door. He snatched one up, formulating the play in his head to make a switch for the one containing the noble's ashes.

On the other side were vials of viscous gel plastered with warning sigils. Nikola scanned the label, surmising that it was some sort of fuel for the cremation furnaces. He picked up one of the vials, too, turning it over in his hands. This could be useful should he

get cornered or need a distraction to get clear with the score in hand.

It would be loud, though, as good as an alarm to any Clan Tariost within earshot. Nikola held on to the hope that he wouldn't have to use it, but stuffed it in his pocket anyway.

A glance over the tattoo on his left elbow showed him that the storeroom was connected to the crematorium by a series of overhead ventilation ducts. Nikola looked up, finding the grate in the ceiling. It was small—too small for a grown man to fit, but *he* would be able to make it.

He did, just barely. With his arms extended straight out in front of him, Nikola wriggled through the duct, trying to make as little noise as possible as he hauled himself through the tunnel of thin sheet iron. Sweat began to stand out across his brow as the temperature rose—a sure sign that he was moving in the right direction.

Soon the faint *whoosh* and crackling sounds of flame reached up into the vent, along with a soft orange glow just around a junction in the duct. Nikola wedged himself around, taking the right branch to bring him directly above the crematorium. He stopped at the edge of a gridded vent cover, peering down to watch the scene unfolding below.

Half a dozen people stood below, wearing finery in the bright colors of Clan Tariost beneath cloaks and shrouds of translucent black. They stood on either side of the short ramp leading to the furnace, flanking the still form of a lady in a dazzling robe of gold and blue.

Even from a distance, Nikola found her striking. On the cusp of her middling years, she bore an elegance brought with time without losing the exuberance she must have held in youth. It provoked a twist of Nikola's stomach to think of what could have possibly transpired for her to fall prey to the machinations of the Silverhanded and what the chem-baron planned to do with her remains.

What made him hate her so?

"Thus we aggrieved," spoke one of the cloaked Tariost mourners, "remember our dearest Aurelie, fourth to bear the name, jewel of noble Tariost. May she stay with each of us, welcome within our hearts, that we might embrace in majestic reunion, when her memory calls to us."

Aurelie, Nikola thought. *What a beautiful name.*

He waited until each of the mourners had said their final words and the body was soberly carried into the flames before he forced open the vent cover. The furnace was quiet—alarmingly quiet to Nikola, when compared to the thunderous machinery he knew from Zaun. One of the Tariosts cast a handful of strange powder into the flames, causing them to change to a brilliant blue that bathed the entire chamber in a sapphire glow. The thief dropped silently to the floor, careful not to throw his shadow against any of the walls.

Nikola did not have to wait long before the body of Aurelie Tariost was reduced to ash. The members of her clan looked on in silence as the flames finished their work, one of them working the controls to extinguish them and cast the crematorium into a sullen gloom. The cremated remains were collected with more reverence than Nikola had seen anything shown in his whole life and placed in a golden box that shimmered with a soft blue energy.

Seeing the box widened Nikola's eyes. *Hextech.* That was an urn. He looked down at the simple ceramic container he held, his plan to switch the two now useless. The mourners poured in the last of the ashes and locked the urn with a sharp electric chime.

That left only plan B, and plan B was a very, very stupid thing to do.

Just beyond the door came the faint tolling of eight bells.

Nikola's new heart throbbed against his ribs with the sound. He had to act fast. The furnace was still hot, its metal cowling ticking from the flames just recently doused. Quietly, he unscrewed the ceramic urn, pouring in the fuel gel and then barely threading the two halves back together. He watched one of the mourners break into tears, the attention of the others diverted to comforting her, before he threw the urn into the furnace.

The residual heat was enough to ignite the fuel, sending a massive fireball rolling up into the ceiling of the crematorium. The mourners recoiled in shock, the closest of them thrown to the ground, and Nikola watched the hextech urn tumble from the hands of the nobleman holding it.

Nikola was on it in a moment, scooping the box up just as the doors were thrown open by the Clan Tariost guards. Retreating back up the ventilation duct was out of the question. Everything was in chaos, and Nikola chose to ride it as far as it would take him.

Before the guards could make sense of the scene before them, Nikola flung himself between them, skidding along the slick floor of the corridor and coming up in a sprint. The soldiers recovered quickly, turning toward the cries of their masters as Nikola flew down the corridor.

Frantically, he checked his tattoos, throwing himself around corners as he followed the path sketched out across the inside of his left forearm. There was an exit coming up, leading out to the street. From there he just had to get clear of Piltover, back down into Zaun, and get this job over with.

Angry words echoed up the corridor behind Nikola as the guards charged in pursuit. Despite the near-constant ache of his chemtech heart, the thief felt energized as he glimpsed the door leading out of the mortuary. Down in the Sump, he could only run so far before his lungs burned and his tongue tasted of copper—up here, the air was so clean, so pure. It made him giddy. He felt like he could run forever. He threw the doors open and went blind.

Artificial light was one thing. That, in all its glittering, flickering forms, Nikola was used to. But this was *sunlight*, pure, unfiltered, direct sunlight. Nikola had never seen it before.

In his youth, Nikola had heard folktales that spoke of majestic, angelic beings, ones so magnificent and beautiful that they left ordinary men blind at even the briefest glimpse. He felt the truth of such stories now, blinking at the blazing orb perched overhead, its light shining and glittering on every gilded rooftop and tower across the metropolis of Piltover.

That was when they caught up to him.

When he awoke, Nikola's arms were manacled in his lap, and his head pulsed with the fresh pain of a blow to the skull—something that was growing worryingly familiar of late. The world shook gently around him, a rhythmic rocking reinforced by the clank and whir of precision machinery. He sat on a bench of padded and embroidered hide, and a quick series of darting glances showed him an opulent cabin with silken drapery and even a small crackling fireplace. Apart from the single Tariost guard sitting before a rear doorway, the only other occupant was an aging man sitting across from Nikola, patiently waiting for him to convalesce.

"Ah, good," said the man as he saw Nikola had gathered his senses, stroking a hand absently down his trimmed silver beard. "I was worried you would sleep the entire ride and we wouldn't have a chance to talk."

Nikola recognized the man from the crematorium, still shrouded in his black cloak of mourning, with the hextech urn sitting in his lap. The thief took a breath, wincing at the agitated birds straining within his chest. "Ride?"

"Yes," the man offered a condescending smile, lifting a curtain to bring daylight and the moving landscape of Piltover into view. "I am Beredai, Grand Consignor of Clan Tariost, and you are

in my personal conveyance, on the way to my home where I have waiting agents skilled in the art of... aggressive... intelligence gathering. And they are quite skilled, I assure you."

Threats of torture in Zaun. Threats of torture in Piltover. Nikola began to question whether he had ever had any luck at all.

"Of course, it need not come to that," said Beredai, dropping his hand and allowing the curtain to fall back and cast the cabin into cool shade. "You attempted to take something tremendously dear to my employer, though something of sentimental rather than monetary value. That tells me you were sent here by someone with their own agenda for you to follow. Tell me who it is, and we can spare my staff the monstrous effort of cleaning up the mess we will make of you."

Nikola glared back at the merchant lord. The man was pompous, rigid, and urbane. He doubted the man's hands ever left the velvet gloves he wore, too proud to ever get them dirty. He looked more than anything to Nikola like a prisoner, content behind a gilded cage of his own making—he was everything a Zaunite despised. Nikola said nothing.

"Very well," Beredai sighed, "I can deduce a certain amount for myself. I see your marks." He gestured to the tattoos on Nikola's arms. "And my agents scrutinized the unnatural heart beating in your chest while you slept. Quite sophisticated for chemtech, nigh impossible to construct for all but a select few artisans in Zaun down below."

Beredai leaned forward, his eyes twinkling in the light of the fireplace, face creased in a smug grin. "So it was the Silverhanded, then?"

Nikola's eyes widened, and he cursed himself for the blatant tell. Beredai chuckled and sat back in his seat, victorious.

"He has ever been a thorn, true enough, albeit an insignificant one. You would think people would learn to know their place. That has always been the problem with you undercity folk, always trying to go where you aren't wanted. Never staying where you belong." He waved a dismissive hand. "Look where it got you."

Nikola's shoulders shook as he laughed. A backhanded strike from the guard reduced it to a wheezing gasp, but failed to silence him.

Beredai raised an eyebrow. "This is amusing to you?"

"We don't know our place, that's our failing maybe. But arrogance is yours." Nikola grinned with blood-pinked teeth. "Your boy here is sloppy, he didn't find it. Look where that's got *you*."

The merchant shot an angry glance at his guard, then back to Nikola. "Find w—"

The Grand Consignor didn't finish the question before Nikola gave the answer, flicking the last small reserve of cremation fuel he had stashed into the fireplace.

A muffled *crump* was all that was heard out on the streets of Piltover, easily lost in the merriment of the crowds celebrating Jubilee. The rear door of Beredai's carriage was flung open as the mechanical beast staggered on its shining back-jointed legs, and Nikola tumbled out onto the street, pawing soot from his face with one hand while clutching the hextech urn tightly against his chest with the other.

The sky opened up over Nikola, blue and infinite and terrifying. It nearly stopped him in his tracks, paralyzed by the sheer endlessness of it. Were it not for the bellowing of old Beredai as he staggered out, roaring for the clan guards

fast closing in on the carriage, Nikola would have been rooted to the spot.

He ran. So hypnotized by the skyline, Nikola only just realized the wondrous, vibrant city all around him. Immaculately dressed people flocked in every direction, strolling or being shuttled about by elaborate machine-powered conveyances like Beredai's. Salons and parlors beckoned to customers with a cornucopia of sophisticated wares, items so fanciful that Nikola could only guess at their purposes.

Everything was awash in color to celebrate the Jubilee. Flowers burst from windows and streetlamps. Revelers sang and played instruments on every street corner, and the air virtually dripped with joy from the heart of each Piltovan. They sang of the dance between the land and sea, like lovers unable to survive one without the other.

Nikola supposed that was true. They survived off the sea, Zaun and Piltover both, and that was worth celebrating. But in Zaun, Jubilee was a somber affair of reflection and remembrance, to give thanks for the bounty of the waves but, more than anything, to pay respect to the sea. Piltover had never felt that lover's embrace turn angry.

Focus took over quickly, shrinking the thief's mind to short, actionable thoughts. He was being pursued by two armed men in a bustling city thronged in celebration. Crowded places were the best ones to shake unwanted followers, so Nikola dived into the revelers' midst.

Losing the Tariost guards was simple enough. Nikola took a winding, circuitous path through the busy streets and thoroughfares, doubling back at random to ensure he broke line of sight and any trace of his direction. It took time, though, and time was something he didn't have.

Nikola stopped at a large, ornate fountain to catch his breath and gain his bearings. The maps inked into his arms could no longer help him now that he was outside the mortuary. He needed to reach the Rising Howl, the quickest and most direct artery between Piltover and Zaun. If he could make it to the massive lift alive and with his score intact, he might have a shot at surviving to see another Jubilee.

The slowly waning light of late afternoon was eclipsed as a long shadow fell over Nikola. He looked up, seeing a figure perched atop the statue at the center of the fountain. She was tall, lean, and bald, her athlete's frame encased in flexible, lightweight armor of gold and blue. A fan of golden blades stamped with the icon of Clan Tariost ringed her back like a murderous flower bloom, a match for two lightning-wreathed ones extending out from beneath her forearms.

She looked like an angel. An angel made of knives.

"I believe you have something that belongs to us," the angel said, her piercing eyes sparking with anger as they glared down at Nikola. "Steal from the clan and forfeit your life."

After a heartbeat of stunned silence, instinct took over, and the thief began to run.

Nikola hadn't survived to reach early adulthood by being caught. A thief could be prime at a heist, but didn't last unless he could get clear with the loot, and at that Nikola was very good.

Two things, however, were making that particularly difficult. The first was the gleaming box of crackling hextech cradled in his arms, as conspicuous a package as he could have ever possibly imagined. Second was the heavily armed killer mere paces away from sinking one of her many immaculately crafted blades in his spine.

The agent of Clan Tariost was as nimble as she was relentless. Nikola used every trick he knew to escape from her, but to no avail. He failed to vanish in a crowd when she could simply vault up atop streetlamps or anchor herself to the walls of buildings with her blades. Her eyes never lost sight of him, piercing through the masses of celebrants no matter where he fled.

As the clock struck nine bells, the sun had fully sunk into the horizon, staining the sky in whorls of deep crimson, mauve, and orange. It would have been a wondrous sight if Nikola had been at liberty to stay and enjoy it.

New strength flooded into his exhausted limbs as he glimpsed the first buildings of the Promenade. They represented the highest peaks of Zaun mingling with lower Piltover in a clash of architectural styles. Nikola flew toward those towers of wrought iron and bottle-green glass.

He reached the Entresol with his pursuer still but a few paces behind. The Rising Howl had to be close. Now he was down in full, proper Zaun, where the ordered grid of Piltover was replaced by a maddening, descending labyrinth of twisting streets that resembled a fingerprint if viewed from above. Entire districts had been washed away and destroyed in the Flood—it was the perfect place to shake loose the angel before his time ran out.

The air became slick and oily, with an acrid tang that coated the tongue and burned the lungs. Nikola had taken his first breath in this air—it was all he had ever known for his life, but he doubted the angel had. A blade sailed a hand's span shy of his head, sinking into the collapsed wall of a tenement house ahead.

She was slowing, her attempts to bring him down getting sloppy. Nikola grinned despite his terror. Right now he would take any edge he could get.

Finally, just after the tolling of ten bells finished sounding across Zaun, Nikola heard the sweetest noise he could imagine. A cacophony of ancient cogwork, gasping hexdraulics, and squealing pullies hauling endless lengths of dense chain. It was the Rising Howl, close enough for the thief to lay eyes on.

An immense mechanical elevator, the Rising Howl ferried citizens of both cities throughout their many levels—a place where Zaunite and Piltovan mingled as they were borne up and down to their desired destinations. The elevator traveled a broad chute, its walls riddled with broken pipework and patches of shattered stone worn away by time and other, more nefarious means.

That was what Nikola was after. He didn't want to ride the Rising Howl—he wanted to find one of the few dozen reliable tunnels leading from the shaft and disappear.

The immense doors of the Rising Howl, all glass and patinated iron, slid shut as Nikola was but a handful of paces away. Nikola banged on the doors, but the attendants within scowled and pointed to their timepieces, shaking their heads in refusal to reopen them. Slowly, with a protesting groan of its grand machinery, the car began to descend. The air just behind Nikola hissed as the angel's blades nearly found him, and with a curse muffled by the wind of the tunnel below, Nikola reached the edge of the shaft and leapt.

For what felt like eternity but was likely seconds, Nikola was in freefall. His new heart jumped in his chest as the urn slipped from his grasp, tumbling for a moment before he snatched hold of it again. Tucking it close to his chest, the thief realized he had been distracted from his fall as it came to an abrupt, painful end.

Nikola's legs buckled under him as he struck the metal-and-glass roof of the Rising Howl. Dozens of pairs of eyes gawked up at him from the riders below, but those weren't the ones he felt most.

Nikola looked back up at the lip of the shaft, seeing the Clan Tariost agent. He watched her exhale, straightening and glaring coldly down at him. She pointed toward her face, a slender gloved finger beneath each eye, and then back at Nikola before the descending car stole him from her sight.

No longer a blade's length from losing his life, Nikola felt an anvil's weight drop from his shoulders. He collected himself, scanning the walls until he spotted a tunnel he had used before, and leapt across to make his way back to the Sump.

Eleven bells rang, clanging from the canyon walls like hammer blows. Nikola's time was almost up.

Navigating the Sump was a perilous task, rife with collapsed remnants of factories and tenements, lakes of caustic sludge, and a myriad of other dangers poised to snatch the life from the careless and the weak. Nikola had done it his entire life, but even he was far from immune to it, especially as he rushed toward the lair of the Silverhanded, counting the last minutes of his life as they ticked away toward oblivion.

He was so caught up in getting to the chem-baron that he didn't even hear the gangers until it was too late.

"Whatcha doing down 'ere, Piltie? What's that flash kit you've got?"

There were nine of them, no older than Nikola. A swaggering pack of patchwork menaces, all threadbare mismatched clothes and predatory grins.

"Now I asked you a question," growled the lead ganger, making no effort to conceal the tarnished dagger he held in his grubby hand. Two more circled behind Nikola, one rattling a length of chain, the other slapping a sawn-off pipe against his palm as the thief looked down at himself.

He realized he was still dressed as a Piltovan in the slums of the Sump and holding a very expensive-looking box. That was incredibly stupid, and down here, stupid got you dead.

"What do you say, lads?" Their leader looked to each of his cohorts in turn. "We just take what he's got and give him the shiv, or see if we can't cut a ransom outta him from his goose-looking friends up top?"

Nikola saw a gap between two of the gangers and made a break for it. Their leader saw it coming, though, catching his collar and hauling him back into a loose chokehold.

"Now that's a very good way to piss me off, little snipe." Nikola felt the nicked edge of the dagger press against his neck. "Maybe we can get a ransom for just his pretty little head."

"Do you even realize who you are stealing from?" Nikola said frantically. "You think this won't end in blood for you?"

Their leader made a show of looking from side to side. "I don't see anyone here to stop us," he said with an exaggerated shrug.

"I would consider looking again!"

How not a single one of the idiots had

heard the footsteps made by rumbling, brass-sheathed chemtech, the chugging cough of expelled fumes, or the rattling of gears as claws rose to strike, Nikola would never know. All he knew was that he was grateful to the horrid brute for his inexplicable gift for stealth.

Bakkens flung two of the gangers clear before the rest even realized what was happening. Their bodies struck the corrugated-iron wall of an abandoned workshop at awkward angles, making short warbles of false thunder as they crumpled to the ground and stayed there. The others rushed the minotaur with their clubs and short knives, provoking a stream of rockslide laughter from him as they clinked and broke against his brass shell. His glee made the punishment he meted out next all the more terrifying.

In case there had been any question, Bakkens was a killer, and Nikola got the distinct impression that he enjoyed his work. His claws tore through patchwork clothing to rend flesh and snap bone like kindling. One jumped on Bakkens' shoulders, scrambling to find a joint for his dagger. The minotaur released a scalding cloud of exhaust from his horns, sending the ganger to the ground, shrieking as his face sloughed away. The leader of the gang had no chance to scream after a clubbing overhead strike compressed him into something like a horrific human accordion. Nikola fought the vomit surging up his tongue at the sight as the shock of the scene rendered him mute.

In spite of their threats, Nikola could not help a pang of sympathy from welling up in his chest for his would-be attackers. He had made a life of stealing, but the urge for bloodletting was just not in him. The lone thought within his numbed mind, as he looked upon the carnage surrounding Bakkens, was how glad he was that he had chosen this job over the alternative that had been offered to him.

The titanic thug tapped his wrist. "Almost out of time." Bakkens gave another tectonic chuckle, a plume of jade smoke coughing from his helm. "You best run along now, little thief."

Nikola pounded his fist against the doors of Karvyq the Silverhanded's tower, shouting to be let in until his voice was hoarse. The birds were close to clawing free of his ribs now, their wings beating thunder against his bones. He felt all of the clocks in Zaun and Piltover perched an inch from his head—none of them more acutely than the Silverhanded's own clocktower, grinning with cogwork teeth as it loomed over him, making ready to strike twelve.

Nothing happened. Nikola jumped up and down, holding the hextech urn up to see as he kicked the door with his foot.

"Come on!" Nikola choked. "I *did* it...."

He *had* done his part. Against everything, Nikola had done it and made it back in time. Now he just needed to get inside and—

A booming peal of thunder struck the air. A second followed, then a third and more after, like the hurried thrum of a dying engine. After the twelfth, the bells ceased, Nikola's death knell echoing through Zaun.

He sank to his knees, forced down by the sound, angry tears streaming down his face as he waited for the clockwork heart in his chest to give its final beat.

"Well, now," came that familiar drawl as the doors swung open. "Don't we look handsome all dressed up?"

"You certainly did leave it to the last moment, didn't you?" said Karvyq the Silverhanded as he led Nikola back up to his sanctum. "A dash of the dramatic, I won't begrudge it."

The chem-baron's voice was low and distracted, his attention focused on the hextech urn he held in his shining mechanical hands. They arrived in the main chamber, where Nikola had first met the Silverhanded. It was less than a day ago but felt like a lifetime. The thief glimpsed Volsk, the chem-baron's surgeon, lurking in a makeshift medical suite. Nikola's eyes fixed on the stained leather chair at its center, almost able to see himself strapped to it when they had cut into his chest.

"Here," said Karvyq, "a reward for a job well done." He pulled a small device from his coat, holding it up for Nikola to see. It was a piece of compact chem-tech, something resembling a trigger assembly. Immediately he recognized

it for what it was: the kill switch for his new heart.

"I fully expected to use this tonight," chuckled Karvyq. "Lucky for you, my clocks run a little slow. Here you are," he tossed it to Nikola. "You can rest easy now. That's the only one."

Nikola looked at the device for a second before hurling it to the ground. It shattered, and he smashed what remained to bits under his stomping foot.

Karvyq laughed. "Enjoy the new ticker, kid. On the house."

Nikola's head was swirling with emotions, but gratitude wasn't one of them. Anger, shock, fear—they all crashed around behind his eyes. He saw the scar along his chest again, beneath the funeral shroud. The angel's glaring eyes. The faces of the Sump gangers as they died. But of all the feelings assailing him, the strongest of them was guilt, a knot of remorse at his very core for doing what he had done.

"She was beautiful," said Nikola quietly.

Karvyq looked down at the urn. "She still is," he said softly in reply, reaching into his pocket. He produced a small gold cylinder, as long as his finger and tipped with a sapphire. He brought it to the urn, and Nikola's eyes widened as a soft chime sounded and the hextech locks opened.

"How did a filthy gutter baron like me get this?" Karvyq held up the key, smiling at Nikola's confused expression. "Easy, I stole it, just like I stole your heart and she stole mine. Unlike me, she never returned what she took."

Nikola felt his confusion surge up, overtaking everything else in his mind.

"Doc?" said the chem-baron, handing the unlocked urn to Volsk before turning back to Nikola. "Stay awhile, pull up a seat, and I'll tell you a story from a Jubilee long past."

The thief and the chem-baron settled down on the worn leather couches beneath the glass dome of the tower. Nikola couldn't help but feel disoriented at how different this meeting with the Silverhanded was compared to their previous encounter. He watched the crime lord roll the hextech key between his metal fingers.

"I've had this key since Jubilee twenty-five years ago," said Karvyq. "Back when I was just the muscle for another chem-baron, just enough experience to think I knew everything and just enough a fool to act on it. We were up on the Promenade, business with the Pilties for some fine, creatively acquired goods, when I saw her."

Nikola's eyes flicked over to Volsk as the surgeon poured the ashes into a vial.

Light seemed to pulse from Karvyq's jade-green eyes. "*Aurelie.* You can't forget a name like that. Just as sure as I couldn't see any face but hers after that moment. How a guttersnipe like me could have gotten her attention, I'll never know. Sometimes, I guess, the stars line up just right for a man, right when he needs it most."

Karvyq rose, crossing the chamber to Volsk as he removed his coat and shirt.

Nikola beheld the tattoos that covered his arms and torso and discovered there was yet one spot untouched. The center of his chest was bare, an island of pale flesh amid a sea of ink. The chem-baron settled into the chair as Volsk slotted the vial into a needle gun and set to work.

"Together we managed to shake our respective entourages and then began a stretch of days that lasted a lifetime and an instant all at once. It was like being in love with the sun, able to see the world around you clearly for the first time because of the light she shone on everything. And I could make her laugh," he paused, looking out through the window with a low chuckle.

The needles thrummed as Volsk ran them over Karvyq's flesh.

"We knew it wouldn't last," Karvyq continued. "She was highborn, a lady of Bluewind Court, her whole future mapped out for her before she was even born. Nobody had accounted for my place in the story, the ganger boy who snuck in and stole her heart. Perfection is the ideal pursued, but without love it's cold and lonely. Together we had both. Soon enough, they tracked her down. Of course, I couldn't let her go, so they took her... and they took my hands." He held up his silver replacements.

"The last thing she said, the last words I'd ever hear from her, were a promise. She made me promise that our hearts would always touch, no matter what. And now, my friend, it's a promise, because of you, that I can keep."

Nikola would never have taken the gangland quack as an artist, but as Volsk worked his needles, the thief watched a careful, steady hand create something beautiful on that last patch of canvas remaining to the Silverhanded. The surgeon took his time, the attention to detail excruciating, but when he was finished, he showed that every second had been worthwhile.

Inked and raw, over the chem-baron's chest was a perfect re-creation of a human heart, laid just above his own. The ashes of Aurelie Tariost had been mixed into the ink, the two now together in her death in a way they had never been allowed to be in life.

Nikola looked up at a cluster of crashes in the distance. The first fireworks of Jubilee burst across the canyon, illuminating Zaun in a riot of glittering color.

"Heart to heart, that was the promise. Now she's back with me, right where she belongs." Karvyq the Silverhanded smiled. "Happy Jubilee, my friend."

Nikola stepped back out into the Sump, leaving the Silverhanded behind. The job was done. There was the reassuring weight of some coin in his pocket and, most of all—at least as far as the past day's events—his conscience was clear.

Dawn was quickly coming. Nikola looked up the canyon walls at the industrial sprawl of Zaun, his home, and cast his gaze up at the Entresol. He felt as though he had earned a good rest, to lay low for a few days in peace, and that seemed as good a place as any.

"Long day?"

Nikola froze. The voice that spoke to him was beautiful, the voice of an angel. An angel made of knives.

He felt the cold flat of a golden blade rest against his collarbone. Nikola looked back over his shoulder, craning his head up to meet the sapphire eyes of the agent of Clan Tariost. With a resigned sigh, the thief offered her a tired grin.

"And here I was, thinking it was over."

IXTAL

Renowned for its mastery of elemental magic, Ixtal was one of the first independent nations to join the Shuriman empire. In truth, Ixtali culture is much older—part of the great westward migration that gave rise to civilizations including the Buhru, magnificent Helia, and the ascetics of Targon—and it is likely they played a significant role in the creation of the first Ascended.

But the mages of Ixtal survived the Void, and later the Darkin, by distancing themselves from their neighbors, drawing the wilderness around them like a shield. While much had already been lost, they were committed to the preservation of what little remained.

Now, after deep seclusion in the jungle for thousands of years, the sophisticated arcology-city of Ixaocan remains mostly free of outside influence. Having witnessed from afar the ruination of the Blessed Isles and the Rune Wars that followed, the Ixtali view all the other factions of Runeterra as upstarts and pretenders, and use their powerful magic to keep any intruders at bay.

Translated from Ixtal's most ancient tongue, this chant is taught to the mages of Ixaocan from an early age, often before they even begin formal study in the arcologies.

I.
The elements of this world are ours
And we strive to unmake all
Understand and master the singular
Control and shape the many
Learn, discover, invent
To create new alloys of our design

II.
Formed by our will and intention
We bend the world to our needs
Temper our hearts with fire
Give breath to our curiosity
Water and nurture our bodies
Ground our thoughts in earth

III.
We are the sons and daughters of Ixtal!
Proud inheritors of mastery
Our skill is our strength
Our creation is our legacy
We are what came before
And the shapers of the future!

Bilgewater

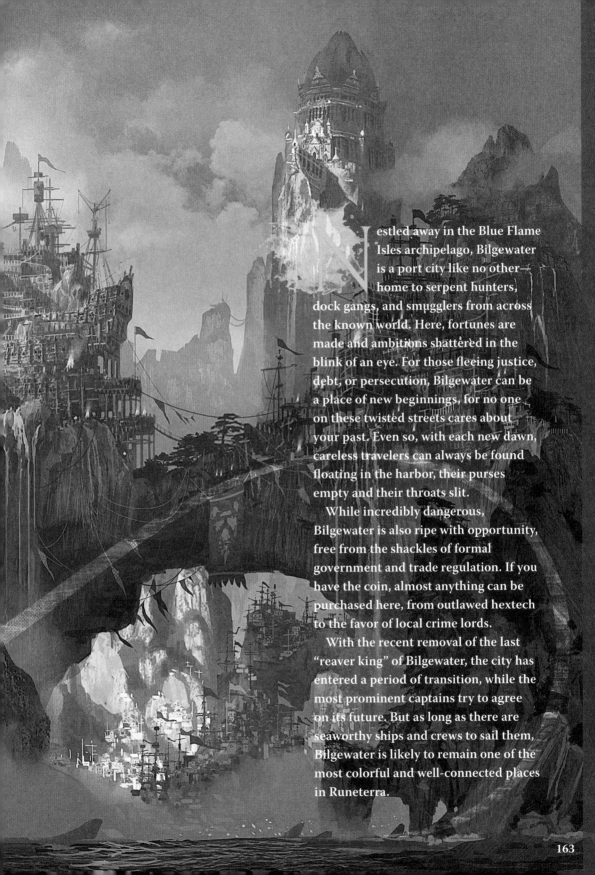

Nestled away in the Blue Flame Isles archipelago, Bilgewater is a port city like no other—home to serpent hunters, dock gangs, and smugglers from across the known world. Here, fortunes are made and ambitions shattered in the blink of an eye. For those fleeing justice, debt, or persecution, Bilgewater can be a place of new beginnings, for no one on these twisted streets cares about your past. Even so, with each new dawn, careless travelers can always be found floating in the harbor, their purses empty and their throats slit.

While incredibly dangerous, Bilgewater is also ripe with opportunity, free from the shackles of formal government and trade regulation. If you have the coin, almost anything can be purchased here, from outlawed hextech to the favor of local crime lords.

With the recent removal of the last "reaver king" of Bilgewater, the city has entered a period of transition, while the most prominent captains try to agree on its future. But as long as there are seaworthy ships and crews to sail them, Bilgewater is likely to remain one of the most colorful and well-connected places in Runeterra.

Living with the Sea

Bilgewater is a place where different cultures merge and meld. The old creeds and faiths of Valoran are often reinterpreted in relation to local customs, since a life on the ocean waves bears little resemblance to the daily hardships of a Demacian ranger, or a Shuriman shepherd.

This aging priest, decked out in his crude sea monster regalia, wanders the quaysides to offer charms and blessings to departing ships' crews, in exchange for a few coins—or a hot meal.

A WATERY GRAVE

In Bilgewater, the dead are not buried—they are given back to the ocean. The port's graveyards consist of innumerable floating buoys, below which are sunk the mortal remains of the recently departed. The wealthy might be interred within expensive caskets with lavish, bobbing tombstones… while the poor are often tied en masse to old anchors underneath waterlogged barrels.

SERPENT CALLERS

Whatever purpose these immense horns once served, they are now used by the people of Bilgewater to drive away sea monsters that wander too close to the shipping lanes.

The Bearded Lady

entral to Buhru culture is Nagakabouros—goddess of life, growth, and perpetual motion. Also known as the Mother Serpent, the Great Kraken, or the Bearded Lady, she is commonly depicted as an enormous, monstrous head with many spiraling tentacles.

Many more strange beings haunt the depths around Bilgewater. Some are from this world, and this time. Others are not.

A PARLEY WITH DEATH

Mortals have precious little understanding of the primal magical forces at work beneath the waves, or perhaps they simply choose not to care. Either way, there is no guarantee that things that "perish" near Bilgewater will stay dead for very long.

THE TITHE

Insisting it is more than mere superstition, Bilgewater locals urge all seafarers to pay the Mother Serpent her due. Whenever they leave port, a ship's captain should throw an offering overboard—or face the ocean's wrath.

HARPOONERS

One of the most important roles on a hunting crew is the harpooner, who hooks and slays the beasts, and entire crews will be built around a veteran who can teach others a thing or two along the way. Many harpooners are marksmen, or particularly fearless free-divers, but few survive long enough for their reputation to become widely known.

TOOLS OF THE TRADE

The most skilled monster hunters know the old ways are often the best. Following the traditions of the Serpent Isles, these cunning traps and vicious hooks are crafted for luring and slaying specific creatures, and such implements are passed down from generation to generation.

Sea monster attacks are a constant threat around Bilgewater, but over the years myriad lucrative industries have grown out of hunting and harvesting the massive creatures. Vessels haul them back to port, to be rendered down into meat, oils, hides, armored scales—even bones and teeth—for sale at the thriving dockside markets.

From MacGregan's Killhouse to the renowned outfits at Bloodharbor, slaughter docks operate day and night to turn death into profit. Only the most successful captains can ever hope to run their own dock, so most are forced to haggle for the best deal before their prize begins to rot in the water.

The Slaughter Docks

The Serpent Isles

While much of Valoran knows them as the Blue Flame Isles, to the indigenous people of Buhru the archipelago has only ever been the Serpent Isles. Buhru's ancient culture is highly respected, reflected, and sometimes imitated in the daily life of Bilgewater—including traditional medicine and monster-hunting techniques. The native peoples' knowledge of the ocean and its denizens is second to none, and few ships are able to navigate the perilous straits around Bilgewater without their guidance.

Bilgewater has no unified central government, making it a place where various gang leaders, syndicates, and power brokers vie for control. However, it is not a totally lawless place—it's just a matter of what you can get away with, and retribution is generally swift and fatal. In Bilgewater, wealth is the true power.

GANGPLANK

As unpredictable as he is brutal, the dethroned reaver king Gangplank is feared far and wide. Once, he ruled the port city of Bilgewater, and though his reign is over, there are those who believe this has only made him more dangerous. Gangplank would see Bilgewater bathed in blood before letting someone else take it—and now with pistol, cutlass, and barrels of gunpowder, he is determined to reclaim all he has lost.

MISS FORTUNE

A Bilgewater captain famed for her looks but feared for her ruthlessness, Sarah Fortune paints a stark figure among the hardened criminals of the port city. As a child, she witnessed the reaver king Gangplank murder her family—an act she brutally avenged years later, blowing up his flagship while he was still aboard. Those who underestimate her will face a beguiling and unpredictable opponent— and, likely, a bullet or two in their guts.

THE BOUNTY BOARD

The closest thing you can get to law enforcement in Bilgewater is the bounty board. Written on it are the names of the most wanted criminals, ranked by how much would be paid for their heads.

It is said that Gangplank regularly added a silver Serpent to his own bounty, as an open challenge to the entire city.

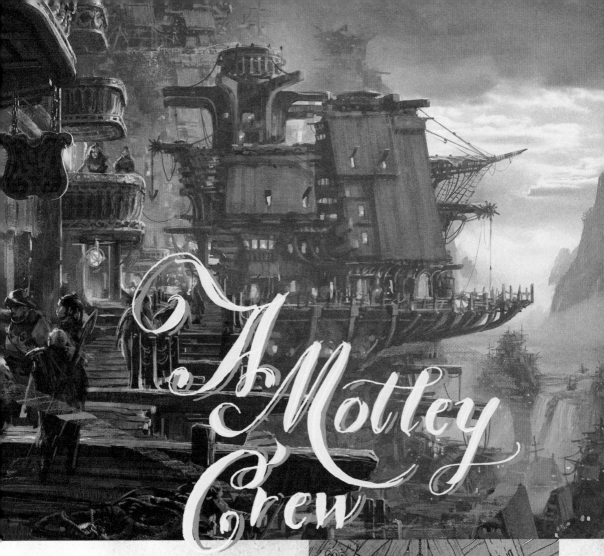

A Motley Crew

A FISTFUL O' KRAKENS

As a trade city, Bilgewater is one of the most amenable to the use of foreign currency, though it also mints its own coins in denominations of golden Krakens, silver Serpents, and bronze Sprats. When a new reaver king or queen rises, they legitimize their hold over the city by putting their mark on each coin— Gangplank was the most recent to do so.

HIGH AND DRY

There is a commonly accepted truth in Bilgewater: The higher you climb, the less likely you are to drown. As the city lacks many natural resources for construction, much of it has been built up with whatever people can bring, find, or steal—be it repurposed masonry, or even the broken hulls of the ships they traveled in.

Those with money in their pocket will frequent the uptown taverns, enjoying fine drinks and merry conversation—even though, in a day or two, they will be back down at the wharf, wrangling a crew for their next dismal voyage.

BLACK MARKET GROTTOS

Bilgewater's lowliest inhabitants dwell in a labyrinth of meandering canals and hidden inlets, with no separation between the homes they build and the sea where they ply their trade. Indeed, traversing perilous waters is not just an occupational hazard, but part of daily life.

I. Conversation in the Dark

Little Lamb?

> *Yes, dear Wolf, o' companion mine,*
> *My darkest friend in all of time?*

Oh, no.
I hate your "water speak."
It is bad.

> *Verse writ by tongue that tastes no flavor,*
> *A riot of colors that none wish to savor.*

Use barks. Or howls.
I like howls. Howls make sense.

> *If Wolf stills his claws and drooling,*
> *His Lamb shall pause her poetic mewling.*

Fine. I will stop.
But what will we do if not chase?

> *There is commotion that interests me.*

I see that motion.
Shapes... bodies!
They make noise, too....

Kindred Eve

by MATT DUNN

Joyous melodies upon delirious tongues.
'Tis a festival in our honor, dear Wolf,
Celebrating the dance of light and dark,
Storm and serene, tooth and arrow.

I want to hunt the festival.
And chase it.

> *Our role is to witness,*
> *Perchance to understand,*
> *Why these mortals worship us so.*

That sounds boring.
How long will it take?

> *Until it ends.*

What if the festival does not end?

> *All things end, dear Wolf.*

No water speak and no chasing... deal.

> *Closer, then, we go together,*
> *o' companion mine....*

> *His Lamb...*

> *... and her Wolf.*

II. The Pale Rider

Every year, those who did not keep faith with the Buhru gathered for a night of exceptionally unfettered debauchery. All who call the ports and islands of Bilgewater home—including those mysterious Buhru worshipping their spiral god, should they ever choose to attend—were welcome. There was no planning committee, yet the riotous jamboree never failed to occur on the final wolf moon of the year.

The revelers, of which there were too many to count, hailed from every culture and class—there were brigands and bankers, captains and cooks, fisher-folk and freelancers. They donned macabre costumes and, by duskfall, packed the docks beyond capacity. It was common for more than a handful of attendees to fall into the waters and perish then and there. It was uncommon for someone to lend a helping hand. What happened this evening, though, was truly rare: not a soul fell from the docks and perished.

Some whispered the lack of early deaths was an ill omen....

All ships were bound for the same destination, and for this night only, no captains charged passage. Once loaded, with folks dangling from mast riggings or towed behind larger vessels on lifeboats, the ships set sail, dotting the eerily calm waters, gliding toward the craggy fang of an island called Witch-Tree Rock.

The outlandishly clad partygoers paired up and filled the beaches. Now that night had well and truly fallen, the crowds amassed to celebrate life's chaotic dance toward death and those who bring that death. This celebration of those eternal reapers was called Kindred Eve.

It was easy to see someone's origins based on costumes: folk of Shuriman stock resembled elegant tusked gazelles partnered with speckled hyenas. Those tracing their lineage across the sea to fair Ionia often had no partner, choosing to represent a snake and a sparrow on their body. There were other odd interpretations, too: a jaull-fish and a minnow, a bloody-antlered stag and a sleek rabbit, a rose and a stinging bee. By far, the most prevalent representation drew from wider Valoran, who dressed as the oldest depiction of the Kindred: a lamb paired with a wolf.

But tonight was special. Amid the costumed revelers were the Kindred themselves. Lamb shone like the palest moon, while Wolf floated like the darkest smoke. Their eyes were the same—haunting and cold, a shimmering ethereal blue. Had the Kindred chosen any other night to reveal their forms, all would have run in terror. But on Kindred Eve, the reapers of life walked among a crowd celebrating the balance of death, disguised with no disguise at all.

The revelers gathered before a torch-lit path that twisted up toward the other end of Witch-Tree Rock, passing through a single shop-lined concourse and ending atop a cliff, from which sprouted a great leafless tree.

"Why do they wait?" Wolf asked, trying to keep his great tongue from licking his lips.

"*They await an invitation, dear Wolf,*" Lamb said, her eyes taking in the island setting.

A bent figure descended the path alone. When the man reached the beach, he stopped and climbed atop a large, flat rock in the surf. Waves gently lapped against its edges. He raised his hands, and silence settled over the crowd. Even those who stood knee-deep in the water stopped kicking away the whisker-eels and ankle-sharks to grant the man their attention.

The man spoke in a high-pitched voice that carried over the water to those still on the moored ships, waiting to wade toward the beach.

"Once upon a long while ago," he said, "there lived a Pale Rider who rode upon a great black beast. Every town shunned him, for they knew that if he rode through their village, any who met his gaze would not live out the night."

"I know this story!" the great shadowy Wolf said. His tongue lolled out enthusiastically.

"And so it happened one night that the Pale Rider came upon a fork in his path. One road led into a deep, dark wood, the other toward a city of light. Faced with a choice, and knowing it would take him twice as long to travel both paths…"

The storyteller pulled a prop axe from his cloak. Moonlight danced along its blade.

"This pale man took his axe," he said, kneeling down, "and knelt before the ancient eldlock tree that forked the road…"

Wolf cocked his head in confusion. "Do I know this story?"

"A tale told throughout time is tainted by each tongue that tells it," the snowy Lamb said. *"We know a truer story, of which this faint dramaturgy projects only shadow."*

The storyteller milked an overly theatrical pause. Thousands of kindred faces hung upon his every flourish. "And cut himself…"

"Right down the middle!" the crowd replied in eerie unison.

The storyteller pressed the axe blade into his brow and jerked his hand backward, slashing his head open from front to back. Rather than sever flesh, however, he merely split a seam sewn into his cowl. Coils of tightly wound ribbon and snowy confetti showered from his head. A large paper lamb, supported by thin bamboo struts, popped up from the top of his hood. It was covered in cotton tufts and painted beamingly white, with hooved legs and the angular snout of a black wolf's mask. The paper lamb's hands held a giant cutlass covered in arcane runes.

In a masterful display of ambidexterity, while the lamb popped out, the storyteller tore his shirt with his other hand. More wooden struts, painted black and affixed to a corset, spread the man's robes out like the dark fur of a great lupine beast, a cherubic lamb face painted on his breast.

"Many miles later, the two paths met again and the Pale Rider regarded the other half of himself. His two halves had grown so different, despite being of one. Together, they drowned his axe in a river and decreed to forever walk side by side…."

"So they would never be alone?" Wolf's eyes were full as he looked upon his little Lamb.

Lamb caressed the wolf mask that covered her true face. *"So they would never be alone."*

"So they would never be alone!" the crowd intoned, finishing the tale.

With the parable's end, cheers rang out, mixed with laughter and the sounds of flintlock pistols fired into the night sky. It was time to walk the path toward the town.

As the crowd marched past the slab of stone, the storyteller swooped and dipped toward his rowdy audience, and they applauded and dodged the lamb's paper sword. Tankards of dark ale and white wine were passed around.

The storyteller did not notice his paper sword pass through Wolf's body as if nothing was there.

"Little Lamb?" Wolf said to his favorite Lamb. "Do you have a sword? Do not hide it from me. I want to see it!"

Lamb looked to her precious Wolf. *"I keep no secrets from my dear Wolf, not now and not ever."*

Torchlight flickered across the sea of kindred revelers as they danced, sauntered, or marched up the path to the town ahead. Pressed tightly together, each shove created a wave that traveled the crowd.

Lamb and her Wolf paid it no mind. Their movements were swift, for they danced upon heads and leapt from shoulder to shoulder—they breezed over the crowd like a zephyr over roiling seas.

All Kindred Eve had begun.

III. Kindred Souls

Slaughtered lambs, hanging by their necks, their heads dyed black with squid ink, decorated storefronts. Every now and then, innkeepers removed a carcass and placed it on a spit to be slathered in salted honey and roasted over an open flame.

Peddlers sold favors to the throngs walking the cobblestoned avenue. Quarrels erupted between the violent halves of kindred pairs—wolves punched sharks, hyenas kicked stags. Wide circles formed around the fisticuffs, which eventually ignited into brawls. Teeth, blood, and wayward bits of costume littered the street. Lovers embraced openly, their lips pressing tightly onto the faces of their partners or whoever had the luck of being in kissing distance.

Perched atop a large cask, Lamb and Wolf watched the heaving gaggle of mortals eat, dance, and shove through the streets of Witch-Tree Rock.

"Look! They knock each other down!"

"They celebrate a crude approximation of a fate none escape. Staving off a common fear through imitation and jest, through purging and release. They see us not for what we are—"

"By the Bearded Lady, your costume is almost the best I've seen tonight!" A female voice interrupted Lamb from the din of celebrants.

Lamb and Wolf looked down from their perch. A young couple peered up at them.

"Isn't that a wonderful outfit?" the woman said to her companion. The man shrugged in reply. Her costume was made up of carefully placed cotton wads and artistically applied white paint. His was a lesser effort: a black loincloth and white face paint applied in sloppy streaks.

"Your *Farya* costume is amazing." She reached up and stroked Lamb's shoulder. "How did you make your fur feel so cold on this late summer's eve?"

The woman's gaze fell on Wolf. "And your *Wolyo* friend's using enchantment? It reminds me of a Harrowing. You should enter the pageant. You'd take third place, at least."

Lamb turned to Wolf. Wolf turned to Lamb. An ethereal blue light shone behind both of their masks, cold and dead and unfeeling, the same and yet… confused. Lamb and Wolf cocked their heads and turned their gaze back to the woman.

"I'm staking gold in the Wolf's wager this year…. Hopefully Lamb's luck winks at me." She blew a kiss at the two of them, then flashed a gummy smile.

"Merry Bloody Kindred Eve to ye both!" The woman waved farewell and sauntered off into the crowd, dragging her loincloth-clad wolf behind her.

"What a weak wolf! I feel sad… and angry, like I want to hunt and not hunt."

"That is called 'confusion' dear Wolf. It is an emotion mortals feel, perpetually and pervasively."

"I do not like this confusion."

Wolf shook his head. Lamb reached out and rubbed the underside of his chin.

"To them, dear Wolf, we bring the greatest confusion," she said.

"Confusion is a hunt, then? A game of knocking down and not getting back up?"

"Not quite, but also yes. Confusion dwells between the knocking down and the not getting back up."

"My claws itch, Lamb, is the festival ended now?"

"For now we keep our pledges, dear Wolf."

"When does 'now' end?"

"Sooner than you know, but later than you'd hope."

Wolf placed his chin on Lamb's lap and listened to the incessant flurry of thousands of beating hearts he could not chase… and then, above it all, a strange sound caught his attention.

"What is that howling, Little Lamb?"

"It is not howling but music, dear Wolf."

Wolf's eyes lit up, his great tongue lolled back out, drooling. "Can I chase music?"

"In a manner of speaking, yes."

IV. The Wheeled Corsair

Lamb and Wolf followed a melodious patchwork to a stage where musicians dressed in black furs played mismatched but complementary melodies. Oddly tuned horns warbled out wavering notes. Percussionists wailed on kettle drums and elongated logs. The music was both uplifting and haunting.

"This sound chases my ears."

"This music is called Dragtime, performed only on this night, to honor tooth and arrow."

Gunshots rang out in perpetual succession. The sound of jeering grew louder, spreading like mist across the Bilgewater folk.

A woman dressed like a corsair captain appeared at the prow of a prop sloop on wheels, pushed and pulled by strong-backed folks. Atop the ship sat a gilded cage with alabaster bars.

"More new things! My head is spun around." Wolf growled at the sight of the ship on wheels.

"That is curiosity, dear Wolf. A closed door ringed in light…. What lies on the other side?"

Lamb leapt onto an awning above a butcher shop to get a better view. Wolf swirled around her.

The crowd parted as the ship grew nearer. The gilded cage loomed larger now. Its alabaster bars caught the glow of flickering streetlamps. Inside, a figure cowered.

"Oy! Make way for the champion of the meek! The lover of the sick!" yelled the captain. "A weaning, mewling mess of a weakling."

The crier's words turned heads. Cheers arose as the revelers saw the pathetic figure inside the cage: a man who had been tarred and covered in cotton. His eyes were wide in fear and panic. He was the only Bilgewater local attending Kindred Eve against his will.

"I present to you the last honest man in our humble stretch of ports… the Lambfool of Bilgewater!"

The crowd welcomed the Lambfool by barraging the lavish cage with whatever bric-a-brac lay within arm's reach. Heads of lettuce exploded on the bars. Overripe mangoes splattered sticky pulp on his tarred and cottoned skin.

"He looks like you!" Wolf said to Lamb.

"Cruelty stuck her deviant thumb in the mortal mold. What a pitiful shape then was wrought."

"Countrymen!" the Lambfool cried. "I beg your mercy. Have I not honored all my debts? Forgiven those who had not a silver serpent? I have committed no crime other than civility and compassion!"

"He sounds like you!"

"Cutting words, dear Wolf. His words nary have I spoken."

The Lambfool shouted louder. "Nary have I ever cheated, stolen, lied, or killed!" His appeal to whatever conscience the revelers had not drunk away proved futile, as he was answered with rousing laughter and mocking imitation.

"Nary, nary, nary! I'm a boring little lamb too!"

The glowing blue light of Lamb's eyes looked downright frigid.

The poor Lambfool was now gnawing at the bars with his teeth, pretending to be a wolf. "Do you want me to be a bastard? Is that it?!" he cried, spitting on the crowd.

"The truest lambs find even the mask of a wolf painfully unbecoming."

Wolf laughed, too caught up in the bloodlust of the night. He turned to Lamb with joy in his eyes.

"I hope they do me next."

"I am sure you will not be disappointed, dear Wolf."

Wolf then threw his head back and let loose a howl, so long and loud it silenced the night entirely. That terrible sound reverberated through flesh and bone, shaking everyone to their core.

V. The Howler, The Hungry, The Hunter

Once the howling faded, midnight tolled. The wolf moon reached zenith, signaling a shift in the mood, the direction of the revels, and perhaps more importantly, the winds.

The procession left the town behind, the wheeled corsair leading the way. A somber, dirgelike mood took hold, in time with the odd rhythms of squeaking wagon wheels, thousands of footsteps, and the whimpering of the Lambfool. The path had narrowed in its incline up toward that great leafless tree, which was lit by two large bonfires.

The road ended here in a large open space. Beyond was only a cliff and a long fall to a grizzly end in the rocks and churning waves.

The two raging fires loomed larger in the darkness, blazing like the eyes of a leviathan rising from the sea. The leafless tree shook in the wind, rattling dead branches like dried bones. Jagged cliffs hewn and worn down by centuries of use formed the space into a rough amphitheater.

"I know this place, little Lamb."

"Roots sprung from seedless fruits strangle the soil."

Three figures emerged from behind the eldlock tree, striking jarring and unnatural silhouettes against the flickering madness—three giant wolf heads, decapitated below the neck. They wobbled forward, fire revealing truth. They were men in costumes. Their torsos were wrapped in thick fur. Feet poked out from below the furry necks. The wolf heads, meticulously and terrifyingly constructed, towered above where shoulders should be.

Each of the three figures' wolflike headdresses was different—one howling with its snout pointed up toward the moon, another with its jaws open and a massive cloth tongue lolling out, and the last with its jaws clamped shut around the carcass of a freshly killed lamb.

"Too many false wolves."

"These are our masters of ceremonies: the Howler, the Hungry, and the Hunter."

The Howler spoke first. "We kindred souls do gather here, under the dread wolf's moon, at the eldlock tree where death itself pledged company."

Next, the Hungry. "Tonight, we mark the day when the wolf conquers the lamb and our liberties run rampant throughout our land!"

Lastly, the Hunter. "Behold the Lambfool! Champion of all weakness, a thing of timid nature and erudite cowardice. We are truly *honored* by his presence!"

A thick metal ring was bolted into the eldlock tree's wide trunk. A heavy chain snaked across the dirt where it was wrapped around the Lambfool's scrawny neck. Upon his head sat a crown of snowy cotton and two little lamb ears. He was truly a pathetic sight—bruised and hungry, wet and soiled from a night of hurled food and drink and other filth.

The gathered audience laughed and booed. When the pathetic man raised his gaze, there was little light left in his eyes. He bowed his head into his hands, resigned to his fate.

"And now," said the Howler. "We present the Champion of Bilgewater..."

"...Strongest of all," added the Hungry, "... and ready to take what is hers by force or cunning!"

"She salivates for the hunt," intoned the Hunter. "She smells blood, she smells death, she smells *freedom*! All hail the Wolfkin Warrior!"

The corsair captain stood proud on her wheeled sloop. She leapt off the prow of the false vessel and addressed the crowd.

"When death comes for us, do we wish to greet it in our beds, ailing and frail, body wasted by disease? A body that can only pull the covers tighter over one's head. Who would die defeated and defanged? Not the Wolf! Not I." Her voice rang with defiance. She pummeled her thighs with her fists. "My legs are strong. They will die strong. Put my boots on and point me to the sea, toward every shark, kraken, and jaull-fish. I'll die on the waves, I'll die with a sword in my gut, I'll die with a drink in my hand and a smile on my face!"

She stripped off her captain's attire. Underneath, she wore all black. Her limbs were thick as ship masts. A pair of tailored gloves with razor-sharp blades sewn into each finger gave her claws. The Hunter placed a terrifying wolf mask over her face, teeth glistening white, completing the transformation.

Wolf's eyes grew wide with excitement. He knew what was happening.

"Little Lamb!" he said. "They are playing us!"

"*We do not fight like this, dear Wolf. And we shall not for a long time. Forever plus a day.*"

"Shhhhhh! Things are happening." Wolf's ears perked up, for he sensed a kill.

The Howler spoke again. "The eternal struggle ends once more tonight, and one of these kindred two shall emerge victorious, as it will be in the final days, when the wolf shall eat the lamb..."

The Hungry spoke next. "Should the Lambfool somehow claim victory—" Laughter interrupted this suggestion. "Then until the next Kindred Eve we will restrain our basest instincts, turn an eye upward from the dregs, and clothe ourselves in manners and honesty."

The Hunter spoke last. "If the Wolfkin Warrior emerges triumphant, we carry on our proud traditions in the name of ourselves and our desires!"

The crowd went wild. Flintlocks were loosed. People threw teeth. Others decked each other in the face, screaming in adrenaline-fueled joy.

The Howler spoke once more. "Dear revelers, friends, ladies, gentlemen, cutthroats, bandits, pirates, barbers, leviathan hunters, jaullers, captains, business folk, cheats, thieves, liars, gunslingers, sailors, soldiers, brigands, rogues, and all who call Bilgewater home—let us watch the Wolf win on this one thousandth consecutive year and reign over all our doings!"

The Wolfkin Warrior, in addition to her claws, received a heavy cudgel ringed with shark teeth. It was a brutish weapon, created to cause the most vicious of deaths.

Someone threw the Lambfool a bow with a broken string and a snapped arrow. He refused them, allowing them to clatter to the ground at his feet. He turned his eyes toward the moon.

"I can hear waves..." the Lambfool said. "This will be over soon."

"No," replied the Wolfkin Warrior with glee. "I will make this last a very long while."

Lamb studied the scene intently. The masked faces in the crowd leaning forward, placing bets—exchanging money, vials of rare beast oils, ornate guns, and glowing gems.

"*By what foolish hand does a rigged bout guide the fortunes of a year? Dear Wolf, they think us a game and try to tell us whom to hunt at least on this one day. They seek to direct our hand, knowing not whose hand they yank. What does all this folly accomplish?*"

In the crowd she saw the scantily dressed lamb from earlier and watched the young woman hand over a sack of gold to her loincloth–clad wolf friend.

"They want to hunt. They want to play. They do not like words or waiting."

The crowd did not want a fair fight. They were not to get one.

VI. Wrath of the Lamb

The Wolfkin Warrior raised her club over her head. Her muscles rippled as she prepared to bring the cudgel down to bash in the Lambfool's skull.

"Blood sport is fun!" Wolf laughed, his eyes getting full.

"*This is not blood sport, dear Wolf. This is mockery. Let them learn the wrath of the Lamb and the might of the meek.*"

Lamb removed her mask. She turned away and hid her true face, even from Wolf. In the distance, there was a sound like rolling thunder. The wind kicked up harder now. A quiet clung to the air, but it did not diminish the fervor of the audience enraptured in a lust for blood.

Few could see the golden trace of strange magic, old and not of the world. Only Wolf saw, and he turned his head sharply to Lamb.

"You said 'no playing'..."

"*I said 'no chasing' and no 'water speak', dear Wolf...*"

The Lambfool felt nothing as the grisly bludgeon smashed into the crown of his head, all the might of the Wolfkin Warrior behind its blow. His spirit, instead of ebbing out of the cracks in his skull, arose in his core like a flame stoked to life by whipping air.

The weakened Lambfool survived the killing blow. And then another. And another after that.

"*Shine on, O defiant spirit who ignores the pains of body, who saw the moon for more than an ill omen and heard the waves above the impending crush.*"

The last honest man in Bilgewater raised himself up on a shaky knee, then up to standing.

The Wolfkin howled and circled the Lambfool. Wolf howled with her, for he was furious at Lamb's breaking the rules. He could not speak, only froth.

Lamb placed an arrow on her bow and drew her deadly aim.

"*...I made no promise to set aside my arrows.*"

She loosed her arrow, and it passed right through the Wolfkin Warrior's heart, tearing soul from body instantly. But the crowd did not see Lamb protect the Lambfool or fire her arrow at the Wolfkin Warrior—they saw a man survive devastating blows.

The gathered clouds loosed a single bolt of fury. The lightning struck the Wolfkin Warrior without warning. She stood a moment as a conduit for forces far greater than her flesh and bones... and then only a scorched husk remained. Her smoking body toppled with a thud.

The Lambfool was utterly befuddled. A godly act had spared him, but no applause erupted. Instead, there was silence—the crowd was dumbstruck. A woman vomited on her shoes. Never before in one thousand years had the Wolf perished before the Lamb.

"Does this mean we must honor our contracts this year?" asked a hook-handed reveler.

"The Lamb won! I am rich!" the scantily clad lamb cheered. She began kissing the revelers around her, but they were far too gobsmacked to react. Tears of disbelief welled up in their eyes.

Wolf pressed his face into Lamb's, their masks almost touching.

"No fair!" he howled with fury. So did others in the crowd. Thousands howled at the moon as one.

Lamb pulled away from her Wolf. She slung her bow on her back and shrugged.

"It must be that once in every long while plus a day, the Lamb bests the Wolf."

"Little Lamb cheated!" Wolf growled. He turned and fixed his gaze on the now terrified Lambfool. "And if Little Lamb wants to play..."

Lamb bowed low to her Wolf. *"...Then it is only fair that her dearest Wolf may play as well."*

The battered Lambfool looked around nervously, but there was no place to hide unless he were to jump from the ledge and plummet to the rocks below.

Wolf pounced upon the Lambfool, knocking him over the cliff and into the churning ocean. When Wolf returned, he was licking his lips, still not sated.

The Howler, the Hungry, and the Hunter shuffled around the fallen Wolfkin Warrior. They conferred over her body, hoping for her to take another breath. But she was burnt and gone. The crowd turned, sorrow and anger boiling over at the thought of a Lamb Year filled with calm and peace....

The Howler raised his hands and commanded silence, which spread like wildfire. One could hear a feather fall.

"For a thousand years, we of Bilgewater have lived in the shadow of the Wolyo, the great black wolf. None command him, and so none command us."

The Hungry stepped forward. "Farya, the educated lamb of light, was afforded the tiniest place in our hearts and in our dealings…"

The Hunter took her turn. "I am here to announce that the Wolfkin's heart still beats! The wolf warrior is the victor! *A thousand years in the shadow of Wolyo!*"

The corsair was clearly dead, and the Kindred two had seen she was the first to fall, but the official proclamation caused an eruption of joyous applause from the revelers. All was right in their world.

"Wolf wins the game!" Wolf laughed.

Lamb cocked her head sideways.

"*The truth is plain as night is dark—*

the avatar of Dearest Wolf expired first. We know this to be true."

"No matter! They said I win. This is their party. They make the rules!"

"*Those who set rules may indeed write rules to rewrite rules.*"

Wolf sniffed at the air. The wind carried the stench of another hunt—one that would end before dawn's breaking.

No one noticed a stray ember leaping from the bonfire to the dried branches of the leafless tree, or how it caught the boughs. None could tell floating embers from the stars in the sky. In the confusion surrounding the Lambfool's overturned victory, none saw the bonfires inching higher and higher.

"Does a parade end, Little Lamb?"

"*All things end, dear Wolf.*"

"Now?"

"*Now.*"

VII. Ashes of Anticipation

> *Dear Wolf?*

Yes, Little Lamb?

> *Of that capricious night's*
> *bouquet of flavor,*
> *What tastes and smells*
> *and sounds did Wolf savor?*

The Lambfool's throat looked weak,
But was filled with juice.

> *Grapes unwilling to leave the vine,*
> *Sometimes produce the finest wine.*

The three wolves.
They were sweet first,
But my tongue turned over.

> *How bittersweet their final moot,*
> *Trampled aflame under many a boot.*

The music-makers,
They popped.
They screamed,
They crackled.

> *Burning players playing burnt songs,*
> *Melodies alight with night's wrongs.*

The pale liar,
Salt on my tongue,
Salt on my fur.

> *A storyteller swallowed by water,*
> *Cast overboard by those fleeing slaughter.*

There was another lamb.
She liked us.
Did she burn?

> *The poor soul wagered a foolish debt,*
> *Hung from the docks on an ill-advised bet.*

It was a good hunt,
Even if we had to wait.

> *Indeed, dear Wolf,*
> *Anticipation heightens rewards.*

Little Lamb,
Do you taste anything?

> *Your Lamb tastes only ashes,*
> *But for one flavor that flashes:*
> *That our prey never gleans our meaning,*
> *They cast us into roles most demeaning.*

We hunted. We chased.
I knocked down so many.
Can we hunt the festival again next year?
They will fear us now.

> *The view of all who survived that now*
> *burnt stone,*
> *No greater Kindred Eve has Bilgewater*
> *ever known.*

SHADOW ISLES

This cursed land was once home to a noble, enlightened civilization, known to its allies and emissaries as the Blessed Isles. However, more than a thousand years ago, an unprecedented magical cataclysm left the barrier between the material and spirit realms in tatters, effectively merging the two... and dooming all living things in an instant.

Now, a malevolent Black Mist permanently shrouds the Isles, and the earth itself is tainted by dark sorcery. Mortals who dare to venture to these dismal shores will slowly have their life force stolen away from them, which in turn attracts the insatiable, restless spirits of the dead. Those who perish within the Mist are condemned to haunt this nightmarish place for eternity—worse still, the power of the Shadow Isles appears to wax stronger with every passing year, allowing the most powerful specters to roam farther and farther across Runeterra.

Hidden from outsiders for many centuries, the Blessed Isles enjoyed a golden age dedicated to knowledge, philosophy, and the safeguarding of magical artifacts from across Runeterra. The capital city of Helia was filled with renowned arcanologists, astronomers, and scholars of every conceivable discipline, while the common people lived peaceful lives of pastoral simplicity in the surrounding countryside.

ARCHITECTURAL PUZZLES

The greatest repositories of Helia were architectural wonders, containing innumerable secret—and sometimes dangerous—treasures. Certain vaults, their decoration laden with hidden meaning and symbolism, would open only at specific phases of the moon, angles of the sun, or alignment of the stars.

BLESSINGS

OF THE PAST

THE WHITE MIST

The lands surrounding the capital were incredibly fertile, and the towns and cities were designed to be secure without giving the appearance of being fortified. Thanks to the confounding magical mist that shrouded the Isles, turning unguided travelers away, there was little need for any standing army.

THE RUINATION

F ar, far from the Blessed Isles, a king and queen ruled over an empire whose name none now recall. When the queen was poisoned, the king sent his best warriors to search for a cure. One of his generals returned with the means to part the white mists of the Blessed Isles, home to the legendary Waters of Life.

Unfortunately, this news reached the king too late. The queen was already dead.

Driven mad by grief and unwilling to listen to reason, the king set out in force for distant Helia. He immersed the corpse of his wife in the healing waters, unleashing a magical cataclysm that laid waste to the Blessed Isles. Every living thing was cursed, transformed into roaming, ravenous spirits caught somewhere between life and death, and the white mists that had once protected them turned black and predatory.

Today, none but the most desperate scavengers and treasure hunters dare to visit the ruins of Helia, in search of the countless arcane treasures that must surely remain buried there. Some mortals have even learned to live close to the shadows and decay... though who can even begin to guess what horrors they might witness there?

The spirits of the dead are often mournfully referred to as "the Lost." For the most part, a dead soul trapped in the Shadow Isles will slowly diminish, forgetting who it was in life. However, the most powerful specters appear to have retained much of their personality and desires even after the Ruination, stalking the weak and vulnerable for all eternity.

The Ruination struck without warning, as farmers tilled their fields and children played games with friends. Some of the spirits fractured during that event were distilled down into echoes of the last emotions they experienced—fear, protectiveness, or the madness of losing one's identity.

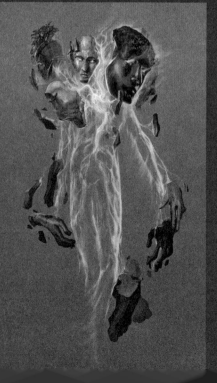

While some spirits are entirely ethereal, and relatively easy to bind or destroy, the most powerful beings of the Shadow Isles have proven themselves to be essentially immortal. Over time, these spirits' appearance will likely change to reflect their most essential qualities.

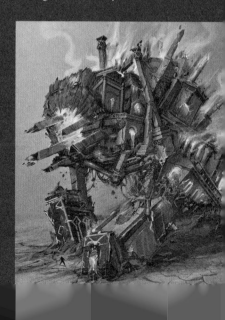

RESTLESS SPIRITS

Many of the humble scribes and archivists of Helia perished at their lecterns, unaware of the disaster that had just befallen them. This poor soul now feverishly scratches descriptions of its torment on an endlessly unraveling parchment.

Many of the Lost are not aggressive or predatory. For instance, an innocent with a good heart who lands on the Shadow Isles may be met by a spirit with a benevolent or empathetic nature, who will try to lead the person to safety.

Similarly humored spirits sometimes merge to form more powerful entities—these five angry souls cling to their hollow existence by clinging to one another, for only the most strong-willed and resilient are able to retain something of themselves in isolation.

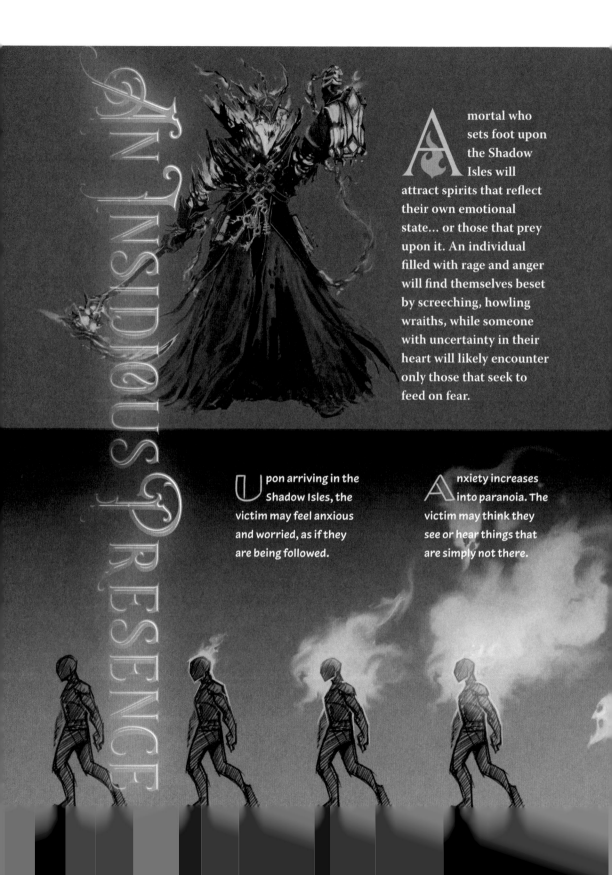

AN INSIDIOUS PRESENCE

A mortal who sets foot upon the Shadow Isles will attract spirits that reflect their own emotional state… or those that prey upon it. An individual filled with rage and anger will find themselves beset by screeching, howling wraiths, while someone with uncertainty in their heart will likely encounter only those that seek to feed on fear.

Upon arriving in the Shadow Isles, the victim may feel anxious and worried, as if they are being followed.

Anxiety increases into paranoia. The victim may think they see or hear things that are simply not there.

THRESH, THE CHAIN WARDEN

The man who would one day be known as Thresh was once a lowly member of an order devoted to the gathering and protecting of arcane knowledge. The masters of this order acknowledged his long years of service, and tasked him with the custodianship of certain hidden vaults. He was methodical and resolute, which made him well suited to such work, but he hungered for greater recognition.

When the Ruination struck, the inhabitants of the Blessed Isles had their spirits torn from their bodies. Thousands screamed in terror and anguish, but Thresh reveled in the undoing of all around him. He rose from this cataclysm as a spectral abomination— unlike many who have passed into the world of shadow, he did not lose his sense of purpose. Now, unbound by mortal concerns, Thresh is free to pursue his cruel ambitions for all eternity.

Abstract noises and visions often begin to take on the forms of people the victim knows to be deceased.

The victim is set upon by one or more leeching entities, until their own spirit cannot go on.

The victim continues to weaken until their material form wastes away, or becomes a mere vessel for another entity to inhabit.

It is worse than we feared.

We know that when the Black Mist reaches across the seas, the spirits of the dead go with it. This Harrowing strikes most frequently in Bilgewater. Living beings that find themselves caught within slowly have their life force sapped from them, until they are nothing but lifeless husks. A truly horrible end, for those slain during a Harrowing are damned, their souls dragged back to the Shadow Isles when the Mist recedes.

Now, it is becoming clear—with every new soul the Black Mist claims, its reach extends.

Also, while the weaker spirits of the Lost may only be able to manifest during a Harrowing, it seems more powerful entities may be able to manifest elsewhere in the world at will.

Thankfully, just as these spirits are many and varied, so too are the ways they can be banished or destroyed. Some are bound to a physical anchor—their armor, a book, or some other talisman, for instance. Destroy that item, and in most cases, the entity too will be destroyed. Sorcery and hextech are known to harm them, as are weapons that are made from silver, blessed or infused with arcane power. Many can be harmed by fire and direct sunlight.

Think on this. We will speak more when next we meet.

THE HARROWING

THE DARING DARLING

by LAURA MICHET

Fayette always warned her guests that the journey from the Shadow Isles back to the Daring Darling's dock would take a whole watch.

The inn sat alone on a tiny rocky island. Fayette had built the inn without a lighthouse, so the place was impossible for predacious ghosts—or treasure hunters, unfortunately—to pick out in the dark. Leave too late, and you'd likely get lost after nightfall, stuck sailing in circles all night long—prey for the wraiths. But if you pushed your boat off the Shadow Isles' black-sand shores early in the afternoon, you'd find the inn's lonely rock outcropping and dock safely long before night came.

Fayette always recommended this plan to the younger and less seasoned guests at her establishment. Leave the Isles *early*. Leave your loot on the shore, if you have to. It was much, much safer to be off the water before night came.

Usually, however, newcomers didn't take her advice. The first boats back to the Daring Darling were always the most experienced treasure hunters. And when they appeared on the horizon, Fayette would go out to help them.

Treasure hunters coming in from the Shadow Isles were always tired, and sometimes injured. They needed someone to catch their dock line and help pull them to safety. Fayette thought of the service as part of her establishment's hospitality: a warm breakfast at dawn, a cold drink at night, a safe place to keep

your goods, and a smiling innkeeper to help moor your vessel.

What more could you want?

"I want a nap," Gavin called to her over the waves.

"Well, you can have one," Fayette laughed. Fayette always enjoyed Gavin's strange levity. It was good to have at least one cheerful friend on this island. The innkeeper held out her hook-arm, waiting for the wiry Demacian treasure hunter to toss her a hawser. She'd been greeting him here at the end of the dock almost every week for the last ten years.

Today, his boat looked empty. "No luck?" she asked.

"Almost nothing," Gavin said. There was no worry in his voice. Sometimes, Gavin came in with a haul of fascinating artifacts, and sometimes he didn't. It never seemed to bother him. You didn't stay alive to loot the Shadow Isles for a decade running if you got anxious about these things. It was about winning the whole siege, not each minor engagement—that was what Gavin always said, anyway.

As Fayette tied his dock line to a cleat, Gavin leapt lightly over beside her. He had a small cloth bag in his hand. It clinked as he landed.

"Sounds like *something*," Fayette said.

"Odds and ends. Nothing for the vault." That meant that after a day digging among those haunted ruins, he'd found nothing touched by magic. Maybe a golden knick-knack, but nothing really interesting.

The vault was only for truly precious, deadly things.

"I'm off to take that nap," Gavin said, before pointing out to sea. "But watch for our holy friend. The priestess and her boys found something *big*."

Fayette turned and saw a familiar vessel on the horizon—an Ionian sail. That Ionian priestess and her acolytes had been bunking at Fayette's establishment for a month, setting off to the Isles every morning to search for something. They'd refused to describe it to anyone, even Fayette.

"So you finally saw it?" Fayette asked.

"Well, almost. They had it under a tarp."

When the Ionians got close enough, Fayette could see that the huge, tarpaulin-covered object had crowded them all out of their seats. The priestess, Madam Saba, was halfway up the mast. Her three muscle-bound students were perched precariously around their find, trying their best to keep mostly inside the boat while their robes and sashes trailed in the water.

"That looks like something for the vault," Fayette called.

It was a huge bell, they revealed to her. About as tall as a young cabin boy. "It's *incredibly* dangerous," Madam Saba told Fayette. Saba's gray hair was plastered to her forehead with sweat, and her reedy voice had a stern edge to it. Fayette couldn't tell whether the rings of white around Saba's irises were a sign of fear or excitement. "Do not so much as *tap* it!"

"What happens if—"

"It flings the spirit realm into chaos," Saba snapped. "Magic rages unchecked.

Then… a vile stillness. Like the crash of a wave, as the toll silences."

Fayette was not quite sure what to make of this. "…Interesting," she said.

"We need to place it in your care. No one may disturb it. Not even you. My acolytes will bear it down into the basement."

The students carefully arranged themselves around the bell and, with a series of grunts, transferred it to the dock. They maneuvered the bell like strange, slow dancers, stepping gingerly over loose planks and gaps in the boards.

Fayette jogged ahead to open the door to the Daring Darling. "Careful," she warned the students, pointing out the jutting threshold plank.

Fayette knew the place better than anyone. Years earlier, she'd built the inn from the wreck of her own ship. She'd come here to the Shadow Isles to hunt for artifacts, and like many, she'd found a bloody lesson waiting for her. Her ship had run aground on the beach. In the week she spent stranded there before she was rescued, she got sick as a dog eating her own seawater-tainted rations, and a screeching wight took her arm off below the elbow.

But this kind of deadly lesson often gifted its students a valuable reward. Fayette had found her own prize half buried in the dark sand beside the wreck of her ship. The rock that had dashed her hull to pieces was actually the corner of a massive, featureless black-steel vault. A delicate key was snapped off in its lock. It took almost a year of digging and hauling, but Fayette finally got the vault onto the shore and opened it.

Inside? Nothing.

But the vault itself was more valuable than any treasure. Only one key could open it. Those who tried to *pick* the lock, or force it open via magical means, would fall dead in an instant. It had happened to Fayette's duplicitous first mate on the return trip—and several others since.

Fayette sometimes thought she could see the cold blue gleam of their souls glinting from the keyhole.

The Ionians walked slowly across the empty dining room, past the bar, and down the stairs into the basement hall. "Stay out here in the hall," Fayette told them. "It will just be a moment." She slipped into the vault room and closed the door behind her.

Then she unscrewed the iron hook from the end of her stump arm. Beneath it, nestled in the empty socket, lay the key to the vault.

Fayette unlocked the vault, then hid the key beneath the hook again. "Come on in," she called.

The Ionians tried to keep their expressions impassive, but Fayette could see their eyes widen when they saw the vault's interior. It held shelf after shelf of glowing relics. A rack of cursed weapons gave off a faint, high-pitched wail. Amulets wreathed with wisps of blue flame hung beside rusted lockboxes vibrating with the energy of furious spirits.

The vault was filled with the finds of Fayette's guests. *This* was the most important service Fayette provided—a safe place for adventurers to store their finds between hunts. None of the other outposts established by Bilgewater folk near the Shadow Isles offered anything quite as secure as this.

"I don't usually let folks place their own stuff in here," Fayette told the Ionians, "but you'd better put that bell down yourselves. Don't touch anything on the shelves."

Saba's students stepped carefully into the vault and set the bell down on a pad of cloth. Fayette watched them like a hawk, but she got the sense they were too frightened of the artifacts to think of stealing them.

"Are any of those *things* hazardous?" Saba asked.

"Nah, it's safe," Fayette said, waving the Ionians back out into the hall. "Been living on top of this thing for a decade, and it hasn't killed me yet!" She put her shoulder against the vault door and heaved it closed.

The click when it shut shook everyone to their bones.

That night, most of the boats came back in. There were a few missing faces, but Fayette wouldn't count them dead until someone saw their specter on the Isles. Instead, she focused on more pressing concerns—some of the guests who were still alive had cornered her behind the bar, and they were arguing with her.

"…You could at least *move* the vastaya," Vaquer begged her. He was a Piltovan fixer, working a job for some clan. He

wore velvet waistcoats, wanted everything *just so*, and was an enormous pain. For the last two months, Fayette had been hoping he'd just die on the Isles.

"Move Kesk? I'd rather move *you* than him, and there are no empty rooms now. We're completely full." Six small ships fought for space on the dock; inside, six treasure hunters, three Ionian students, and fifteen sailors were packed into an inn with only twelve rooms.

"Kesk stamps his scratchy chicken feet directly above my bed," Vaquer whined.

"You should talk to him yourself!"

"We've tried," said Jolera. She was a Noxian merchant. At least, everyone assumed she was. She had a Noxian accent, and she *dressed* like a merchant. Jolera mostly just huddled in a corner, poring over notebooks. Fayette was surprised to hear her complaining.

"You can hear the vastaya, too?" the innkeeper asked.

"Me and my whole crew. He sings marching songs. From the war."

"Oh."

"*Ionian* marching songs."

"There's nothing wrong with Ionian marching songs," Saba called from the other side of the room.

Jolera whirled on her. "The entire song is about killing my people!"

"Please!" Fayette exclaimed. "No fighting in the Darling!"

"Well, they're not actually fighting yet," Vaquer pointed out. He adjusted the focal distance on his clockwork goggles, a smile oozing across his face.

"Though that's something I'd like to see."

Just then, Gavin came down the stairs from his room, flashing Fayette a quick smile. "What's all this about?" he asked. Immediately, Jolera and Saba began yelling.

With a sigh, Fayette grabbed a pan and rapped it with her hook. "*Hey!*" she shouted. "Hey! Save it for the wraiths, will you?"

"Agreed," Gavin laughed.

"Does anyone need anything locked up?" Fayette asked. "Last call for the vault before I cook supper."

Fayette saw Vaquer's goggles flash in the candlelight as he looked from guest to guest. He was just as curious as she was about the artifacts they'd found.

"I don't have anything serious," Gavin said.

"Ours is already stored," Saba added.

This seemed strange. "Nobody else?" Fayette asked.

"A bad day on the Isles for me," Vaquer sighed. "I have nothing."

"What about the other guy?" Fayette asked. She kept forgetting his name. He'd barely come out of his room since he'd arrived. "The aristo fellow?"

"The rich Noxian?" Vaquer asked. "I haven't actually ever seen him."

"Me neither," Gavin said. "And I bunk next door to him."

Fayette shrugged. "All right, I'll cook—"

Outside, someone screamed.

Fayette and the guests all rose from their seats at once and hurried out to the dock. They found one of the Ionian acolytes frozen there, pale as a corpse,

pointing toward the Shadow Isles.

Where Fayette usually could see a thin strip of black hills against the steel-gray horizon, she instead saw a mountain of pitch-black mist rising into the sky.

Mother Serpent have mercy.

The Harrowing.

No one had to give the order—every treasure hunter on the dock immediately dashed off. Some went to grab their luggage. Others hurried to collect their sailors and prepare their vessels for departure.

Fayette's sloop, however, was already prepared to leave. She checked it every morning. You didn't make a living off the coast of the Shadow Isles without being ready for the Harrowing.

Besides, according to tradition, she had other things to prepare right now. As the guests scrambled about and panicked, Fayette just cleared her throat.

"Meet at the bar in fifteen minutes!" she shouted.

When the Harrowing came, all the resupply stations between Bilgewater and the Shadow Isles cleared out as quickly as they could. Artifact hunters grabbed their loot and fled. Innkeepers locked their doors—and hoped everything was still in one piece when they returned.

And before they all went, each of these small communities made sure to complete the Final Toast, a celebratory ritual unique to those desperate adventurers who came to hunt on the Shadow Isles. Before everyone boarded their ship to leave, they gathered to drink to one another's continued survival. Some, of course, had their fingers crossed behind their backs when they raised the glass. If a treasure hunter didn't survive, that was just more loot left for the ones who did.

Fayette took this ritual very seriously. She took a dusty bottle out from behind the bar and poured a drop out for each living soul in the inn. Six treasure hunters, fifteen career sailors, three Ionian acolytes, and one Fayette. Twenty-five cups lined the bar.

One by one, her guests gathered for the Toast. She could see fear in their eyes—even in Gavin's, and he'd survived plenty of Harrowings. But he gave her a smile and gripped his glass in a steady hand.

"This again," he sighed. "How many has it been for us, Fayette? Four? Five?"

"I've never seen it before," said Kesk, the vastaya everyone seemed to hate. He was originally from Ionia, but he'd introduced himself to Fayette as a Bilgewater captain, and he certainly dressed the part. "I only started docking my boat in Bilgewater this year, so I've never seen a Harrowing."

"Your crew can handle it," Gavin told him. "They've seen Harrowings before."

"Your *crew* has seen a Harrowing, but *you* haven't?" Vaquer snorted. "Why are you in charge?"

Fayette was certain that Vaquer hadn't seen any Harrowings in Piltover, either. "Keep the peace," Fayette ordered. "Tonight is important. This hardly ever happens, but when it does, we do it right. Oh, one last thing—does anyone need anything from the vault?"

"No time to move my whole haul," Gavin said. Gavin had found a lot of interesting artifacts this season. Enough to weigh down a couple of Demacian draft horses.

"There isn't time for us to move the bell, either," Saba grumbled.

Vaquer turned to Kesk. "What about you, bird boy?"

"Oh, I didn't find my thing yet," Kesk said, innocently tugging at the extravagant, lacy neckline of his shipmaster's frock.

"And what was it, captain?" Vaquer asked.

"An amulet that holds the spirit of a Blessed Isles sea captain who knows where treasure's hid! My old captain said *his* old captain had it, but he died on the Isles at—"

"Hush, boy," Gavin grunted. "Don't tell 'em *all* your secrets."

Kesk blinked.

Unperturbed, Vaquer turned his smiling face to Jolera. "And what about you, Noxian?" he asked. "What do you have in the vault?"

"Nothing," Jolera grumbled. "I haven't found anything."

That's a lie, Fayette thought. Jolera had asked her to lock up a box after her last haul. But she kept her mouth shut. Her customers had the privilege to lie, if they wanted to.

"And our host?" Vaquer asked, turning his flashing goggles toward Fayette. "Do you ever take anything from the vault during a Harrowing?"

"What about you?" Jolera interrupted. She was pointing at Vaquer. "So eager to ask everyone what they found—but what about *you*?"

"Oh, I haven't found what I'm looking for, either," Vaquer said. "I'm…"

He fell silent. There were footsteps coming down the stairs.

It was the silent aristocrat who bunked in the room next to Gavin's. He was very fair, with long silver-white hair draped over his shoulders. It stood out bright against his maroon velvet robe. His expression was weirdly calm.

"I see the Harrowing has come again," he remarked, as if he were simply talking about ordinary weather. "Shall we all leave now?"

Gavin guffawed. "You better. Or the wraiths will drown you."

"Not so many of them are drowners," the aristocrat corrected. "Most of them simply… rip people apart."

"So you're an *expert*?"

"Stop it." Fayette raised her glass. "We're all here. Gavin?"

As the oldest treasure hunter there, the honor was his.

With a smile to Fayette, the grizzled Demacian raised his cup. "Let's toast," he said.

But before he could begin, the candles and lanterns guttered, then all went out at once.

For half a moment, nothing happened. Then the room erupted in screams.

Fayette ducked behind the bar. Fumbling in the dark, she found her sword-arm hidden back there, and with a few deft twists, she replaced her hook with it. She was just in time, too—someone rolled over the bar, wildly kicking and punching as they fell. She grappled with the body in the dark, found their neck, and pressed her blade against it.

"Everybody stop," she shouted. "Stop!"

A light flared up, and the fighting ceased. Fayette released the throat of the sailor she'd pinned, stood, and saw the Noxian aristocrat idling calmly in the middle of the room with a lamp in his hand.

Around him, however, reigned chaos.

Vaquer was crouched on the floor, surrounded by glowing… *bear traps*? One of the Ionian students and two of Jolera's sailors were hunched over on the floorboards nearby. Blue-green jaws of light held their ankles tightly. When they tried to crawl away, they grunted in pain.

One of Kesk's sailors lay dead on the floor, a dirk clutched in his hands. Gavin stood above him, a pair of bloody daggers in his. "He came at me," Gavin said, a note of dismay in his voice.

Jolera was hiding under a table. Kesk was hiding on *top* of one. Saba was dusting off her knuckles, surrounded by a heap of groaning seamen.

"What are *those*?" she demanded, pointing at Vaquer's traps.

"All right, I lied. I found what I was looking for on the Shadow Isles today." Vaquer waved his hand, and the traps released their victims. They fell to the ground, groaning. "My clan is looking to reverse engineer these contraptions and manufacture more of them. Rather than the physical body, they bind the spirit."

"They disturb the *spirit realm*," Saba shouted.

"You killed *Davy*," Kesk screamed at Gavin.

"He tried to stab me!"

"Who turned out the lights?" the Noxian aristocrat asked. And although his voice was quiet and measured, everyone stopped to listen. "Everyone is here. Twenty-five cups. Twenty-five souls." He nodded at the corpse at Gavin's feet. "Including… Davy. So who turned out the lights?"

Jolera was already peering at the extinguished candle on the end of the bar. "Blood," she grunted. Fayette recognized that Noxian frankness in the way she confronted these signs of death. "Look. Blood."

Fayette bent close. A splash of blood was still pooled around the cold wick.

"This was a distraction," Jolera said.

She ran to the door. The rest of the guests followed.

Outside, each one of the ships moored at the dock was bound and wrapped with red-black chains of—*something*. Seething, roiling, snaking ropes of it.

Gavin stepped forward toward the ships—and Fayette grabbed his arm. "Don't," she warned her friend. "We have no idea what's doing this."

"Dark magic," Jolera said. She was almost too furious to speak. She turned toward the group with her fists balled and her teeth gritted. "*Disgusting* magic."

"You've seen it before?" Vaquer asked.

"I've read about it," Jolera said. "It's not from the Shadow Isles at all. It's ancient evil—from *Valoran*."

Back inside the Daring Darling, Vaquer accused the Ionians. "You lot are all sorcerers!"

"I'm a priestess," Saba said. "And they're students!"

"Students of dark magic?"

"Students of *religion!*"

Gavin gathered with most of the sailors at the far end of the room. The seamen often kept themselves separate from their clients, the high-and-mighty treasure hunters, though they'd long welcomed Gavin as a practical fellow. "We're going out to try to release the boats," he announced. "Anyone's welcome to come along and help us sort this out."

"Wait," Fayette said. "We shouldn't split up! There's a saboteur among us."

"We're going outside, too," Saba said, and crossed the room with her students. "We have to release the boats."

"Well, I'm not going with *you*," Vaquer snarled. "Damn Ionian sorcerers." He wrapped his Piltovan jacket tightly around his shoulders, as if the finery would protect him from the mist.

Kesk was shaking hard, the feathers on his captain's hat quivering. It was a wonder the vastaya could still stand. "I'm— I'm going to my room," he stammered.

"As am I," Jolera said.

"There's no point in hiding in your rooms!" Fayette cried. "We've got to leave the island as soon as we can!"

Gavin looked out the window. "Based on my experience, we've got about an hour until the Black Mist gets here," he said.

"Then I'm going to my room, too," Vaquer snapped.

"Don't!" Fayette shouted. But the group split—three upstairs and the rest out to the dock. The only one left was the young Noxian noble.

"They are all in danger," the aristocrat said. His voice was serious but calm. "You are right—there is a saboteur on the island. Whoever they are, they will attack again."

"That'll barely matter when the mist arrives," Fayette snapped.

"True," the noble admitted. "I am a bit of an expert on the Shadow Isles. I have been studying this place for years." He produced a small book from a pocket of his robe and flipped idly through it. Fayette caught glimpses of drawings and scraps of ancient script. "We are quite doomed if we stay. I am sure you have heard of the Iron Order? And the—"

"I've heard the stories," Fayette interrupted. "And I've survived my share of Harrowings. Have you?"

"This will be... the first Harrowing I experience. But then you know that this unnatural mist threatens us with more than just your average wraith. There are ancient horrors out there on the Isles against whom we would not stand a chance. Relic weapons might aid us, though. If you have any in the vault, we should get them."

Fayette felt a hot rush of indignation. "Take my guests' things?" She couldn't imagine sacrificing her reputation as the trusted guardian of the vault. It would be such a waste—like throwing the vault back into the sea!

"The guests cannot trust you if they

are dead," the noble pointed out. "And we are wasting what little time we have to sail clear of the mist."

"I can't do it. Stop asking. Let's just go get these fools before something kills them." She started toward the stairs, then stopped. She couldn't remember the aristocrat's name. "What are you called again?"

"Oh, me?" The aristocrat asked, mild as ever. "I am called Vladimir."

Gavin had guessed that the Black Mist was an hour away, but the first wisps of it were already creeping across the surface of the sea. As Fayette and Vladimir hurried up the stairs, she spotted fingers of it swirling toward the island through a window.

The second floor of the inn was dead silent. Jolera and Vaquer's doors were shut tight. She made for Vaquer's door, but Vladimir grabbed her arm and pointed at the floor.

She squinted at the wooden boards. Some kind of magic warding blurred them from her vision, but she could see the traps lying in front of the door.

"Gods below," she groaned. She reached out across the traps to tap on Vaquer's door. "Come on, man! We've got to stick together!"

"Absolutely not," came Vaquer's shrill reply. "I'm perfectly safe in here."

"Spirits can go through walls," Vladimir reminded him.

"Well, these traps catch spirits and mortals alike!"

"I am saying the spirits aren't going to come through the *door.*"

"*Leave me alone!*"

"Let's check the trader," Fayette suggested. But Jolera's door was locked, too—the cranky Noxian merchant simply didn't answer the innkeeper's knocking.

"These people *want* to die," Fayette seethed. "That's always been a problem here. Dilettantes from Piltover and Noxus playing at treasure hunting on the Isles—no offense."

"None taken," Vladimir said, smiling faintly. "But one of these two might be the saboteur… playing the fool."

"No proof yet," Fayette said, though the thought was gnawing at her, too. "Let's check on Kesk."

Fayette and Vladimir hurried up the stairs to the third floor—and nearly tripped over the corpse of a sailor halfway up.

"Gods," Fayette yelped. In the dim light, she could see deep cuts in the man's chest. Threads of smoke rose from the slashes in his clothes. "What did this?"

Vladimir crouched over the corpse. "A spirit weapon." He took out his little book and started quickly flipping through it. "Let me see…"

Squeak! Above them, at the top of the stairs, someone stepped on a loose board.

"Who's there?" Fayette asked. "Kesk?"

Kesk's voice was small and terrified. "*Stay back!*"

"We're coming up," Fayette warned.

Vladimir gave Fayette a worried look. "Do be careful."

His concern was rather charming, Fayette realized. It had been a while since a handsome young man expressed worry over her safety. She found herself smiling back.

"I can handle him," she said, and sprinted up the stairs.

It was lucky she had her sword-arm raised. On the top step, *something* came down heavy at her head, and she barely blocked it. "Stop!" she shouted. "We're trying to help!"

Kesk was hunched halfway down the hall, but something lurked between him and Fayette. A dim shape of a man, visible as a nervous trembling of air—as if the shadows had been frightened into the form of a human.

Vladimir hurried up the stairs with his lantern, and then Fayette saw it clearly— the specter of a burly sea captain wielding an enormous cutlass. His clothes were torn, and his translucent flesh hung off his hazy bones.

Fayette saw something cradled in Kesk's hand: a glowing locket. "You liar! You found your artifact!"

Kesk rubbed the locket. "I didn't want anyone to know," he said. His eyes were rolling in their sockets. "There's all sorts of things people shouldn't know. I looked out the window… I… looked out…" He shuddered.

"He saw something in the mist," Vladimir muttered. "He has gone mad."

"Banish the spirit!" Fayette said.

"I don't want to!" Kesk bared his teeth at the two of them. As he huddled on the floor, Fayette saw that his sweat had soaked clear through the back of his grandiose shipmaster's frock. His voice grew shrill with despair. "You trapped us here!"

Fayette frowned down at the vastaya. "Don't make us do this, Kesk!"

The sea captain swung his shimmering cutlass at them, and Vladimir and Fayette leapt backward. As she moved onto her back foot, however, something strange came over Fayette. She'd been tending bar, cleaning rooms, and locking the vault over and over for the last ten years… but the old fighting instinct must have been hibernating in her bones.

All at once, it woke.

As the cutlass swept past them and the ghostly captain turned into the end of his swing, she saw a gap and lunged forward. Before he could react, she spun around the drowned spirit and dove at Kesk, her sword-arm raised.

Vladimir followed her like a purple velvet dart, dodging around the sea captain's other side. He seized Kesk's arm and shoved the vastaya against the wall.

"The spirit!" Vladimir shouted.

Fayette whirled around with her arm raised and barely deflected what would have been a killing blow from the sea captain. He leaned forward and screamed in her face, rotten lips parted in a maggoty wail she felt in her bones. His claw-like hand grasped at her throat, but she turned, using the spirit's momentum to fling him toward the nearest wall—

—where he burst like a shimmering bubble and vanished into the dark.

Vladimir laughed and dropped Kesk's lifeless body to the ground. The locket hung in his hand, its light gone. Kesk's blood pooled at his feet.

"Good work," he said, admiringly. "But this locket seems linked to the wearer. Its magic vanished when his breath did." Vladimir slipped the amulet into his pocket. "We should seriously consider opening that vault," he said. "The Black Mist will bring worse."

Fayette leaned against the wall to calm her heart. She couldn't tell whether she was out of fighting shape after all, or just faint from the excitement. She'd forgotten how *wonderful* it was to win a real fight. "We're not opening that vault. My guests trust me."

Vladimir shrugged. "But if they are all dead…"

Fayette felt herself growing frustrated with this mild, elegant aristocrat. "It's not just the people *here* whose relics I'm holding. There are folks at other outposts too. And there are hunters still out on the Isles who have treasures in my vault. They might be alive!"

"That seems… *optimistic*, considering the circumstances."

"Let's just meet up with the others," Fayette said.

Vladimir followed her obediently. It wasn't until they were down on the ground floor that Fayette realized she hadn't actually seen how Vladimir had killed Kesk.

Interesting, she thought. *He's not even holding a weapon.*

As Fayette reached the inn's door, her heart sank. Out on the dock, sailors and treasure hunters were hurrying back toward the entrance. Behind them, at the far end of the dock, a strange commotion was brewing.

The flat gray gleam of the sky was giving way to the pitch black of the encroaching mist. Black tendrils snaked across the water between the moored ships. There were large, dimly glowing shapes moving below the surface.

"Get back inside," Gavin shouted at her. "They're here!"

The whole crowd piled inside the Daring Darling. Saba was unharmed, but only two of her students were left alive. Four or five sailors were missing too. The remaining ones rushed to grab tables and chairs and stack them against the door.

"That may not accomplish much," Vladimir sighed. "They saw you out there. They'll come through the walls."

"They put a hole in Kesk's ship," Gavin said. "Where's Kesk?"

"Dead," Fayette said. "Completely mad. He attacked us."

"Then it's the Piltovan or the Noxian who trapped us here," Saba spat. They're the only two not with us. One of them must be casting the spell."

Fayette frowned. It seemed doubtful. But it was possible, wasn't it?

"It's *gotta* be one of them," Gavin said. "I mean, it seems likely."

"They're both locked upstairs in their rooms," Fayette said. "We could get them—"

"I want my weapon," someone shouted.

The whole group turned to look at the stairs. With the worst timing in the world, there stood Jolera. She looked madder than a blood-hungry sluice shark.

"Open the vault," she told Fayette. "I want my weapon, and then I'm leaving."

"I thought you didn't have any treasure," Saba snapped.

"And leaving on *what*?" Gavin demanded. "The ships are still all tied down!"

"Just give me my weapon," Jolera yelled—but then the sailors were on her. They dragged her to a chair, and Saba's students tied her down with their sashes.

"Let me *go*," Jolera shouted. "You'll pay for this! My allies—they're powerful!"

"Cut her throat and see if the spell lifts," one of the sailors suggested.

"That's not necessary," Saba said. She approached Jolera with her hands raised. "I will sense if she's in communion with the spirit realm."

Gavin rolled his eyes. "Really? You can sense mages? I don't believe it. I've seen people sense mages. Back in Demacia they had a boy who could tell, but he—"

"Magic connects everything," Saba insisted. "My order maps it. We can feel... changes. Whorls. Perforations."

"Show us, then," Fayette said.

The room fell silent. Even Jolera quieted herself, more intrigued than afraid. Saba held her hands near the merchant's head and whispered words Fayette didn't know. For a moment, she tasted hot metal.

Then Saba pulled away. "Nothing," she said. "Her link with the spirit realm is superficial. She cannot use magic."

Gavin shook his head. "I dunno," he said. "I bet she can hide it from you. Back in Demacia—"

"Untie me, or you'll regret it," Jolera blurted. She looked Fayette in the eye. "*You* untie me. You're in charge around here."

But before Fayette could decide what to do, the floor behind the bar exploded—and spirits emerged.

It was hard to tell exactly what was happening. A scrambling madness of ghostly limbs and wailing voices rose from the basement. Fayette saw twisted, wrathful faces full of fangs boiling over the top of the bar like foam over the lip of a forgotten pot. Drowned sailors, ancient soldiers, legless wraiths hauling themselves upward with skeletal arms—

"Run!" Vladimir shouted, dragging her back toward the stairs.

Fayette ran. A ghostly warrior bearing an axe longer than she was tall hauled itself out of the basement and swung it at her, but she leapt over the arc of the blade. It obliterated a table behind her and kept swinging right into the crowd of sailors gathered around Jolera.

Fayette and Vladimir scaled the steps to the second floor in an instant, then ducked into Jolera's open room. Fayette turned to watch the stairs, but nobody was following them. There was just screaming, smashing wood, unearthly roars....

Vladimir reached past her and slammed the door shut.

"I thought doors don't keep spirits away," Fayette said.

Vladimir didn't answer. He was flipping through that little book again, dragging his finger down lines of ancient script. "That axeman," he murmured. "Not Iron Order. Maybe Helian city guard? Have you heard of the Horseman?" He looked up at Fayette with a wild, euphoric stare—his serene calm gone. "This is a *proper Harrowing!* They will be here, all of them. The Horseman. The Torturer. The Harbinger, maybe. Powerful beings. Death hasn't defeated them!"

He seemed oddly excited to be obliterated by ancient ghosts, Fayette thought. "We need to get off the island," she said.

"That's right," Vladimir said. "You are lucky I am here to help. I and my benefactors know quite a lot about the Shadow Isles—I might be able to tell what the artifacts in your vault do. One of them could be capable of lifting the spell on the ships."

Fayette felt sick. "I can't... I can't open the vault...."

Vladimir drew close and showed her a page of his book. It was filled with intricate illustrations of ancient devices and weapons—and script in a language Fayette did not recognize. "My benefactors sent me here to find these powerful items. Just *show me the vault*, Fayette—"

Anger swelled in her chest again, and before Fayette could stop herself, she'd shoved Vladimir away. "Never," she told him. "How many times do I have to tell you?"

But Vladimir didn't seem intimidated. His elegant smile had twisted into a strange frown. He seemed... disappointed? "Fine," he said. "Whatever you say. Head back down and fight with what we have, then. If you think that's so clever."

Seething, Fayette turned to the door.

And when she opened it, she found a *wave of blood*.

It filled the entire hall outside, floor to ceiling, and it crashed into her with a force like a swinging sailboat boom. She felt herself thrown back against the far wall, blood in her eyes and her mouth—then, dark confusion. Muddled thoughts. Had she hit her head? She wasn't sure. A strange weight settled around her neck, like someone had locked an iron collar there.

Almost as quickly as it had arrived, the blood flowed away from her. Surprisingly, she was standing up good and straight, which was very odd, because she wasn't *trying* to stand up. And she was walking, which was even stranger, because her eyes were closed and she *definitely* wasn't trying to walk.

She peeled her blood-gummed eyes open one at a time and saw that she was walking with jerky steps... straight down the stairs and back into the fight!

And no matter what she did, she couldn't turn around.

Some horrible spell had settled on her. Fayette couldn't turn her face away, either. She saw spirits boiling out of the basement and flinging themselves at Saba and her students. She could see Gavin, daggers out, dodging the swipe of a bony claw. She saw Jolera splayed on the ground.

Then she noticed a dampness in her shoes and a gurgling sound. Though she couldn't turn her head, out of the corner of her eye she could see streams of blood unnaturally flowing down the stairs with her. *Animate blood.*

She'd seen something like this recently. She'd seen—*oh, by the* Bearded Lady.

This was what she'd seen holding down the boats. Chains of blood.

In the dining hall, it rose to fight for her. A spirit lunged, and the blood darted forward to impale it. Another spirit flung a beam at her, but the blood welled up in a sheet and knocked it aside. With uncharacteristic poise, Fayette watched herself walk straight along the wall of the room, past her screaming and dying guests... right up to the shattered floor behind the bar.

Then she jumped down.

She landed with a splash in the basement below. There was a good foot of water on the floor and the sound of more pouring in somewhere. As she stood, something swung out from below her chin. She glimpsed it for a moment: a glowing gem hanging on a simple leather thong.

An Isles artifact? Is someone con-trolling me?

In the vault room, her good hand began to creep toward her sword-arm. She pulled it back as hard as she could, but the gem around her neck flashed brighter, and her hand jerked toward her elbow and unscrewed the sword fitting from the metal cap of her elbow.

She watched herself loosen the vault key from its hiding spot and saw her hand move toward the lock. That hot rage boiled up again. She focused all her will on her hand....

And it stopped moving.

Her jaw was clenched. Her face was hot. She could feel sweat beading up on her brow.

You won't open that damn vault, she thought. *Whichever depths you crawled from, you won't.*

But something burbled at her feet. A fountaining column of blood rose from the water. It narrowed to a delicate arm, then congealed into a graceful hand.

It took the key from her fingers and put it in the lock. The door clicked.

Fayette, overwhelmed, passed out.

When she woke, she was slumped in the mouth of the vault, and it was empty.

The hooks for hanging amulets were bare. The weapons rack was quiet, all the screaming prizes it held gone. The shelves were swept clean. Only the bell was left.

The amulet that had controlled her hung inert around her neck. Furious, she ripped it off and crushed it beneath the heel of her boot.

I can't trust anyone, she realized. *How long have I been unconscious?*

She screwed her arm back on and staggered through the deepening water toward the stairs. It was rushing in through the back wall, behind the vault. The spirits had thoroughly wrecked the place. There were scorch marks on the steps, claw marks on the walls—but no ghosts.

They were gone from the first floor of the inn, too. Shattered tables and chairs lay in heaps. Fayette saw Jolera lying still beside the chair she'd been tied to. Two more dead sailors lay draped over the bar.

And in the middle of the room, Saba stood victorious over Gavin.

"Fayette!" she gasped. *"He cast the spell!"*

"I didn't do anything," Gavin groaned. His hand clasped over his gut. Blood trickled between his fingers.

"He's a *mage!*" Saba shouted. "I felt his connection to the spirit realm!" She hefted Gavin into a sitting position by his collar. "It's twisted. Dark!"

He cried out in pain. "I'm a mage, but I didn't do it!"

Fayette froze. *"What?"*

"It's why I left Demacia," he groaned. His face split with a nervous smile—and a trickle of blood crept from the corner of his mouth. "I'm a mage, Fayette. How do you think I stayed alive on the Isles all this time?"

"You… you *lied* to me?" She'd called him her best friend. She'd tied his boat to the dock every day. *How did he hide it so well?*

"I didn't lie to you," Gavin coughed. "I just didn't tell you the whole truth."

A high, cruel laugh escaped Saba's lips. "We'll kill him, Fayette, and the spell on the ships will lift." Saba sent Gavin sprawling to the floor with a thump. "Where are your daggers, traitor? I'll cut your throat."

Fayette felt numb. *Why didn't he tell me?* It was damning.

But he was hurt near to death. If he was the sorcerer behind this blood magic, why hadn't the spell lifted already?

Saba turned to search for Gavin's daggers in the wreckage. "Watch him for me. We'll slay this dark mage."

Fayette did watch him. She looked Gavin in the eye.

They had shared each other's company for many years and often knew what the other was thinking—Gavin knew what she was thinking now. He nodded, then turned his head. Fayette followed his gaze, and there it was: one of his daggers lying hidden under a shattered chair.

Silently, Fayette bent to pick it up.

With three quick steps, she crossed the room… and stuck it into Saba's back.

Saba tottered and fell, hands grasping helplessly.

Fayette rushed to Gavin's side. "I'm sorry," he said. He was crying.

"Don't be," she said. She was crying, too, she realized. Red tears fell on Gavin's shoulder, scouring the blood from her face.

"We were good friends, weren't we?" Gavin said. He gripped her hand—a weak grip. A dying grip. "I didn't tell you. I was ashamed. In Demacia… they scare you when you're a kid like I was. I was so ashamed. I never told anyone."

"Don't be sorry," Fayette told him. "We'll get out of here."

"We won't," he whispered. "Those dark sorcerers. They're still here."

"Sorcerers?" Fayette asked. "More than one?"

"Oh, *bravo!*" someone exclaimed.

A loud, clear, triumphant voice. It was the haughty tone of a man with an ironclad belief in the magnificence of his own scheme.

"You finally figured it out," Vladimir said.

Vaquer and Vladimir descended from the second floor together.

They were armed to the teeth with glowing amulets and wailing swords. Vaquer carried a sack stuffed with artifacts. Vladimir's handsome, pale face was topped with a spiked silver crown wreathed in ghostly flame.

Fayette wanted nothing more in life than to rip that sneering head from his shoulders.

"I am genuinely impressed," Vladimir told her. "Most mortals lack the will to do what you have done."

The polite aristocrat had been replaced by a cruel, snarling demon of a man. His eyes glinted bloodred like rubies, and his lips were twisted in an ageless smile.

"My benefactors would love to meet you, Fayette," Vladimir said. His voice seemed richer and louder than it had before. He seemed *taller*. Fayette felt as if some hateful radiance were shining from him—some deceptive magic she didn't have the knowledge to puzzle out.

But she said nothing. This was a monster, not a man. She was checking her exits.

"I call them *benefactors*, but they are partners. As ancient as I am, and just as powerful," Vladimir said, slinking toward her. A whirling mass of blood followed him. When he raised his arm, the blood danced around it.

Vaquer bowed. "You *are* powerful, milord."

Vladimir bent close, bringing the stench of blood. "My partners and I have an interest in the Shadow Isles. We are searching for certain powerful artifacts to aid us against our enemies. We would *love* to have you, Fayette. You have such deep knowledge of the region."

Fayette could barely breathe. The smell of blood was overpowering. She looked away.

"Ahh, so that's how it is," Vladimir sighed. "You are the last one left now. It's a shame to waste that survivor's spirit."

Fayette looked down at Gavin. He was cold. *Drained.* She glanced up just in time to see the last of his blood flow up to circle around Vladimir.

"I reward those who join my… circle. That's all hemomancy's about, really. They tell all these scary stories, but it's just about staying young and strong… and looking good, of course."

There was so much hate storming in Fayette's heart, she could barely decide what to yell at him about. "*You*—you forced me to open the vault!"

"Of course I did! Vaquer here has watched this place for weeks. He plays a good Piltovan. A disarming dandy. But he uncovered what everyone was looking for." Vladimir produced Kesk's amulet. "Every ancient charm, every rusty weapon. Everything in the vault… all part of our plans. Gavin found the amulet I used to control you *just today*, you know," he added. "Silva's Madstone. The one that brought you down to the vault. He didn't trust you to hold it—I imagine he thought the Ionians would relieve him of it. But I picked it from his pocket while he was accusing the Noxian."

Oddly, Fayette was offended. *He should have told me*, she thought.

"I was most impressed by what that Noxian found, though. We didn't expect she had the ingenuity!" Vladimir raised a wickedly barbed iron spear. "I would not be surprised if she were working for my organization's enemies. This is a spear of the Iron Order… I wonder if it pierced Vengeance herself?"

Behind Fayette, someone spoke. *"You'll learn soon."*

Fayette turned to see Jolera hammer a chair leg onto the mantelpiece. She was… *nailing something?*

The Noxian merchant clung to the mantel just to keep herself upright. Her voice was ragged. "I invoke thee, Lady of Vengeance!" With trembling fingers, she put another nail above—

Is that a little model of a man? "Vladimir I name my betrayer." She hammered again.

Vladimir was shocked. "Wait—"

"Vladimir!" *Slam!*

"Stop that," Vladimir snapped.

"VLADIMIR!"

With the final blow, Jolera dropped dead on the ground.

Fayette rushed to the window. Outside, the Black Mist was whipping by faster than ever. The waves were dotted with the glowing forms of spirits, racing past her little island and toward Bilgewater—ignorant of the few humans left hiding inside the inn. They roiled over the dock and around the ships.

But something out at the end of the dock was standing still. A tall, luminous figure in dark and slender armor with long black hair trailing in the wind.

Vladimir spat a curse in a language Fayette had never heard before. "Kalista," he said. "Vengeance!"

"What do we do, master?" asked Vaquer, a trembling note in his voice. Now that he'd dropped the Piltovan character, he was all passive subservience.

But Fayette saw—Vladimir's chains of blood were gone!

She bolted out the Daring Darling's door and ran for her boat.

Behind Fayette, Kalista thunked one of her spears into the wood of the dock. "Vladimir," she bellowed. "Betrayer!"

Fayette *tried* to ignore it. She dodged the slow, hulking spirit of a Bilgewater butcher-master and dashed toward a little cove on the side of the island.

Vladimir's voice rose up behind her. "You're a dog," he shouted. "Servant of foolish mortals. Go bark elsewhere."

"She pledged to me," Kalista howled. "Jolera of the Warmasons."

Fayette found her sloop but skidded to a stop on the beach. The sand was swarming with glowing spirits bumping mindlessly into one another.

The shore was thick with wraiths, half of them carrying weapons taller than Fayette. *I should have opened the damn vault*, she thought. But there was nothing left now. Nothing but…

…*the bell!*

Fayette turned on her heel and ran back toward the inn. She arrived at the dock just in time to see Kalista's charge connect with the Darling's front door.

It blew into smithereens. So did most of the inn's front wall.

Kalista flung a spear at Vaquer—*through*

Vaquer. Vladimir just peeled himself out of the wreckage of the doorway and gestured with his hand, calling Vaquer's blood to himself. He was sparkling with artifacts. "I've waited for a moment like this for *centuries*," he laughed.

Vladimir leapt at Kalista. Fayette leapt under the dock.

Above her, a battle for the ages commenced. Blood spattered. Ships cracked in half. Ancient amulets vomited fountains of ghosts. Fayette waded through salt water—heading toward the back side of the inn.

Once on the far side of the building, she hauled herself out of the sea and shimmied along a ridge of broken rock. These spirits didn't care about doors or windows, even though they sure seemed to like breaking them for effect—they'd come through the basement because it was closest to the water. They must have broken through the back wall behind the vault. Fayette jumped down into the waves, dodged a grasping spirit that looked suspiciously like Saba, and—*yes!*—hauled herself into the basement through a ragged hole in the wall.

Gavin's spirit was waiting for her there.

It raised its hands for an embrace. Its glowing green flesh was already melting off its bones. "Fayette," it howled. The voice was *not* Gavin's. "My friend—"

Fayette recoiled. This was a mockery of the man. Gavin didn't deserve this grotesque parody.

She gritted her teeth and brought her sword-arm down in a firm, clean cut, and the spirit dissolved into scraps of gleaming air.

Then she grabbed a loose board and swung it at the bell.

Chaos, Saba had said. The bell filled the spirit realm with energy. Fayette wasn't sure what that would mean for the wraiths outside, but she knew she wanted to shuffle them around and send them scrambling.

First, though: the ring. The effect was instantaneous. Outside, ten thousand souls wailed at once, and then the walls caved in.

The spirit of a bloodthirsty shark smashed headlong into the vault.

Splinters flew, and Fayette dashed up the stairs. On the inn's main floor, specters were crawling out of the dead sailors. Fayette dodged her resurrected guests, leapt over Kesk's still-wailing form, and skidded outside.

Vladimir was crouching on the far end of the dock. His velvet robes were torn, and his skin was gray and withered. Kalista lunged, stabbing him with her spear again and again, empowered by the strength of the bell.

For a moment, between the blows, Fayette saw his hateful glare turn in her direction. *Gods below. He's seen me.*

She jumped off the dock and dashed to her sloop—and just as she arrived, there came the crash of the wave—and the horrible silence after.

All at once, every spirit in the place fell as still as a statue. The only sound was the wind, rattling and whining through the docked ships' broken rigging. The spirits on the shore were frozen, mid-step and mid-scream, like wax figures in an unusually good Bilgewater spook-house. Fayette gingerly edged around the somnambulant spirits, slipped into her hidden sloop, and set her small sail.

Before the Black Mist closed between her and the island, Fayette saw Kalista, sluggish and stooped, lunge again toward Vladimir. *I hope he dies,* she thought. *If he can die at all.*

The wind bore her swiftly through the mist. Soon, she would be out at sea, on course toward Bilgewater. For half a minute, it was strangely silent.

Then—*clang!* The sound of the bell rang louder than a cannon shot.

It was followed instantly by a deafening roar, like a Noxian man-o'-war's entire powder magazine catching on fire at once. Fayette could hear the island's bedrock cracking. The inn's dock rained down in splinters around her... and from below, there rose a mass of glowing, grasping, clawing wights.

She grabbed her oar and started battering them as hard as she could. She snapped fingers and stove in soggy skulls. Deep under the waves, a horrible voice boomed, and with each percussive syllable more wights sprung up to grab her sloop. It tipped almost clear over on its side, and Fayette was forced to drop her oar and wrap an arm around the mast.

But then the sound of the bell faded. And as suddenly as they'd attacked, the ghostly horrors fell back. She saw them, frozen, plummeting to the ocean's floor like stones.

Fayette collapsed on the bench in the back of her sloop and tried to catch her breath. Her whole body was sore. Her sword-arm was cracked. Her bloody limbs were studded with splinters from the dock.

Then she heard it. Something was approaching the boat.

A man, standing on a sheet of flowing blood.

"Curse you, Kalista," Fayette muttered.

Vladimir stepped into Fayette's sloop without a single Shadow Isles artifact left to his name. He dripped with his own blood. There were lines on his face she hadn't seen before.

"That damned bell works just as well on Lady Vengeance herself, if you hit it hard enough," he said.

"Get out of my boat!"

He gave her a faint smile. "Oh, please. I'm harmless. You shall sail us to Bilgewater."

Fayette felt sick, but as the sloop hurried onward toward the moonlit open ocean, each of the exhausted killers on board knew they were too tired to bother killing each other.

"And I *told* you we would have to open the vault," Vladimir said.

SHURIMA

The empire of Shurima was once a thriving civilization that spanned an entire continent. Forged in a bygone age by the mighty god-warriors of the Ascended Host, it united all the disparate peoples of the south, and enforced a lasting peace between them.

Few dared to rebel. Those that did, like the accursed nation of Icathia, were crushed without mercy.

However, after several thousand years of growth and prosperity, the failed Ascension of Shurima's last emperor left the capital in ruins, and tales of the empire's former glory became little more than myth. Now, most of the nomadic inhabitants of Shurima's deserts eke out a meager existence from the unforgiving land. Some have built small outposts to defend the few oases, while others delve into long-lost catacombs in search of the untold riches that must surely lie buried there. There are also those who live as mercenaries, taking coin for their service before disappearing back into the lawless wastelands.

Still, a handful dare to dream of a return to the old ways. Indeed, more recently the tribes have been stirred by whispers from the heart of the desert that their emperor Azir has returned to lead them into a new, wondrous age.

Though the empire's first capital was Nerimazeth, far to the west, a second, much larger city was raised above the legendary Oasis of the Dawn, where the great rivers of Shurima converged.

For countless generations, the Shuriman emperors ruled from this seat of power. With each new conquest or alliance, the empire grew, and older nations such as Ixtal, Kalduga, Targon, and Faraj were welcomed into the fold.

However, when the noble emperor Azir was denied Ascension, all Shurima's hopes died with him. The royal line was broken. Rivers ran dry, leaving the land barren and desolate, and the Sun Disc sank beneath the sands.

The remaining Ascended could not agree on how to preserve the empire's legacy, eventually fighting among themselves in a war that ravaged most of the known world.

A LOST CITY

Now that Azir has risen, life is slowly returning to what was once desert. In the throes of rebirth, Shurima struggles to balance the return of this ancient power with the disparate cultures and ways of life that ensured survival in its absence.

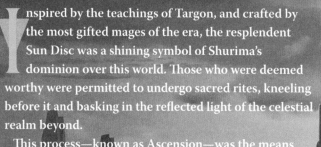

Inspired by the teachings of Targon, and crafted by the most gifted mages of the era, the resplendent Sun Disc was a shining symbol of Shurima's dominion over this world. Those who were deemed worthy were permitted to undergo sacred rites, kneeling before it and basking in the reflected light of the celestial realm beyond.

This process—known as Ascension—was the means by which Shurima created its renowned "god-warriors," each one of them blessed with powers beyond mortal understanding.

THE SACRED 8

The Ascended were mighty heroes, peerless tacticians, and cunning sorcerers chosen to lead the armies of Shurima in battle. It was said that entire campaigns could be won the moment a god-warrior took to the field, because their foes chose to turn and flee rather than face them directly.

THE SPURNED

hile the secrets of the Sun Disc were fiercely guarded by the Ascended Host, it was not an exact science. Those mortals who underwent an Ascension ritual but emerged flawed or incomplete were known as "Baccai," and it was considered a kindness to end their inhuman suffering as quickly as possible.

The people of Shurima have been emperors and warriors, slaves and scholars, enduring beneath the glare of the desert sun. Through their knowledge of the sands, their strong family bonds, and sheer determination that history will not forget them, they have survived wars that spanned many centuries.

When Azir fell, his empire was shattered. From every fragment emerged claims—divine, inherited, or otherwise—to rule, and it was a power struggle that almost destroyed Shurima's people. Today, every claimant, successful or not, has their own legend for why they alone should govern, in luxury and wealth.

Every Shuriman knows their empire was once the greatest in the world, but that distant glory is bittersweet to those being paid a pittance to haul sand for outsiders. Even so, when porting water, digging irrigation, or performing other menial labor, they remember their golden past.

SAND IN THEIR BLOOD

Where outsiders see only desolation, the merchants of Shurima see opportunity. From ancient artifacts pried from lost tombs to singing crystals of inestimable magical power, these shrewd traders know—to the smallest coin—how much to charge the stream of foreign explorers who hunger for the desert's riches.

There are countless ways to die under the burning Shuriman sun, yet these hardy nomad scouts call the Great Sai home, guiding Piltovan expeditions or Noxian agents between the lonely settlements and oases of this desert.

The expedition out of Urzeris has likely been lost.

GATEWAY

THE GOVERNOR AND GOVERNESS OF NASHRAME

Marriages between Shurimans and Noxian nobles were once matters of political convenience, as they often yielded better results than any general's declaration, or some meaningless missive from the Immortal Bastion.

TREASURE

After Azir's passing, Shurima became a very different place. The southern deserts of Kahleek and blighted Icathia began to encroach upon the once-verdant landscape, forcing the population to migrate widely and often in search of water.

Shurima's population declined sharply, year after year. Nomadic life was hard, and often very short. There were still many wonders out there, certainly, but fewer and fewer Shurimans left to behold them.

Trade and travel became a way of life. The old nations of the empire were gone, with everything north of the river now swallowed up by the treacherous deserts of the Great Sai. It fell to the nomad caravans to establish and maintain overland routes between the scattered settlements.

Also, as explorers from distant lands began to seek Shurima's lost wealth, there were many Shurimans who were only too happy to act as guides, in exchange for foreign gold. A number of ports and cities in the north were voluntarily assimilated into the ever-expanding empire of Noxus. The original inhabitants of these settlements live in relative peace with their Noxian counterparts, seeing the exchange of food and preferential trade as a price worth paying for military protection from raiders.

From the wastes of the south to the so-called "Endless Plain" of the Sai Faraj, the deserts of Shurima are filled with dangers beyond the arid climate. While most trading posts uphold their own customs and laws, there is little to protect those who wander outside the jurisdiction of local enforcers, and unwary merchants do not often last long in the wilderness.

THE GREAT SAI

THE ZOANTHA CASCADE

The shifting erg-tides of the desert have been known to carve paths even through bare rock. Traditionally, Shurimans have traveled here, to the Zoantha Cascade, to toss beloved objects into the sandfalls as offerings to the Ascended.

As a result, such locations often become dangerous yet lucrative haunts for scavengers and treasure hunters.

While many fierce predators are drawn to the oases and wasteland settlements where prey is more plentiful, the deep deserts are home to some truly deadly creatures—venomous arachnids, blind sand-snakes, and even the unearthly xer'sai.

Hardy beasts of burden, skallashi are ideally suited to Shurima's harsh environment. Though notoriously bad-tempered, they are treated with great reverence—their hides painted with sacred symbols of protection, their horns hung with totems and charms—and to own one is often considered a sign of prosperity.

Shuriman raiders survive not through trade, but violence. These bands of marauders often attempt to blend into the environment in order to lure unsuspecting travelers into traps before killing them, taking their belongings—and in very rare cases, eating them.

This band call themselves the Shakkal; they are known for their incredible agility and unparalleled cruelty. Employing hardened bone-braces and long polearms, they vault toward their victims at terrifying speeds, howling their battle cries as they go.

SURVIVAL UNDER AN ETERNAL SUN

WATER & SHAPE TO YOU

by GRAHAM McNEILL

For the first time Khari could remember, flowers grew on the street leading from the town square to the Cut. To the people of Saikhal, this street was known as the Path of Dust, though Khari's *bibi* said it used to be called the Water Road in the olden past. Not in her time, not even in her own bibi's time, but a time long before even that.

To a girl of eight summers like Khari, that might as well have been in the time when the Great Weaver spun the world into life.

The bowl she carried was fashioned from clay, with an ugly crack that snaked its way around its edges and which had been crudely repaired with hardened blobs of resin glue. Its sides were painted cornflower blue with an enameled sun disc at its base, and when it was filled with gritty water from the cavern wells, the ripples on the surface made it look like the sun was dancing.

But now the river was back, and the Cut was no longer a dry, sunbaked gouge in the rock that curled around their town. Water flowed along it, and it wasn't the hard, gritty water from the wells. It was clear as blown glass and didn't make you want to spit as soon as you took a mouthful.

At night, when the old men gathered around their pipes, they whispered that it was the Hawk Father who had brought the waters back when he lifted his city up from beneath the sands. They spoke of pilgrims flocking to that golden city, but from their furrowed brows and the tone of their voices as they shooed her away, Khari wasn't sure if they thought that was a good thing or not.

Khari paused to smell one of the flowers, a conical bloom with long, oval petals the color of milk and honey. Bibi called it a starbloom and, like the water, said it hadn't been seen in these parts since she was a girl of Khari's age. She loved its rich, musky smell, but the spicy pollen suddenly made her want to sneeze. She closed her eyes and tried to hold it in, first turning her head to sunrise, and then to sunset. Bibi said it was bad luck to sneeze before

midday, and she was the oldest person Khari knew, so there wasn't anything she didn't know.

The urge to sneeze passed, and Khari opened her eyes in time to see *Maza* Isza limp from her home of sunbaked brick with a handful of greenleaf rushes to spread before its entrance. It was too late to get away without her seeing Khari. The old woman was the town gossip, and when Maza Isza decided to talk to you, it would be sundown before you got away, but at least you'd know everyone in the town's comings and goings.

"Water and shade to you, Khari," called Maza Isza. "Is Anhay's child born to the sun yet?"

"Not yet, Maza Isza," said Khari, holding up the bowl. "Bibi sent me to fetch clean water!"

Isza nodded and pointed to the Cut. "Be sure to get it cold and fresh from the river, child! New life oughtn't greet the sun bathed in dirty well water!"

"Yes, Maza Isza," said Khari, grateful for this chance to get away.

She continued on, skipping down the road and taking the winding path from the edge of the town. In truth, she'd been pleased to be given a way to escape Anhay's birthing screams, and she had gladly taken Bibi's cracked bowl to the river.

It still felt odd saying that. *River.*

There hadn't been a river flowing

past Saikhal for many generations, at least nothing beyond the few weeks in Cloud Season when it rained over the summits of the soaring mountains to the south. Rainwater poured down the Cut in powerfully brief torrents, but it never lasted, and then Saikhal's people were back to relying on water from the cave wells that tasted like biting on metal.

Back when the rivers had dried up, Saikhal's inhabitants had stubbornly refused to leave and follow the remaining waters. Those ancient settlers had chosen to remain in the mountains, but no one now remembered why they'd decided to stay.

Khari left the edge of the town and the rock upon which it was built, winding down the switchback path to the river. Once it had been paved with smooth glass mosaic tiles, like a river itself, but now only a handful of faded blue chips remained. Beyond the shade of town, the sun was a searing golden disc, now almost at its zenith, and Khari looked forward to reaching the cooler riverbank.

From here, the river was a wonderful silver ribbon that tumbled down the mountainside, clear and cold and tasting of nothing at all. Its banks were green with new growths: berry bushes, acacia saplings, and riotously colorful swathes of wildflowers.

Beyond the river, high clouds gathered over the titanic mountains rising on Shurima's western coast, and an ocean of sand stretched to the north and east as far as the eye could see. Dust devils capered over the crests of the dunes and blew curiously regular patterns in the sand, like a grazing sandswimmer in search of insects just below the surface.

She lifted a hand to shield her eyes from the sun as it glinted on something golden by the river's edge. It was too bright to see clearly, and whatever was down there was hidden by the swaying branches of a new-blooming palm tree. What was it?

A wandering skallashi stopping for a drink? Nomads, Shakkal bandits?

Or maybe it was some ancient treasure washed down from a tomb somewhere high in the mountains? When Khari was in her third summer, her father had found a golden-bladed dagger half buried in the river mud, its grip so large it was almost a sword. No one knew where it had come from, but in the years since then, it had never lost its edge and never tarnished.

The weapon of a god-warrior, her father always claimed.

The old men talked about the mighty god-warriors of ancient times, towering hybrids of beast and man, who once led the armies of lost Shurima. Ancient wars were said to have destroyed them, and their remains were sealed away in lost tombs guarded by spells and monsters. Treasure hunters, scavengers, and grave robbers traveled the length and breadth of Shurima's burning sands in search of these riches. The old men said it brought ill luck to hunt the resting places of the dead, but when she had been younger, Khari had always imagined herself as a fearless adventurer.

At least until her father told her there were rich hunters and old hunters, but no old *and* rich ones.

She carried on toward the river, passing through a patch of wildflowers with petals of vivid blue and crimson. Clouds of pollen rose up, and she hummed along with the lazy droning of insects as they flitted to and fro. The splashing of the river drew her on, and she took a deep breath, tasting its crisp sharpness and the warm scents of the flowers.

Emerging onto a wide patch of earth beaten flat by the feet of Saikhal's water-bearers, Khari took a moment to savor the view, all thoughts of washed-down treasure forgotten at the wondrous sight of the river.

The Cut was a gorge around fifty feet wide and—when it was dry— around ten feet deep. The children of Saikhal took shade in it when they had time to play, but now there was no shade to be had, for the Cut was filled with fast-flowing water that ran like molten silver from its source high in the mountains. The river spumed at its banks and swirled with endless spiraling patterns where it eased past outcroppings of red rock. Dartflies skimmed the water's surface, and Khari felt droplets misting on the mahogany skin of her arms.

She knelt on the bank and placed the bowl beside her before plunging her arms into the river. After the heat of the day, the icy cold was welcome. Khari scooped the water into her cupped hand and took a long drink… so different to the taste of the cave wells.

This must be what kings and gods drink!

Once she had slaked her thirst, she dipped the bowl into the water. She grinned and tipped the water over her head, gasping at the biting chill of it. Again, she filled it and poured it over herself, laughing at the sheer extravagance of what would have been unthinkable only a few years ago.

"Refreshing, isn't it?" said a deep voice from farther along the riverbank.

Khari jumped and almost lost her grip on the bowl. She caught it just before it hit the ground and let out a long breath of relief. Bibi had been so angry when she'd dropped it last summer and tried to hide her mistake instead of just admitting to it.

She looked up in annoyance, again seeing the golden glint between the tall grasses crowding the riverbank.

"Who's there?" she demanded. "You almost made me drop Bibi's bowl again. If it broke for good this time, I'd tell her it was *your* fault. And then you'd be in real trouble!"

"Apologies, child," said the voice. "I did not mean to startle you."

Khari carefully set the bowl down and peered into the undergrowth.

"Who are you?" she asked.

The rushes parted as a tall figure rose from its crouching position, and Khari felt as if the breath was being squeezed from her chest.

Clad from head to foot in golden warplate with a polished gemstone the color of spring sky set at the center of his breastplate, the armored warrior was taller than anyone she'd ever seen. Much taller than even Kadidu the metal-smiter, who everyone agreed was part Ascended. The warrior's shoulder guards were carved in the form of spread wings, from which a tan dust cloak and streamers of gold-edged crimson cloth were hung.

She couldn't see his face behind the beaked and winged helmet he wore, but his eyes burned with the pale glow of a rising sun. She knew she ought to be scared of this warrior, for he was clearly dangerous, and she could sense the terrible power lurking beneath his armor. But his manner wasn't threatening, and he hadn't done anything to make her afraid.

Only then did Khari notice that his thickly muscled legs were not those of a man, but had the reverse-jointed form of a hunting hawk. One hand was wet with river water, and the other held a giant staff with a heavy spear tip atop a haft of brightest gold.

"Aren't you *hot* in all that armor?" she asked.

Those sunlit eyes narrowed, and his head cocked to the side as he regarded her quizzically.

"I suppose I should be," he said, his voice rich and its accent unfamiliar. "But no, I do not feel the heat as I once did."

"Why not?"

"The Sun Priests remade my body," he said. "Their fire wrought my flesh to be stronger and all but invulnerable. It enhanced my being into something even I do not fully understand."

"Are you one of the… *Ascended*?" asked Khari. "I've heard about you. Bibi used to tell stories about them. She said you were men once, but you were turned into monsters and killed each other."

"We called ourselves god-warriors," he said sadly, "but perhaps monsters is more accurate."

Khari glanced across the river as she saw something moving beyond the lushness of the far bank. For a second it had looked like figures moving through the dunes, but when she shielded her eyes, they were gone, almost as if they'd sunk into the sand.

"In truth, I no longer feel anything as I used to," he said, squatting by the river's edge and letting the water run playfully over his fingers again.

"Why are you here?" asked Khari. "Are you looking for a lost tomb?"

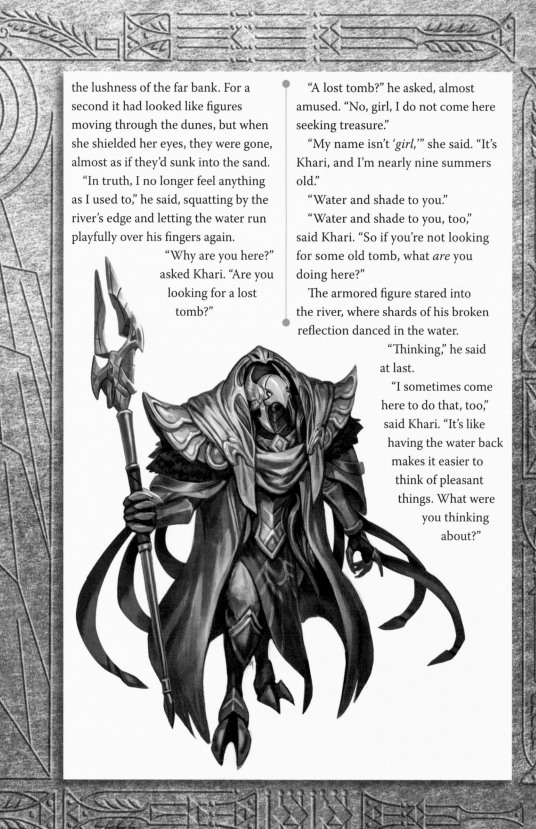

"A lost tomb?" he asked, almost amused. "No, girl, I do not come here seeking treasure."

"My name isn't 'girl,'" she said. "It's Khari, and I'm nearly nine summers old."

"Water and shade to you."

"Water and shade to you, too," said Khari. "So if you're not looking for some old tomb, what *are* you doing here?"

The armored figure stared into the river, where shards of his broken reflection danced in the water.

"Thinking," he said at last.

"I sometimes come here to do that, too," said Khari. "It's like having the water back makes it easier to think of pleasant things. What were you thinking about?"

"Many things," said the armored figure with a heavy sigh. "And none of them pleasant, Khari of Saikhal."

"Wait, you know Saikhal?"

He nodded and said, "I do indeed, Khari. I knew it when it was no more than a few crude huts beside the riverbank. I knew it when it grew to a town, and I knew it when I traveled here as a guest."

"You must be very old then," said Khari.

He laughed. "Yes, I am *very* old. How is it you do not know me? Great gulfs of time have passed since I last walked my domain, but I am told my name has not been forgotten."

"So who are you?"

"I am Azir, Blessed of the Sun, Emperor of Shurima."

"You're the Hawk Father..."

"I am," agreed Azir, and again Khari saw more shapes moving across the river.

She sensed movement beneath her and looked down as the sand rippled between her sandaled feet. Looking back up, she saw what might have been the outline of another man through the tall grass, but it faded with a hiss of falling sand as soon as she looked at it.

"Is there someone else with you?" asked Khari.

"I am an emperor," said Azir. "And emperors seldom travel alone."

"Did you really bring your city up from underneath the sands?"

"I did, yes, and it cost me greatly."

"What does it look like?"

"It is a golden city of wonders and magic," said Azir, holding up his hand and letting the water run between his clawed fingers. "Its rise brought the rivers back to Shurima. This tributary flows only because I have made it so."

Khari's mother had raised her with manners enough to say, "Thank you. We used to have to rely on cave-well water, and it's *nasty*. All red and cloudy and full of sand. This is *much* better. I have to get some clean water, you see. My cousin Anhay's having a baby, so Bibi sent me to the river to get clean water."

She turned from Azir and scooped up fresh water in the bowl.

"Wait, stay awhile," said Azir as she turned to go.

"I... really have to get back," she said. "The baby could come at any moment."

"I could command you to stay," said Azir.

"Would I have to stay then?"

"If your emperor commands it, yes."

"Are you *my* emperor?"

Azir crouched and briefly placed a heavy, clawed hand on her shoulder. His skin had a ripe, animal reek to it, like a skinned hide just before it was cured. She felt the power of his grip as talons dug into her skin, an awesome strength that could crush stone and bend iron.

Despite that, she still felt no threat from him, only a strange sense of loneliness.

"I am your emperor," he said.

"Very well, I'll stay then," said Khari. "But you have to tell Bibi it's because you told me to."

"That will not be necessary," he said.

"You don't know my bibi," said Khari, looking back up the hillside to the town.

Smoke curled from cookfires readying meat for the evening meals, and the sound of livestock vied with the clang of metal from Kadidu's forge. Someone was singing an old water-finding song, and Khari smiled as she thought of the newest addition to her town's family.

"Tell me, what do you know of Saikhal's history?" asked Azir. "Do you know how special it is?"

"Special? Really?" said Khari. "I don't think so. Not much has ever happened here. Bibi says it's been here centuries, but all the best stories are about things that happen far away."

"You are wrong about that," said Azir. "The best stories are the ones that unfold right in front of us, even if we do not know it at the time. And something of great import took place in this very town, not long after it first grew from the river folk's dwellings."

Now Khari was intrigued. "Really? What was it?"

"Saikhal is where Xerath was *born*."

"Who?" she said.

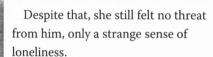

A flock of hookbills took flight across the river, and Khari scooped up more water from the river to splash in her face. It was getting hotter, and the sun was directly overhead now.

Azir looked at her expectantly.

"That name means nothing to you?" he said.

She shook her head. "Was he a friend of yours?"

Azir turned to look out over the sands, and she felt the tension rise in him, like the sinew of a bowstring on the verge of snapping. The shapes in the sand shifted again, and Khari saw just how many of them there were. Dozens at least, probably more. She took an involuntary step back in the shallow water, at last feeling the onset of fear. The claws on Azir's slender fingers arrested her in place once more, biting through her thin tunic.

"You're hurting me," she said, and he immediately released her.

"Truly, the name means nothing to you?"

"No, sorry."

Azir knelt before her, and a great weight seemed to settle upon him. He swept his staff out across the endless expanse of desolation, to the invisible horizon where killing heat rippled the air and strange creatures of obsidian lived beneath the sands.

"All of this," said Azir with great weariness, "was *his* doing. His ambition and his hate drove him to betray me at what was to be my greatest triumph. Or at least that was what I told myself. The truth is, it was at the moment of my greatest hubris, my greatest blindness, that he struck."

"I don't understand what that means," said Khari.

"No, I suppose you wouldn't," said Azir. "Time has changed Shurima beyond all recognition and wiped away the memory of our triumphs and our defeats. Only legends remain. The people of this new Shurima speak of our lost greatness as stories to tell children, believing it gone forever. Did you know my empire once stretched from ocean to ocean, across this entire continent? That golden outposts were built amid the jungles of the east? Three score satrapies sent tithes and warriors to the capital, and wealth flowed to its coffers in a river of gold. The Shuriman Empire spoke in a hundred languages, with art and music from cultures beyond number."

Azir paused, looking up at Saikhal. Khari couldn't read the face behind his helmet, but his pale eyes burned with cold fire as he spoke again.

"But it was an empire built on the bloodied backs of slaves; those our armies took in conquest or who broke the law or were born to that fate. And ours was an empire that reveled in cruelty. Slaves were denied any names but those we chose to give them. We exploited their skills and rewarded them with suffering. We used their bodies until their flesh gave out, and when we were done with them, we cast them aside."

"Was Xerath a slave?"

Azir nodded. "Yes. He was taken by the host of Renekton at Nerimazeth to the northwest, but *this* was where he was born. I met him in the great library of my father's capital, and we soon discovered our shared love of history and mathematics. We met in secret, for a member of the royal bloodline could not consort with a slave, poring over the library's many scrolls and books. We grew up together, and after I became emperor he brought me here, and we lay by this very river to look up at the stars, just as we had when we were children."

"It doesn't sound like you were cruel," said Khari. "It sounds like you were friends."

"I believed we were, and perhaps even he did for a time," said Azir. "But I was royalty with other slaves, and I was not kind to them until much later. Xerath knew that every moment we were together, I held his life in my hands. On a whim I could have had him killed, and he knew it. That I would have never thought to do so was irrelevant. He was a slave, and our

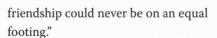

friendship could never be on an equal footing."

"What happened to him?"

Azir laughed, but it sounded bitter and hollow to Khari.

"As my arrogant dream of becoming emperor came closer to reality, Xerath's ambition swelled, and so too did his ruthlessness. I saw it, I *knew*, but his plots were paving my way to the throne… so I chose to ignore it."

Azir stood and planted his staff in the earth beside him. The sunlight gleamed on his armor, and though he towered over Khari, he suddenly seemed somehow *diminished*.

"On the day of my Ascension, just as I planned to free Shurima's slaves, he betrayed me. He cast me into the killing fire as he took my place on the sun disc to steal my godhood. I was supposed to ascend that day, but instead Shurima fell and devastation swept over the land. An empire that had ruled the known world for centuries was wiped out in the blink of an eye by a terrible cataclysm that laid waste to the earth and burned away the waters."

"Is that why Shurima's a desert?"

Azir nodded.

"I kind of feel bad for him," said Khari.

"For Xerath?"

"Yes. I mean, it's bad he betrayed you, but how could he *not* feel the way he did? He was a slave, and he had to do whatever you said all the time or else he'd be killed."

She felt his anger but couldn't tell if it was for her or Xerath or even himself.

"You speak with a child's understanding," he snapped, "and I have tarried too long with you. It is time to set my hands to purpose here."

Khari backed away from the risen emperor, suddenly fearful as he turned his gaze on Saikhal.

"What purpose is that?" she cried. "*What purpose is that?*"

"I feel you in the winds, in the water, and upon the earth," said Azir, but Khari knew he wasn't talking to her, only to a ghost. "I stood in the ruins of Vekaura, the city of my *mother*, now a blasted, corpse-choked ruin, and felt your spiteful magic. The age I spent in formless oblivion and the years since my rise have not been spent in vain, my *brother*. My power grows with every rise of the sun, and as the land awakens, so too am I reborn. But there can be no future while you still live, so I will draw you from your hiding place in the shadows with the fire of the sun."

Golden light burst from the blades of his staff, so bright Khari couldn't look at it. Its wrathful heat forced her to take a step backward. She looked across the river as the sand there shifted again, and the shapes she had glimpsed in the depths were finally revealed.

Warriors rose from the dunes; tall and broad, armored in the manner of their master, yet rendered entirely of sand. They came in the hundreds, sand spilling from their warplates as they marched in perfect synchrony that no mortal soldiers could ever hope to match. They carried long lances with blades that glittered with flecks of crystal mixed with the sands of their undulant bodies.

Khari felt a terrible, knotted fist of anguish in her gut at the sight of them.

She jumped as the earth around her cracked and more of the horrid warriors of sand poured up out of the ground. They carried the stench of the deep earth with them, dry and dusty, like the rotted robes clinging to skeletons sometimes uncovered by winds over the dunes.

They came on in serried ranks of windblown sand, moving up the slope toward Saikhal with murderous purpose in every stride.

These were not warriors who fought to protect their loved ones or defend the weak, but terrible killing things of magic whose only purpose was to destroy. Khari had heard the old men tell stories of terrible wars in far-off lands, and even as horrible as some of them were, she knew they were fought by people who might know mercy and forgiveness.

These blank, soulless warriors knew nothing of such things.

"What are you doing?" Khari demanded. "Where are they going?"

Azir looked down on her as if debating whether to even answer her.

"I cannot build Shurima anew with the chains of the past still binding me," said Azir. "Xerath must die so I can move forward. I mean to purge him from this land, root and branch, and where better to start than where his poison seed first emerged?"

"You're going to destroy my home just because this is where Xerath was born?"

The emperor nodded. "That is exactly what I am going to do."

He moved past her, heading with slow, deliberate strides toward the path uphill.

The knot of fear in Khari's gut uncoiled like a snake, and she gagged at the acrid taste of bile in the back of her throat. She felt it slither through her body, as if paralyzing her with its venom.

But what did Bibi always say about snakes?

Stamp on them, hard. Right behind the head so its fangs can't bite you!

Bibi's words stole away Khari's fear in a heartbeat and replaced it with an anger that burned the snake in her belly away. She turned to Azir and threw the only thing she had at him.

The bowl flew through the air and smashed against the back of his head. The broken pieces landed at his feet

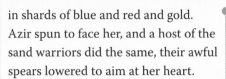

in shards of blue and red and gold. Azir spun to face her, and a host of the sand warriors did the same, their awful spears lowered to aim at her heart.

"Entire tribes were wiped out for less, girl," he said.

Khari stared, aghast, at what she'd done. The broken pieces of the bowl reminded her of how it had been the lie that caused the most hurt to her bibi, not the fact it had cracked. Looking up from the smashed pottery to Azir, she was struck by a sudden thought.

"How did you come back?" she said.

He paused, her question surprising him as much as it did her. She didn't know where it had come from, but she knew it was important. The army of sand paused in its advance on Saikhal, and her mind raced as she tried to think of how she could stall the emperor a little longer.

"You said Xerath killed you," said Khari. "Pushed you into a fire, yes? So how did you come back? How are you alive now?"

At first, she thought he wasn't going to answer, that his moment of introspection by the water's edge was over. Then the cold fire in his eyes flickered, and she felt the presence of the man he once had been.

"Blood of my blood brought me back," he said at last. "A daughter of the sands, many centuries distant. She too was betrayed and left for dead. Her blood soaked the sand of my death and brought me back as a phantom of ash and dust."

"But you're more than that now, aren't you? Ash and dust, I mean?"

"I am Ascended."

"How? How did you go from dust to... *this*?"

"I... She..."

"You saved her, didn't you? You came back, and you saved her somehow."

Azir took a step toward her, a golden killer looming over her. "How can you know this?"

Khari took a breath, tasting the heat and fury within him, but also the soul that had made him befriend a slave boy in a library, the part that still burned with the pain of that friend's betrayal.

"Because it's what I would have done," said Khari. "You saw she needed help, so you helped her, didn't you?"

Azir nodded slowly. "She was dying, and so I bore her to the Oasis of the Dawn," he said. "Its waters were long since dried, but with every step I took toward it, clear water bubbled up from below. I laid her down in the clear waters, and as they washed over her, they restored her to life. And as her eyes opened, the power of the sun lifted me up in its fiery embrace and renewed me. It burned my old form away and remade me into something new, something greater than I could ever have been before."

"That's it! Don't you see?"

"See what?"

"You were brought back because you saw someone who was hurt and needed help," said Khari. "I bet if you'd left her to die, you'd still be a ghost haunting the ruins, if you'd be anything at all."

Azir looked to his sand warriors, who still stood poised to run Khari through with their spears.

"I have sacrificed so much…." he said, as Khari bent to lift one of the broken pieces of the bowl.

"You see this?" she said, holding up a bladed shard of pottery. "I broke my bibi's bowl last summer. I dropped it and cracked a piece off the side. It was her favorite bowl, so I tried to hide what I'd done by gluing it back and hoping no one would notice, but I only ended up making things worse."

Khari stood and held the fragment of the bowl out to Azir.

"We can't take back the mistakes of the past, but we can learn from them," she said. "Killing my town isn't learning from the past, it's making the same mistake Xerath did."

For long moments, Azir was silent, and she saw the turbulent emotions warring within him echoed in the tremoring sand warriors around him.

His helm rose, and he fixed her with his pale gaze.

"You speak with a child's understanding," he said.

"You told me that already."

"But this time I do not mean it as an insult," said Azir. "I only mean that your words are uncluttered with greed, ambition, or thoughts of some grand destiny. You speak with an innocent heart."

Azir knelt, and she met the sunlight behind the metal of his helm without flinching.

"You are wise beyond your years, Khari of Saikhal," he said.

"Does that mean you're going to leave my town alone?"

"Yes, Khari, it does."

And with a hiss like sand through an hourglass, the army of sand sank back into the dunes.

Khari let out a sigh and bit her bottom lip as tears of relief threatened to spill down her cheeks.

But she didn't want to cry in front of an emperor, so pressed her chin down into her chest.

Azir lifted her head and said, "You have her eyes, you know. Blue, like sapphires."

"Whose eyes?" asked Khari.

Azir ignored her question and reached down to lift the broken pieces of Bibi's bowl. He turned the shards of broken clay over in his hands, and Khari's eyes widened as clouds of sand lifted from the ground at Azir's feet.

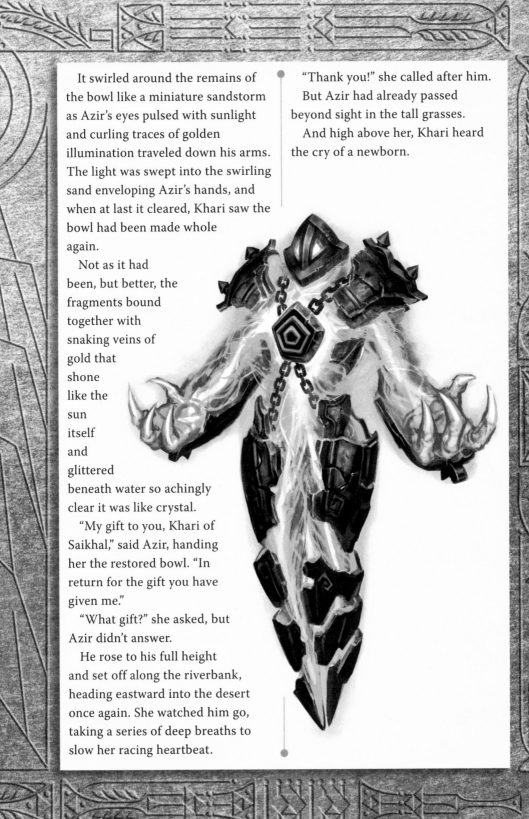

It swirled around the remains of the bowl like a miniature sandstorm as Azir's eyes pulsed with sunlight and curling traces of golden illumination traveled down his arms. The light was swept into the swirling sand enveloping Azir's hands, and when at last it cleared, Khari saw the bowl had been made whole again.

Not as it had been, but better, the fragments bound together with snaking veins of gold that shone like the sun itself and glittered beneath water so achingly clear it was like crystal.

"My gift to you, Khari of Saikhal," said Azir, handing her the restored bowl. "In return for the gift you have given me."

"What gift?" she asked, but Azir didn't answer.

He rose to his full height and set off along the riverbank, heading eastward into the desert once again. She watched him go, taking a series of deep breaths to slow her racing heartbeat.

"Thank you!" she called after him.

But Azir had already passed beyond sight in the tall grasses.

And high above her, Khari heard the cry of a newborn.

Screaming into existence with the birth of the universe, the Void is a manifestation of the unknowable nothingness that lies beyond. It is a force of insatiable hunger, waiting through the eons until its masters, the mysterious Watchers, mark the final time of undoing.

To be a mortal touched by this power is to suffer an agonizing glimpse of eternal unreality, enough to shatter even the strongest mind.

Mistress,
Pleased to note, caravan skirting the site revealed something new. As reported, these creatures appears to "seize" into reality. Form abstract at first, likely not original, individuals assume solid shape then feed voraciously on anything nearby. Such immense strength, hunger, I can scarcely imagine results if directed against our enemies. Will advise captain moves outpost closer to ruins.
I remain your servant.

Mistress,
No creature movement in last four days. Many in outpost camp complain of mild headaches, aversion to light. Some appears lost in thought, cannot readily remember own name, rank, close family, or purpose of expedition. Feels somewhat infectious.
I remain.

Others gone into ruins.
Memory. Memory? Like trying to hold on to water. Not entirely unpleasant. Not. Not entirely. Are these my hands? I can't. Hard to remember.
Must fight. Fight it. If you don't fight, it washes you away. Nice. To be washed away. When I close my eyes, close, my eye. Nothing.
Go to back, go to, go back now. Ieathia awaits me.

Opinions differ as to where exactly the true home of the yordles is to be found, though a handful of mortals claim to have traveled unseen pathways to a land of curious enchantment deep within the spirit realm. They tell of a place of unfettered magic, where the foolhardy can be led astray by myriad wonders, and end up lost in a dream.

In Bandle City, it is said that every sensation is heightened for non-yordles. Colors are brighter. Food and drink intoxicates the senses for years, and once tasted, will never be forgotten. The sunlight is eternally golden, the waters crystal clear, and every harvest brings a fruitful bounty. Perhaps some of these claims are true, or maybe none—for no two taletellers ever seem to agree on what they actually saw.

Only one thing is known for certain, and that is the timeless quality of Bandle City and its inhabitants. This might explain why those mortals who find their way back to the material realm often appear to have aged tremendously, while many more never return at all.

I who walk the realms have heard of death's strange and opposing world.

254

Watch for the hunter half part, half beast, and for the one who bears its mark.

Bandle City

ACKNOWLEDGMENTS & CREDITS

Story Editorial: Michael Haugen Wieske
Background Editorial: Laurie Goulding
Editorial Support: Abigail Harvey,
Thomas Cunningham, Laura Michet
Creative Direction: Ariel Lawrence
Production: Omar Kendall, Ghiyom Turmel
Art Direction: Bridget O'Neill, Laura DeYoung
Localization Consultation: Addie Sillyman, Petros Pantazis
Head of IP/Creative: Greg Street

Special thanks to Ryan Rubin and the Worldbuilding team, Christian Bayley, Peter Yoon, Xiaolu Li, Brandon Meier, Yula Chin, Jerod Partin, Stephanie Lim DeSanctis, Dan Sutton, Glenn Sardelli, Brian Chui, Section Studios, Andrew Silver, Chris Cantrell, Prashant Saraswat, Larry Colvin, Ryan Rinkle, Jason Chan, Alex Shahmiri, and all the other folks who helped make this book a reality.

This book was produced by

 MELCHER
MEDIA

124 West 13th Street • New York, NY 10011 • melcher.com

Founder, CEO: Charles Melcher
VP, COO: Bonnie Eldon
Executive Editor/Producer: Lauren Nathan
Production Director: Susan Lynch
Senior Editor: Christopher Steighner
Designer/Editor: Renée Bollier

Melcher Media gratefully acknowledges the following for their contributions: Chika Azuma, Camille De Beus, Shannon Fanuko, Luke Gernert, Nicky Guerreiro, Michael Szczerban, Megan Worman, and Katy Yudín.

All images are copyrighted by Riot Games except for those on the pages in the following list. Adobe Stock: Ever (30–31, 40–41), pamela_d_mcadams (32–39), DavidMSchrader (44, 46–48, 50–51, 53, 66), Sonate (54–65), prachaubch (70–71), ParinPIX (72–73, 76–77), naiaekky (74–75, 78–79), Mandrixta (108–115, 118–119), kurapy (113–115, 118–119), Charlie's (116), Sergey Pristyazhnyuk (116–117), Jag_cz (120–121), jpramirez (122–137), grasycho (163, 166, 168, 171–172, 175), vellot (165), natali_mya (176–177), korkeng (178–189), darkbird (200), bartsadowski (204–205, 210–213, 216–219, 222–223), Ivan Kurmyshov (206–207), James Carroll (208–209, 214–215), morkdam (220–221); Dreamstime.com: Pixelshow1 (130, 132–133); Shutterstock.com: YamabikaY (44–51, 80–95), Guenter Albers (53–65), Bas Meelker (98–105), Denis Galushka (108–119), siloto (134–137), foxie (138–157), basel101658 (164, 172–173), Ullithemrg (168), goldnetz (174–175).